Mary La Chapelle's HOUSE OF HEROES

"Mary La Chapelle, a cool and compassionate voice from the Midwest, comes as a refreshing novelty these days when so much new fiction is self-absorbed and stylistically derivative. Her lack of pretension, her honesty, her eye for the odd and illuminating detail, her humor, and interest in the idiosyncratic behavior of others so different from herself, all presented in smooth narratives, indicate the arrival of a substantial talent. If our luck holds, she will be rewarding us with that talent for years to come."
—Donald Barthelme, Roger Groening, Toni Morrison,
judges for the PEN/Nelson Algren Award

"Extraordinary...*House of Heroes* is a wonderful gift, a treasure... The stories are some of the most moving, meaningful, beautifully crafted, and memorable I have ever read."
—Susan Dodd,
author of *Old Wives' Tales* and *Mamaw*

"*House of Heroes* is one fine response to the current argument that the short story should be an express train to despair. La Chapelle shows that evil is never so visible and real as when surrounded by light. These are splendid stories. Read them. Breathe them, like good air."
—Sharon Sheehe Stark,
author of *A Wrestling Season*

"The title story is the shining gem around which the other, semiprecious stones are set. And, as with any artfully composed piece of jewelry, the surrounding stones set off the luminous center one and reflect its glow. Accrues in subtle power and carries the intimacy of a journal entry or private letter."
—*Philadelphia Inquirer*

"With Raymond Carver and Richard Ford, La Chapelle helps bring the frank, ruefully compassionate view of small town America into the 1980s. One is moved by La Chapelle's wisdom and subtlety."
—*Providence Journal*

"Rich with detail and refreshing in the number of risks La Chapelle takes. This book shouldn't be skipped."
—*Milwaukee Journal*

"These ten stories, set in and around Minnesota, are as deep and clear as that state's northern lakes. Hauntin
—*St. Louis Post-*

HOUSE
OF
HEROES
AND OTHER STORIES

Mary La Chapelle

Vintage Contemporaries

VINTAGE BOOKS   A DIVISION OF RANDOM HOUSE, INC.   NEW YORK

FIRST VINTAGE CONTEMPORARIES EDITION, FEBRUARY 1990

Library of Congress Cataloging-in-Publication Data
La Chapelle, Mary.
   House of heroes and other stories / Mary La Chapelle.—
1st Vintage contemporaries ed.
   p. cm.—(Vintage contemporaries)
   ISBN 0-679-72457-5
   I. Title.
[PS3562.A13H68   1990]
813'.54—dc20   89-40105
                                                      CIP

The author is grateful for permission to reprint stories that
appeared, sometimes in slightly different form, in the following magazines: Northern Lit Quarterly ("Homer"), Sing
Heavenly Muse ("The Gate-House"), WARM Journal ("Superstitions"), Redbook ("Accidents").

Manufactured in the United States of America
10 9 8 7 6 5 4 3 2 1

TO MY PARENTS,
CATHERINE REARDON LA CHAPELLE
AND
JAMES MICHAEL LA CHAPELLE

CONTENTS

HOUSE
OF
HEROES

ANNA
IN A SMALL
TOWN

I'm waiting in the car outside the Waupaca County jail. My cousin Anna left me here five minutes ago. She needs to check on Mike's bail and to see if she can talk with him awhile. I had started to get out of the car to go with her, but she said, "Wait here, Jane. I feel so bad about your being involved already." I couldn't be sure what she really wanted, or what I wanted, so I made one of those faces I know how to make, where each of my eyebrows goes in a different direction.

And after she got out, she came over to my side of the car and bent far down to peer into my window. "Really," she said. "He's so hung over, he won't mind sleeping until the bail comes through. Besides, Sunday is the best time to see the zoo; I'd still like to give you the tour."

She straightened up, and all I could see were her log-size legs until she walked away. Her softball jacket was shiny blue and said BALDY'S AND MARY'S on the back. I thought about how there wasn't much reason for her to wear it anymore, and then I could see her from behind pulling at the material in the front of her jacket. Adjusting, not because she was cold, or because it was raining, but because adjusting was second nature to her, always making herself fit, into her clothes, into other people's cars, or the next room she might enter.

My cousin is a giant, and you can't forget that fact while looking at her. I watched her set her feet on the steps to the jail with a sliding motion, smoothly and softly, the way I imagine Indians were taught to step so as not to disturb the forest. Her purse looked like a toy over her wrist, and she took the steps two at a time. But these are details anyone might notice.

There are yellow leaves stuck to the windshield. One leaf is sliding down a drip of water. It could make me think of a tear, but I don't want to think about tears, or the gloom inside this car, or the gloom outside of it. I want to know how I got into this? I came here to see Anna; well, this is partly true. I came to direct a mime workshop at the college in Stevens Point, which is only a stone's throw from Waupaca. The two of us have exchanged a few cards, but basically we haven't seen each other since her sister's wedding six years ago. She urged me in every one of her cards to stop in Waupaca if I should happen to pass through. I never encouraged her to visit me, however; I suppose because I was doubtful about her fitting into my little box of an apartment, but also because I am on tour so much of the time.

Anna called me a week ago. My sister, she said, had mentioned in her last note that I would be coming through. I had forgotten about her voice: it's like birch bark, rough and smooth at the same time. And we chatted together with the strained feelings of two people who were once close and now aren't sure why. Finally, she talked me into driving up for the weekend since my workshop didn't begin until Monday.

We estimated that the leaves would be peak color for my drive from Chicago, but I was disappointed. The trees were undramatic. If they had changed at all, it was only to a dull yellow like these leaves on the windshield—no reds, no ambers. In fact, there wasn't a tree along the road that didn't seem somehow listless in its response to autumn.

I had hardly come onto her property and out of my car before Anna was there, bending over me. She gave me a kind of hug by putting a hand around each of my shoulders. "Sorry about the leaves," she said.

"Why?"

"Because the rain's been bringing them down before they've had a chance."

"That's not your fault, Anna. It's been raining in Chicago too."

I'd forgotten how different she was from anyone else. She was standing back from me, smiling, but trying not to smile too much. Sometimes her body has an enormous energy of expectation you can almost see, like mercury in a thermometer. It makes me very uncomfortable. When she sensed I was feeling this way, she let go of her excitement and became still before slowly bending at the waist into the trunk of my car. I noticed once again how the movements of her hands were delayed, as if it took longer for intentions to travel the lengths of her arms.

Her fingers were too large to fit into the grips of my suitcases. And after she had gathered up all my bags under one arm, I had to tell her I only needed one for the weekend; she blushed and put two of them back. "This is it," she said, extending her other arm over the property. Three years ago she sent me a card on which she had sketched a picture of her land. It was drawn as if from an aerial view, a square, cut into the front of a forest of small, friendly pine trees. Standing in the lot, I could see the pines were not as proportionally small as they had been drawn, and they weren't friendly. They were stiff and had been planted in rows. The bottom branches were scraggly on every tree, creating, at eye level, a scratched, gray haze. And the upper bulk of the trees was massed together in a unified plan to keep the light out.

If I ever lived in a forest—and I have thought about it—I wouldn't live in a pine forest. I've never seen much else grow in pine forests, except pines. Whether this is because of the piles of needles, or the lack of light, I don't know. The kind of forest I would live in would be a great mixture of plants and trees. And if I couldn't identify everything that grew there, I think I might even find a comfort in that.

I didn't know what to say to Anna, so I said, "Just smell that pine."

We walked up to the house, which isn't quite a house yet. She had explained this on the phone, and now she was explaining it again. "Everything's in the basement while the rest of the house is being built. It's sealed off, though, and warm."

A door was cut into the front blocks of the basement, which were all exposed. It was too small for Anna, as most doors are, so she needed to bow her head and pull in her shoulders to go through. I stopped behind her and waited. When she was inside, I said, "Anna, look." Then I imagined a door much smaller than my body, and I mimed my way through it. She was laughing as she watched, but her eyes were troubled. My imitation wasn't right; I could feel it, and she knew it too. And I imagined, even in this case, that she probably felt it was her own fault.

I tried to smooth it over by switching my attention to her place. Since it wasn't completely a house yet, it seemed to me a basement apartment. The floors and walls were cement. She had tried to warm it up with rugs and hangings, but still the color and the smell of basement blocks were everywhere.

"This is nice, Anna. And look! A wood stove."

"This little fellow," she said, tapping her knuckles on the pipe, "is going to heat the whole house eventually."

"Really!" I made a big deal of it because I knew she must have paid a lot of money for it, and because it was an uncommon thing in the city.

We drank Leinenkugels, brewed locally. The afternoon was so gray, we needed to turn the lights on, and I wondered if I could already feel so fuzzy from the beer. There was an illustration of an Indian maiden on the label with her arms winding up toward the neck. I was sitting on the couch, and Anna was sitting on an unpacked crate of books she had pulled up to the coffee table, her legs set wide apart with her feet flat on the floor. This is the way I remembered her sitting whenever she had pants on. After many of our exchanges she would say, "God, it's been a long time." She would punctuate this by jabbing a little knife into a nut-covered cheese ball she had made, spreading the cheese over another cracker. "Your hair's so short," she finally seemed comfortable enough to say to me.

"Once a harlequin, always a harlequin," I said deadpan.

"Harlequin?" she said. "I forget what that is."

We talked about Chicago, her old neighborhood and my old neighborhood, high school, and the times we slept at each other's houses. We didn't talk about her being a giant. In my family the policy was not to call attention to her differences, but we talked about her among ourselves. Grandma would cluck, "Poor Nanna," after each visit. I was only eight months younger than she, but even when we were babies, Anna was three times my size. I can still hear my aunt, calling after her as she ran into the yard to play, telling her to be careful of the other children, as if she were a Great Dane loping into the midst of us.

After Anna told me about her promotion and transfer to the post office in Waupaca, and I tried to explain the different ways I was able to make a living as a performer, there was a lull in the conversation, and the noise of Anna shifting her weight on the book box sounded the way a tree groans just before it falls.

"I hear you have a boyfriend." I knew this was going to embarrass her, but I didn't know how else to break into it.

She put her hands palms down on her knees. "Mike," she said.

"Tell me about him."

"He was one of the carpenters working on the house. We got friendly, and then we got close."

"Close?"

She hugged her knees, looked down, and smiled, like it was high school and this was her first boyfriend. I was the one with boyfriends in high school, not Anna. When I slept at her house, she'd pump me for every detail. "What did he say? What did you say?"

And when I first learned to kiss, I promised I would show her. Setting the stage for her that night was far more dramatic than any real kiss I'd had up to then. I put some red gym shorts over the lamp and a 45 on the player called "The Look of Love." Her cocker spaniel, Puddles, named because his eyes were muddy pools of devotion, watched the record go around. I had Anna sit on the edge of her bed while I went out of her room to come back in again. Then I walked up to where she was waiting and put a hand on each side of her big face, looked into her eyes and said, "I'm going to kiss you." She fell backwards on her bed laughing, which was a long fall for her and hard on the bed. Puddles jumped onto her stomach and barked at her. I climbed onto her and tried to throttle her, pleading for her to get serious. The needle came to the saddest part on the record. She sat up and set Puddles on the floor. I imagined I was the most serious kisser. I put my face close to hers. "The first one is the most important. Dry your mouth on your sleeve like I am; our lips have to be dry. Don't open your mouth and don't breathe."

Even then I knew it wasn't experience that Anna needed. She never had a boyfriend, she didn't pretend that she didn't want one. She approached her makeup like a science. She set her hair, painted her nails, pulled away her eyebrows with melted wax. I remember her identifying the shape of her face from a makeup diagram in *Seventeen* magazine. She was pleased to find that hers was heart-shaped and from then on would point out other people with heart-shaped faces whenever she saw them.

I looked at her with her tiny knife poised in the air. She was looking back at me, as if to say, "Don't think what you're thinking." She picked at the label of her beer bottle, sucked in her breath, then let it out. "None of you ever thought I'd be with anyone, did you?"

"Well, I think we expected it would be harder for you than for some people."

"It was. Mike's the first one, and Mom and Dad won't admit he exists."

"Why?"

"Because he's older, because he's been married more than once, because he's had some trouble along the way."

"He's not what they expected," I said.

"They didn't expect *anything*. But now that I have someone, they don't approve. They're looking into some book for the right person for me. You'd never find me in those books in the first place. But that's enough, we don't have to spend our whole wad on this kind of talk." She dug into the cheese ball. "It'll be good just to have some time together. I planned things out. We can change anything you don't like. Tonight I'll take you to a good fish fry."

"When am I going to meet Mike?"

"He's hoping to make it to the fry, but he's always stuck with a lot of overtime this part of the year, trying to get things built before the cold sets in. Tomorrow we're going to play an out-of-season softball game."

"Why are you going to play out of season?"

"Baldy's and Mary's, the bar that sponsors us, is having a closing-out party tomorrow night."

"A what?"

"When a bar closes, they can't sell their liquor to the next owner—tax reasons, or something like that. So they have a party and serve it free."

"Sounds as though people may be getting a bit drunk."

"A bit," she said. "Then on Sunday I want to take you to the zoo."

"Waupaca has a zoo?"

"Well, it's a little one, but yeah. It was a community effort. The Lion's Club sponsored the lions. Other groups sponsored other parts. The hardware store donated cans and cans of paint. The high school kids have done a lot of the painting and help keep up the grounds. I'm surprised you didn't hear about it in the papers last year."

"About what?"

"Someone tried to kill one of our elks."

"I'm not sure what elks are."

"They're like deer here, only bigger. I think these came from Wyoming."

"Someone tried to kill one?"

"Yeah, it was in the paper here for two weeks. A twelve-point male, a gorgeous animal, something they could have used in a beer commercial. Everybody was shook up. Someone went out there in the night and filled it full of arrows. Three of the high school kids found him when they were doing their chores in the morning. He was still alive, heaving with all these arrows in him, and blood coming out of his nostrils. One of the high schoolers ran to get help. When the vet and the sheriff and the kid came back, they found the other two kids fighting with each other. One of them, it seems, had been running in circles, trying to find a rock or something to end it for the buck. The other one was standing his ground over the thing, telling him he wouldn't let it be killed . . ."

"So the buck's okay?"

"Well, he's alive."

I'd been looking forward to a fry at a Wisconsin tavern: the knotty-pine kind we found when we summered at the lake as kids. I'd even mentioned this to Anna on the phone. But she chose a more modern place in Stevens Point, something I might have found on any strip in the Chicago area, a place with anchors on the walls, a circular salad buffet, and a huge fish-tank wall that separated the bar from the restaurant.

Anna had dressed up in an orange silk top she had sewn for herself, and orange earrings that looked diminutive on her ears. While she took great care to make up her face, I decided to follow the cue and bring my black suit out of the car, along with an orange bow tie I use in some of my performances.

We went together as an odd couple to the Schooner Inn, where it seems the locals were proud to come. Many of the ladies looked as though they had had Friday afternoon hair appointments. Anna, who wears a hairstyle reminiscent of the bouffant she wore in high school, had fluffed hers up, too. She didn't try to understate her visibility in the way she used to. She did not slouch or talk softly. And there was even one point where she spoke up to me as if I had said something on the subject that needed to be corrected. "All the upstairs doors in my house are going to be custom fit. It's expensive, but Mike figured out a shortcut, some way that he can use standard doors and add on to them." I realized she was still troubled by my imitation of her that afternoon.

In the salad line, she introduced me to two married women with perfectly stiff hairdos. She said, "This is my cousin Jane from Chicago. She's a visiting teacher at the college." She didn't tell them I was a mime, but I had a great inclination to waddle away from the buffet like Charlie Chaplin. When the ladies returned to their table, I could see they were telling their husbands what the story was. The husbands nodded, chewing, and went back to their steaks, reassured. I had the keen feeling throughout the evening that we were being watched, but whenever I looked around, people would look away.

Anna went into the bar several times to call Mike. Each time she came back to the table flushed. And when I finally asked her what was wrong, she said there were troublemakers in there. I tried to look through the aquarium wall of the bar to see who these troublemakers were, but all I could make out were the reflections in the glass of all the people in the lighted restaurant, as if they were sitting at little tables inside the tank, and the fish were swimming around them.

"I'll go make the call for you."

"Not with the bow tie and all," she said. "They're tanked up. They'll give you just as much of a hard time." So neither of us made another call to Mike, and he must have gotten tied up, because he never came.

I slept on the couch near the stove that night. Before I went to sleep, my thoughts wandered through the reasons I felt Anna had been showing me off at the restaurant. Maybe Anna thought that if the people in the restaurant could see that we had known each other for a long time, it would make her more real to them.

But did I know her? When I tried to do her in the door-way, it wasn't her *at all*. I realized it was only the smallness of the doorway that I had been imitating. I've done so many people and animals and household appliances, she should have been an easy subject.

When the adults weren't around, my brothers and sisters used to say, "Do Anna! Come on, do Anna!" But walking into a mime is like walking the length of a diving board. On the first bounce you know if you're going to pull it off. I tried a few times to make the approach with Anna, but couldn't get her. At the last minute, I would be unsure, and the sense I had of her would swell into something impossible and painful. I couldn't contain her. I fell asleep with that idea of standing on the edge of the diving board.

I've slept on couches before, in many people's houses, so when I heard Mike come in, I barely stirred. I heard the talking, and later I heard the bed moving in the other room. It registered that two people were making love. But in the dark there, almost asleep, I wasn't expecting to hear Anna's voice. I don't suppose it was so different from other women's cries at those times, but it was surely Anna's voice, and then I was awake and disturbed. For all the pleasure associated with it, there is also a beseeching quality in this sound. It has to do with coming to the edge of loneliness, being helpless in the face of it. There is that moment where you can be every-thing—or nothing—depending on how the other cares for you.

Even after they were quiet, I couldn't go back to sleep. What was it like to sleep with Anna? I should know; I'd spent enough nights in her room. I'd hook my arm over the side of her bed to avoid rolling into the crater her weight made in the mattress. Her bed was really two mattresses, a double bed and a single bed strapped crosswise to the end of it. Puddles would try to sleep between the two of us, but he would be delegated to the bottom of my side of the bed, since there was still a lot of room left there, and even though it was hard to see him in the dark, it seemed that he would be sitting up and watching us, as if he could make sense of our conversations.

She'd ask me questions, not wanting me to fall asleep. Questions about what I thought of her, and if I thought there was a way she could make friends. Because of her longing, I found the simplest ways to mislead Anna about the world. I painted possibilities for her that I didn't believe. It was just a matter of people getting to know her I would say—just a matter of time.

I had stopped sleeping over by my sophomore year. I was involved with my own friends. In Anna's junior year she maintained that her height was seven feet six inches. But I'm sure she was at least eight. She stopped going to school. My mother would say, "Call your cousin. She's depressed." I hated this. Sometimes my aunt would call. "Talk to Anna," my mother would whisper with her hand cupped over the phone. But I'd shake my head and wave her away.

Close to that time we were all shocked by a feature story about Anna in the *Tribune*. My mother saw it first. She pushed the paper in front of me at the breakfast table and stood up abruptly to call my aunt.

GIANT GIRL RESOLVED TO BECOME MONUMENT AT EL was the headline in the local section. My mother was on the phone, "Helen, they say she has been loitering in the El station for weeks. The same stop every day."

I stared, bleary-eyed, at a photograph of Anna in the paper. Anna, whom I had never thought of as part of the world, had been photographed at the busiest El stop in Chicago, and this picture was printed in hundreds of thousands of newspapers across the state.

"Helen!" my mother hissed into the phone. "You knew she wasn't in school. Didn't you wonder where she was? They say she stands right where the doors of the train open up. People have to walk around her to get off and on. She won't answer the guards when they question her."

I won't forget that photograph, Anna's back to the camera, her head and shoulders standing out of the crowd like a tree in a marsh. The absurdity—what made it a good photograph, and perhaps also a good story—was that not one face or body in the crowd was acknowledging Anna's enormous presence amidst them. Only the photograph recognized her power—the frozen image of the impression she made in a crowd of bodies, and how the crowd had no choice but to stream around her.

I still have that photo tucked away in my performance scrapbook. Even when I was sixteen, looking at that picture for the first time, I wanted my cousin to turn and face her photographer. I wanted to see her realize that, at least for that moment, she was being understood.

The publicity caused the police to be involved, and she ended up in a psychiatric unit. I don't know if they talked to her about the difficulties of being a giant. I'm sure they talked about "fitting in," because her behavior turned around. She got a starting position at the post office through Job Corps. While I went to college, Anna started a checking account, got raises and promotions. Eventually she was transferred to Waupaca in a supervisory position. I received a card from her in my dormitory one day. "Puddles died," she wrote, "and I'm still sad about it. I won't be getting another until I'm more settled here. This is a very small town. I see the same people over and over again and they see me. I figure eventually they're going to get used to me. . . ."

Anna and Mike were up before I was. They were making breakfast sounds, and the smell of coffee eventually drew me out from beneath my covers. The stove had gone too far down. I put my coat on and my wool socks because the cement was cold.

"Here's Jane, Mike," Anna said with great enthusiasm.

He was perhaps in his mid-forties, stout in his work clothes. His hands were short-fingered and ruddy around his coffee cup. I think he probably thought that he smiled. But it was really just a quick nod.

"Hello," he said, clearing his throat.

My short hair, after it has been slept on, tends to resemble that of a hedgehog's. I wished I could look less bizarre.

"Why don't you stoke that thing, Mike, while I start the eggs," Anna said.

The smell of bacon frying and the burning of new wood in the stove began working against the dampness of the cement, making it more like a home.

After breakfast, Anna showed me some wooden figures Mike had carved. Most of them were of wildlife: a squirrel running over the branch of a tree, a duck in flight. He was very good at conveying the motion in the bodies. Mike stood near the stove with his coffee cup and thumbed through the morning paper while we commented on each figure. But he was paying enough attention to realize we were finished because he pulled out another shoe box. "I've started to do some people too," he said. They were not as true to form, but there was an earnestness in some of his detail—an apron bunched in a woman's hand, a boy with bulging pockets—that made the figures appealing in their own way.

The Waupaca Township field is like other small-town athletic fields. It is in a prominent location on the highway into town. The town marker (POPULATION 3,862) is directly across the road. Except for the two cyclone-fence backstops, the two diamonds, two trash barrels, and a pair of six-tier bleachers, the park is grass. Standing in the field, one can see the surrounding businesses: an auto body shop in a large aluminum prefab building; a house with a lot full of school buses; a co-op with two grain elevators like shoulders on either side of it. Nothing was too far away. As people began gathering in the field, I imagined I could almost hear the doors of their houses slamming and cars starting as they left home to come there.

The sky was a gray canopy, bulging, heavy, and holding water over our heads. The few spectators and the team members stood in hopeful but uncertain postures; it could so surely rain in the next minute. Some of the people dusted the paths between bases with sand to make them less muddy.

Anna started the women's softball team three years ago. That was how she made her first friends in town. Mike is on the men's team. Since they were playing a casual game, the two teams mixed together. Mike and Anna were split up, so one or the other came to stand with me while they waited to bat. Mike brought me a plastic cup filled with beer, which was cold in my already cold hand. Anna was playing first base. She stood with her feet wide apart, calling at plays, yodeling and yelling, having a good time.

"How'd she ever find a mitt to fit her?" I asked Mike.

"Had it custom made," he said.

I was having trouble thinking of conversation. But there was always the game to watch, and Mike, though taciturn, was comfortable to be with. He had the slightest overbite, giving a touch of vulnerability to an otherwise rough face.

"She looks absolutely frightening," I said.

"Yeah." Mike laughed for the first time, letting his teeth jut out. "You gotta believe. No batter can run as fast as he might when he's got Anna waiting for him on first."

"You should carve her like that," I said.

He looked out at her from underneath the visor of his cap. "No," he said. I knew he wasn't finished. He seemed to need to spend a certain amount of time between words. "It would have to be Michelangelo," he said. "I bought a book of him in Milwaukee. It cost a hundred and twenty-five dollars."

He was right. We could see it in the muscles in her legs, as she strained forward waiting for the next play, and in her hands, which were both like a man's and a woman's and then like something else. Mike couldn't carve her into a figure that fit into a shoe box any more than I could make my own hands resemble hers simply by copying the movement of them.

When I was nine, I used to stand on the sidelines with my friends and watch her play touch football with the older boys. She was fascinating to all of us, and I played the part of her representative. "She's only ten," I would say, defying our family taboo about calling attention to her size. "She ate forty-seven pancakes for breakfast last Saturday." Anna stood for the possibility of myth in our daily lives. And for a while, I earned a certain admiration from the others because I knew her. This was when I first realized that I had a special knack for pointing out certain details in life. But eventually Anna was no longer an amusing wonder. She was as real and floundering in her adolescence as we were. And I suppose, where she was once an ideal, she later became only an exaggeration of what was painful in ourselves.

A thin man with long sideburns got caught in a pickle between first and second. Anna had the ball and shuffled toward him. He headed back to second. Anna whipped the ball over his head. He spun round and made it back to first before she could touch him or the base.

"Go, man! Get past that big hog!" A fist came up out of a group of five men standing on the sidelines.

"Jesus, what's he doing here?" Mike muttered.

"What? Who?" I said.

"The guy in the letter jacket."

After some of the men in the group shifted their positions, I could see the man in the letter jacket. Levis, boots, about thirty years old. The men around him were different ages, mostly older. Some wore hunting clothes, a couple wore jeans and flannel shirts like Mike. All of them seemed affected by the diffuse charisma of the younger man. One would chuckle and pass some joke on to another, who would laugh and spit on the ground. But the flow of their interaction seemed to originate always from this young man, who was very handsome. He stood with the tips of his fingers in his jeans' pockets. He kept his eyes on Anna, and he must

15

have been saying things under his breath, because the others would laugh and look toward her.

"What does he have to do with her?" I asked.

"Good question," Mike said. "He's a troublemaker. He's out for her. He was at the Schooner Inn last night. Didn't she tell you? This has been a problem since she came."

"What do you mean out for her?"

"Out for her. Can't let her be."

"Why?"

"Who knows? Anna's convinced herself that the guy applied for a job at the post office and didn't get it or something. That's not it, though. There've been others like him, drawn to her in a hateful way."

The game ended in rain, with Anna standing on first base. She stood out there longer than anyone, as if the umpire might change his mind. Her wet clothes were becoming translucent and defining the lines of her body. Her makeup was running. She would be embarrassed, I thought, if she could see how she looked. Mike and I waited for her, getting water in our beer. The man in the letter jacket stood around. The blond hair on his head got dark in the rain. His friends shifted their weight on their feet, blew on their hands. It was getting colder by the minute.

I took a Saturday afternoon nap in Anna's room, while she and Mike watched a football game on TV. I think the smell of the cement made me dream about the El station. I was walking along the tracks. Someone had sent me to find Anna. I still hadn't found her but met the man in the letter jacket everywhere, coming down the stairs, hoisting himself up onto the platform from the tracks. I spent the whole dream trying to get to her before he did.

Anna woke me hours later. She had a bag of burgers and some milk. "You've slept a long time. Fill your stomach now, or you won't keep up with the drinking tonight."

It was dark, and I was groggy and disoriented. "Where's Mike?"

"He has a roof in Stevens Point to finish. He'll meet us later."

Anna and I went early to the closing-out party. This way we were able to get a table before the crowds piled in. I thought I had known what to expect: there would be more men than women, many farmers and mill workers. I expected that people would get very drunk, and I'd get a little drunk and watch them. I looked forward to it. I hadn't expected to get involved.

Baldy's and Mary's was downtown. When we came to the door, Anna stopped for a minute and adjusted herself. She brought out a mirror that looked as tiny as a postage stamp in her hand, checked her lips, her eyes, and the blush on her cheeks. Cars, driving by, made a sticky sound on the wet pavement. A banner cut out of a bed sheet with the word WELCOME hung over the door. The paint was running. Pale red drops of water beaded from the edges and dripped on the sidewalk. When Anna opened the door, there was a vacuum sound like one's ears being unclogged.

The bar was dark. We were the first ones there. As we walked, the sound of our heels echoed over the wooden floor. There was one long bar with a mirror behind it. The bartender was bald, as I would have expected. He watched Anna and me as we came in. "Wait, I'll introduce you," she said. During her introductions, Baldy looked at me with the studied indifference I've seen in many bartenders. But he had small, brown, wary eyes. Mary, a wiry, middle-aged woman, wearing a T-shirt and an apron, pointed her finger like she was shooting us and went on working at a grill behind the bar. I expected this was another friendly sort of bartender's greeting.

"Baldy, your bottles are already gone?" Anna said, gesturing toward the empty shelves in front of the mirror.

He looked up at Anna. "We'd a gone crazy—pouring out individual drinks. We made Wapatui."

17

There were five tables on the floor constructed out of wooden cable spools. Two stacked together made them high enough to put stools around them. In the center of each table was a steel tub. We walked over to one of the tables and looked into the tub.

"What's in here?" Anna called back to the bar.

"Everything," Baldy answered.

It was hard to tell what color the punch was. It seemed a sort of amber red. Maraschino cherries and canned pineapple rings floated in it. As we settled onto stools, Anna pulled two plastic cups from a stack and filled them with a ladle. It tasted sweet and very strong.

We were joined shortly by three young women, each of them wearing a shoulder bag. They didn't remove their purses, as if they hadn't decided they would stay. Anna knew one of them slightly. A young man, whom no one knew, and his girlfriend sat down. The last two stools were taken by an older man and his wife.

People kept coming through the doors. I realized I'd better pace my drinking. The liquor was much stronger than it tasted. Anna huddled over me, and we were able to talk in the privacy of the noise. We became used to people standing near our table reaching around us to fill their glasses.

"What do you think?" Anna asked.

"It's wild. How come they're selling out?"

"Baldy's had two heart attacks. Mary gave him an ultimatum—no bar, or no wife."

Sometimes we were quiet, and I could listen to the snatches of conversation about gardens, or factories, or casseroles. Sometimes there would be hick Wisconsin syntax shouted across the room. "Com'on over—why don't cha, hey?" and I'd want to nudge Anna to share the distinction between this place and Chicago. But then I remembered that Anna felt no kinship for Chicago. She was less a part of that than I was of this.

"Do you like Mike?" She was bending close to my ear.

"Yeah," I shouted.

I was telling Anna about the Mardi Gras in New Orleans,

because the crowd reminded me of my time there. She began to seem distracted as I was talking. We were facing the bar, and she kept looking in the mirror behind it. I finally looked into the mirror too. It was the man in the letter jacket. He was leaning over his glass on the bar, but he was watching Anna. She had turned away from him and was laughing with the girl next to her—trying to ignore him. His cronies were standing around him on the floor, but he had his back to them. They were all laughing and drinking together. One or another would look over at him, make some mental note, and then look again into his drink.

Anna seemed resolved to ignore him. She had struck up a conversation with the husband and wife. I stared at him, trying to lock his eyes, the way people will do with cats. But his eyes wouldn't leave Anna. I looked around the room. Little dramas were developing throughout the crowd that wouldn't have happened an hour ago. A woman crying in her hand while her boyfriend tried to talk to her. A young man pleading into the pay phone, waiting, nodding his head, opening and closing his fist against the wall. Many people making a point with each other, emphatically pointing their fingers, carefully slurring the words, trying to explain something.

Anna wasn't drunk. It took a lot to get her there because of her size. I was on my way. So was the man in the letter jacket. Now he was leaning his back against the bar and facing us. He had begun to mix with his friends again. They all seemed glad of it. Then I heard what he was saying.

"What a sow! Look at her. They shouldn't let things like that out of the cave."

Anna's hand was tight around her glass. He was getting louder.

"Hey! You big sexy thing. Hey! Look at me when I talk to you." Anna wouldn't look up, but I did. He was quiet, weaving a little on his feet, waiting for Anna to look at him. He began chipping little pieces off his plastic cup, throwing them in her direction. The woman next to me was murmuring her disapproval to her husband.

"Somebody should round that fellow up," the husband said.

The young couple watched the man in the letter jacket the way they might watch someone on TV. The three women next to Anna looked down at their hands.

The little pieces of plastic were collecting in Anna's hair. I looked over at Baldy. He had decided he wasn't going to do anything yet. He had a heart condition. The man in the letter jacket had chipped away his entire cup—started a new one. Anna's hair was full of the pieces. She wouldn't look up. People all around us were getting drunk. Perhaps it seemed this was just a part of it.

Anna clamped the table edge so hard there were white streaks on the top of her hands. I felt sick.

"I have to go to the bathroom."

Anna pinned my wrist to the table. "Don't go."

I broke away, grabbed my bag, and pushed through the crowd to the ladies' room. A woman was coming out of the stall. I shoved ahead of the other women in line, said, "Let me by. I'm going to be sick!" Closed myself in the stall, leaned over the toilet. Nothing would come. There was sweat in my eyes, my face was burning. I kept thinking about Anna and how she would bear anything—she would bear it until he was all played out. She had hopes for this town, thought she could rely on her own durability, just like she relied on that little stove to heat her house. I'm sure she believed it was just a matter of time before most of them stopped being afraid of her. But it was taking too long; it hurt her. It was hurting me, and reasons as simple as these are the reasons that make you brave.

Mime is an art of absorption. If one day I find that I imitate a rooster rather well, it means that somewhere along the lines of my life I have seen roosters and taken in the impressions they have made. But I mustn't think too much about those roosters, not about why they lift their feet in a certain way or what they can see out of each side of their head, because all those thoughts confuse me and cause me to lose confidence in my particular talent. This has seemed excuse

20

enough for my detachment. But there's been another reason—I've been afraid that if I somehow let what I watched become a part of me in more than a superficial way, I would find too much there to absorb to know what to do with and it would hurt me.

I left the stall and pushed ahead of the women at the sink. I rubbed cold water over my face, dried it with my sleeve. In my bag I found my tin of whiteface, my grease pencils. The white spread quickly, changed my face to nothing. A girl in the corner said, "What's she doing?" I put the little bit of red on my mouth, a long vertical line through each of my eyes. I pressed my bag into the arms of a girl in the corner and told her to watch it for me.

I moved through the crowd quickly, before anyone had a chance to really see me. I'd see surprise begin to register on a man or woman's face; then I was past them.

The man in the letter jacket was still standing a few paces in front of our table. His feet were apart. He was pointing at Anna. His friends had backed away from him. His litany sounded frightening, even from a distance. My face was turned so he couldn't see it. One of the girls at the table gasped and covered her mouth when I stepped up from the rung of her stool onto the table. "Hey!" he shouted. I stood with my back to him facing Anna.

The voices in the crowd were still rubbing together, like pieces in an engine. She looked up at me. With my hands, I made a square around my face. A face just for her. I made the sign for a tear. I gave my face the expression of great sadness, none of which could be said in words. It was all in my face, what I gave to Anna.

He was shouting into my back. I could hear him. As I looked at Anna, he seemed so weak compared to her. But I didn't think so much about him. I wasn't thinking about how some people need to be the master of their world—not just their life, but their little world and every perceivable object in it—and how that is another difference between people and animals. An animal would never just destroy something because he didn't understand it. Or misunderstand it only because it was different, or because it was something great and beautiful, but not exactly the same as itself. Or how the difference can be as small as the difference between a man and a woman. But the differences were all there, and they made up the engine in that room, and that was the sound like a roar in my ears. I was standing, drunk, on a table in a Wisconsin bar. Not too drunk to know it, but drunk enough to do what I was doing. And everyone else was drunk. But I didn't think about everyone else, how all of us in that room, including me, are unsettled by our own humanity, how we bleed it but can't stand the sight of it.

So, I have to say again that, standing there facing Anna, I wasn't thinking. I was a mime, on the edge of the diving board, poised for a backward dive. And when I had looked at her long enough, I was ready to take in the man in the letter jacket. He kept shouting. I could feel him behind me. But it really didn't matter, because many of his traits I'd absorbed before I'd ever seen him. I mean they weren't unique to him. I was ready to do him. As I turned, I felt I had his body now. And when I faced him, I *was* him; if a man could be a clenched fist with white knuckles that held nothing, that's what he was. It was right.

I hadn't seen anything after I had turned on the man. In that moment my vision had reversed, like a movie camera turned into a projector. I became a short film of his miserable life. I became handsome, gave myself a letter jacket, stood in the center of everything, just the way he did; and then slowly, I became ugly, just the way he was, the way a lot of us are. The engine sound died. No crowd, just one man screaming— a faraway call like an angry crow's. The air was being pushed out of me. I felt faint, then weightless.

Anna said he had lunged for my legs. She had picked me up by the waist and carried me out the backdoor of the bar. She carried me to an abandoned pickup, which was leaning against a wet telephone pole. She pulled me up with her into the back. I had to hang over the side to vomit something that had been creeping up my esophagus. I coughed and cried, came back to where Anna was and punched her in the chest. She laughed and put her hands around my shoulders.

"That was good," she said.

I was still crying. "When are we going to be happy, Anna?" I was trying to find a place in the truck bed to lay my head. And I think I was trying to find a way to ask her forgiveness. But all I could say was, "I hate the rain. It feels like it's been raining for weeks." Sometimes I cry like that when I've been drinking and when I become too much a part of the world.

Now I'm sitting in the car in front of the Waupaca County jail. And I'm waiting for Anna. For a moment I had a fantasy that she might come back down those steps as an average-sized person, and I tried to imagine what would be different about the way we were together. But I realized that was a trick I was playing on myself, as usual, making things simpler than they are or even should be.

Mike's in jail because he and some of his friends went back to the bar to fight for Anna. The man in the letter jacket had already vanished before he got there. So they ended up fighting with everyone, making it into a kind of free-for-all. Anna says he feels like a jerk. But I think if he had the option, he would have made a life-size sculpture of Anna as beautiful as a Michelangelo and set it up in the middle of Baldy's and Mary's. I know how it feels to want to show everyone exactly what is so hard to see.

Those who were in that crowd at Baldy's and Mary's will be talking about this for weeks. Most of them will say the man in the letter jacket started it. Some will think it was me, or they'll think it was Mike. No one would blame Anna, but many are angry with her without knowing why. "My God! She's a human being," my grandmother used to say. It was a refrain we heard so regularly it stopped having meaning. And as long as she was out of our lives, in some other place, the enormous fact of her couldn't hurt us. But the fact has always been in us.

And whatever is happening with Mike, Anna still intends to show me the zoo. "I'm so tired," I'll tell her, "and don't feel like looking at another thing." But I know her heart is set on showing me these places. The leaves are still dripping down the windshield, gathering one by one in my view, and it's all silence here except for that dripping. She tells me that the kids have painted everything on the zoo grounds bright colors, the picnic tables and even the tree stumps. We'll see lions, she says, peacocks, reindeer, the heroic elk.

SUPERSTITIONS

Frances slept in her clothes. This was a recent practice she had adopted from Jimmy after finding him one morning under his covers outfitted in his miniature army costume. As he popped out of his covers and swung his weedy legs over the bed, his sister was further puzzled to see his feet still shod in his little army boots.

"Jimmy, they're muddy."

He had looked at his dangling feet and reached down to flick a piece of dirt encrusted in the soles of his boots.

"Why did you wear play clothes to bed?"

"I always do." He hopped off his bed and began tapping his boot against the bedstead, causing the mud to flake off in a pile on the floor.

"Well, I know you didn't always. Why do you want to?"

"Simple, Franny, that way I'm ready to play as soon as I wake up."

Now for the last three days, Frances had slept in her red Buster Brown shirt and her light blue cutoffs. As she meandered into wakefulness, she found a specific comfort in fingering the familiar clothing.

It was an early June morning, a week into the summer vacation. Frances held on to her sleep even as the sun came into her bedroom and lay across her forehead like a warm rag. But when the light became so bright that she needed to cover her eyes with her arm, she woke up and rolled onto one elbow so she could rest her chin on the window ledge by her bed. She blinked her eyes. From two stories up the grass looked wavy like water.

Frances turned from the window and looked around the squareness of her room. Reassured that she had gone no-where else in the night, she slipped out of her tight covers from the top. This was another time-saving trick Jimmy had taught her. He theorized that little kids who got in from the top and out from the top never had to make their beds. "Just punch the pillow and that is that."

She stood for a moment by the bed and looked out at the day-to-be. In the sky two swallows spiraled erratically down-ward. They looked more to be falling than flying. Away from the window she turned to face the half-open door.

She closed her eyes and touched her fingers to the wall just above her bedpost, then walked like this, eyes closed, her one hand guiding her along the wall out of her room and down the hall. She was apprehensive as she brushed on toward the attic, because if she were to find it had been left open, it would be a bad sign that she couldn't change. Her hand hesitated at the doorway molding as a draft wafted over the little hairs on her wrist. The door was open. She passed her hand over empty space, making believe there was a door there. This didn't help, and the panic she had dreaded surged up from her stomach, making her run blindly down the hall until she was at the opening of the stairway. She bent over to feel where the first step began and sat down on the landing. Her eyes were still closed, she pressed them against her knees, and the pressure created white lights under her eyelids.

This ritual of the blind walk through the upstairs hall was one Frances had adopted herself. She had not taught it to Jimmy because it made no sense. Just as it made no sense to be afraid of an open attic. It was something she had begun, and now she was compelled to continue.

Frances sat at the top of the stairs with her eyes pressed against her knees. Something bad was going to happen, and there was nothing she could do about it. She was trying not to think about the attic, and she wished she had never made up the rule. She muttered aloud, "I just made it up. It's silly, so nothing can happen."

Frances found no one in the kitchen, but she heard sounds indicating that the others were out of bed. Her father was at work. Her mother was in the sewing room in the basement. She could hear the steady whirr of the machine, and then it stopped, shortly to be replaced by the sound of scissors snipping. The racket of cartoons was coming from the TV room along with Jimmy's shrill giggles. Frances chose a firm banana from the bunch on the counter and went to join her brother.

Frances once heard her mother confide to Mrs. Benson that Jimmy was hyperactive. Her grandmother called him high-strung. Frances liked to watch his green eyes when they danced on the wake of one of his ideas. His freckles, too, they danced. Or it seemed to Frances, at least, that they moved about on his face, and as long as she needed to blink she would never be sure.

Jimmy's black hair was controlled by some strange static that caused it to stand up in little tufts, always, as if he had just taken off a wool stocking cap. His father would wet it and comb it, saying, "Kiddo, we are going to train your hair to stay put." But half an hour later Jimmy's hair would be sticking up all over again.

Frances believed that Jimmy had more God-given life than she had. It was the bravery that made the difference. He had more life to risk than she had, and she stayed close to him for need of the bravery.

Of the two, Frances thought she was the stronger. She was tall with the dark skin of her Indian grandmother. Jimmy was fair, his skin translucent, the veins lying close to the surface. He was slight and smaller than he should be for his age. Sometimes she would use this against him and say, "I'm ten and you're a puny eight-year-old." But that was only when she felt the least brave in the face of him. The times she did feel truly stronger, she said nothing. Sometimes as they sat arm against arm on the sofa, and he looked ahead distracted by the TV, she would trace the veins in his fine hand with her finger, and that quiet tenderness would come over her. She would move closer to him and cover his whole arm with her own, laying her brown hand over his so each of her fingers covered one of his, and nothing was left exposed.

His energy overflowed the confines of his body sometimes, like popcorn popping out of a pot too small. On the day that the Bensons' cat had kittens, Jimmy had come running up the back-porch steps where Frances and her mother sat trimming rhubarb. He stopped, breathless, on the top step, making little hops and shaking in the shoulders. He opened his mouth but could only stutter, "The, the ca . . . c."

Their mother said, "Now, Jimmy, calm down."

He made a short whistling sound through his skinny nose and tried again. "Th . . . th . . . th . . . ."

"Jimmy," their mother said crossly. "Stop. Think about what you are trying to say."

Then he did stop, stopped hopping; he stopped shaking, while his eyes ceased to dance and rolled back as though to see what he was trying to say. He fell then, crumpled down like a kite that lost its wind. His tremors began before their mother reached him, and she hesitated as though she was afraid to touch him. Frances looked down from the top step at her brother's closed eyes. She could see violent movement beneath the faint blue skin of his eyelids. In a moment he was calm. When he opened his eyes, they were dull, duller than the time he had been sleeping and Frances had peeled his eyes open to see what was in there.

Jimmy took two different pills now to control his seizures. Their mother kept the bottles stored in a square Tupperware container up in the kitchen cupboard next to the

Kool-Aid packages and the Green Stamps. Twice Frances had climbed on the counter to look at the pills. She took them out of their bottles to touch them, and the second time she almost took one, but she decided against it and put them back.

Jimmy didn't have any more big seizures. But once in a while he had a little one, and he would nod over his dinner plate. He'd snap his head up just in time and then just go on as though nothing had happened. Sometimes his eyes would close while he was watching television, and if Frances saw him, she would wonder how much he had missed. Jimmy himself seemed the least concerned about it.

Their mother worried, and she let Frances know that it was the daughter's job to worry when the mother was not around. So Frances put this worry in the back of her head with all her other worries. Though, after a while, she did not think specifically about his seizures, the fear she felt that first day she had seen him lose himself hovered in her dreams—dreams of reaching for him before he fell into some blackness and out of her dream. Her nightmares were forgotten in the daytime, but she began to feel more irritated with him, concerned about his uncontrollable ways. And he didn't like it when she cared so much, called her "Bossy" and "Miss Big Business Beeswax."

Frances leaned against the TV room doorway. She peeled her banana and watched her brother's back. He sat forward in the rocker, his boots just touching the floor. A large bowl of cereal was perched on his knees. She couldn't see his face, but she knew what he looked like. His eyes were opened wide, absorbed, connected to the action on the television, and his mouth was the part of him eating cereal, eating vigorously. Sometimes he would forget, laugh at the cartoon, and milk would dribble out of the corner of his mouth.

Frances waited for Jimmy to finish with his cereal. Then she placed her banana skin in the wastebasket by the door, crouched over, and crept up behind his rocker. Gently, she took hold of the top of his chair and placed each of her bare feet over the rockers. She leaned back, causing her little brother to slide back in the chair and look up at her. "Gimme a ride, Jimmy."

"Well, Jell-O, Franny. It's about time."

She moved about the room, then stopped to stand a bit in front of the television so he would pay attention to her.

"Is it going to be a TV day?" she challenged.

"No way, Ray!" Jimmy twisted around in his chair so that his head was soon hanging where his feet had been and his skinny feet were poked through the back rungs of the chair. His hands, still holding the cereal bowl, dangled close to the floor. Then he rocked himself just enough to set the bowl down.

"What are we going to do?" She was getting impatient.

"War games," he said.

"What kind?"

"We're going to take an important bridge."

"Jimmy, there is only one bridge, and we already took it."

"Not this one, we didn't."

"Where is it?"

Jimmy gave an upside-down smile, grunted; his face was red with little white patches where the veins stood out on his forehead.

"Is it over the river? Jimmy! Stop doing that! You're all purple. Answer me, is it over the river?" She grabbed his arms, pulling him out of the chair onto the floor. He breathed heavily and giggled a bit as his face faded to a more agreeable shade. Frances plopped herself into the rocker and began rocking, giving his bony butt a light kick every time she rocked forward. "For the last time, is it over the river?"

"Don't worry. I'll show you," he said, a smug expression on his face.

"So I suppose that means you are going to be the leader?"

"Yeah," he said, grabbing her ankles and pretending to bite them.

"Jimmy, you were the leader yesterday."

"No, I wasn't. Scotty Tanner was."

"Well, let's both be leaders," she said.

"We can't both be. I'll be the leader before the bridge, and you be the leader after the bridge."

"We need more men," she said, as she fantasized being the leader of a larger group.

"Nope. This is a secret maneuver. We can't have everybody in the neighborhood knowing about it."

"Oh, big deal."

"Hey! You're supposed to obey me now."

"Okay, okay, so let's go," she surrendered, giving him one last kick from the rocker.

This last kick spurred Jimmy, and he blasted up from the floor in one swift movement. He stood in front of Frances, his legs spread with his little knees hyperextended in back. She knew immediately, by looking at him, that he was already playing. He was playing soldier.

He pulled his thumbs through the empty belt loops of his fatigue pants and pressed his other four knuckles into his hips. As he stared her down, Frances resisted. Her eyes started to laugh at him. She wanted to protest and call him silly. But the largest part of her wanted to be drawn into his fantasy, and this turned her expression to expectation. She waited.

Jimmy leaned her chair back. "All right then, we're going to take an important bridge today. It's over the river, like you thought, but it's not a common bridge. I think, mostly, that people don't know about it. So once we take it, it'll be our bridge, and the territory on the other side'll be our territory. Now, I'll get the supplies, and you tell the home office."

Frances went down the basement stairs to her mother's sewing room. Her mother, the home officer, surveyed Frances from across her sewing table and then bowed to her sewing again.

"Frances, when are you going to change your clothes?"

"I don't know."

"Well, I hope you'll know soon."

Her mother concentrated on changing the needle in her machine.

"Mom?"

"Mm, hmm?"

"Jimmy and I are going out to play."

"Where is out?"

"Oh, you know."

"I know that you are to stay away from the banks. Stay up on the trails. Before you go, take this up to Jimmy." She handed Frances an old leather belt of their father's, trimmed down with extra holes poked into it. "Tell him to wear it. I have had enough of droopy drawers and everybody in the neighborhood seeing where his legs begin." Her mother looked over her sewing glasses to make the point, then resumed her work.

Frances held the belt in her hand. But instead of moving away, back to Jimmy, she waited as though her mother might have something more to give her. She leaned against the sewing table.

"Frances, don't jiggle the table. How can I sew a straight line?"

"Mom?"

"Hmm?" Her mother now had pins between her lips.

"Sister Margaret Therase said that God knows all our thoughts the very second that we think them."

"Mm, hmm." Her mother bent her head close to the sewing machine needle and pushed a black thread through the tiny hole.

"Sometimes I have bad thoughts. I don't mean to think them, but, you know, they just come to me, and then, I suppose, He knows. I try to take it back . . ."

"Take what back?" her mother mumbled, with the pins still between her lips.

"The bad thoughts." Frances moved up to her mother and plucked the three pins altogether out of her mouth. "Now, talk to me."

"Well, Frances, if it's important, why don't you start

from the beginning and try to make yourself a little more clear?"

Frances sighed, closed one eye, looked at her mother. "Sometimes I have bad thoughts." She announced this sentence, each word stated loudly and with long pauses in between, as though her mother might be hard of hearing or slow-witted. "I don't think them on purpose, and I wish that God would just forget about them so that I won't be in trouble."

"Well, just tell God you're sorry. Go to Saturday confession." Her mother smiled at Frances.

"Nooo," Frances bleated. "Not those kinds of bad thoughts, not sinful or mean ones."

"Are you talking about impure thoughts?"

"Ahh!"

"Well, honey, you're not being very clear then. Can't you give me an example?"

Frances cleared her throat. "Okay, we'll be riding in the car. We're passing underneath the stoplight, and just then the stoplight changes to yellow. Well, the first time that happened to us, I got the bad thought."

"What bad thought?"

"Just that it is bad luck to be under the light when you can't see it change to yellow, and if I ever do that again, something bad will happen."

"Like what will happen, Frances? Would we be in a car accident then?"

Frances pictured in her mind what a car accident might be like. She looked up at the ceiling to see what else the bad thing might be.

"I don't know, Mom. Bad is bad. I just get scared. I think the thought about something not going the right way, and then the next thing I think is, Oh, no, now God knows it, and he is going to make it a rule."

"A rule?"

"Yes, a rule! A rule!" Frances pulled at the bottom of her red knit shirt with her hands and stretched it almost to the bottom of her shorts as she strained to be clear. "I make the rule up first, which isn't so bad, but if God hears it, and you know he always does, he's the one that can make the bad thing happen. Do you see?"

"No."

Frances leaned her elbows on the sewing table and cradled her forehead in her hands. She thought about lying in her bed at night and how the hall light shone in through her door. She couldn't sleep with the light shining in her eyes, but she was afraid to sleep in the dark, too. She remembered when she had first found the solution to the problem. She had gotten up and moved the door to the position of being exactly half-open and half-closed. But as soon as she had done that, a new rule had entered her consciousness. Exactly in the middle, that was what the rule had been after that. From then on she had to remember to keep the door exactly in the middle when she went to bed, or somehow it would be bad luck.

Frances felt her mother touch her elbow, and she heard her say, "Tell me."

She looked up, still holding her chin in her hand and said, "Like for instance, the bedroom door has to be half-open. That's not a bad one though, not as bad as the stoplight one anyway. I suppose the bigger the bad luck, the worse the bad thing that is going to happen. I think little ones hardly count, but I do them just the same to be safe."

"Give me an example of a little one."

"Eating M&M's."

"What about M&M's, for heaven sakes?" her mother asked.

"I have to eat them in order. I lay them all out in rows by color. I eat the M&M's from the longer rows until all the rows are the same length as the shortest row." Frances was finding this a difficult process to explain. "In other words, until there is the same number of each color left. Then I eat one from the red row, one from yellow, one from the brown, never changing the order, until they're all gone."

"Frances, look at me. Those rules you are worried about

are just superstitions, like walking under ladders and breaking mirrors. Lord knows why you have to make up your own. Maybe we all do at one time or other."

Frances looked at her mother, and her mother looked back kindly through her sewing glasses. Frances looked down again at Jimmy's belt and felt the sadness of being misunderstood. "Mom?"

"What, dear?" she said as she leaned toward the sewing machine and pushed the blue fabric under the needle.

"I had a bad superstition this morning, and I just can't help feeling that God is going to take me up on it."

"But God is good," her mother said. "Don't worry about that."

Frances heard Jimmy rattling the basement stair railing, sending her signals that he was waiting for her to join him. Their mother heard him too. She raised her head from her work and shouted above to the first floor. "Jimmy! There is no point in sneaking around. I know about your little expedition to the river, and all I can say—and I've told Frances, too—is that you are to stay on the upper trails."

Jimmy made high, whining noises like the sounds of radio frequency and shouted back down the basement, "I can't read you—am experiencing interference."

"Well, you better read me, fella," she called back.

They heard Jimmy shout, "AWOL!"

"When you go up there, tell your brother no more shouting."

Frances didn't answer her. Still leaning on the table, she spent a lot of time sticking each of the pins that she still held into her mother's pincushion.

Her mother glanced up. "You're such a moody bird, Frances." Frances rolled her eyes and walked away from the sewing table with a sort of underhanded wave. It was a wave to half-say good-bye and to half-say get lost. She stomped up the stairs to let her mother know that she was leaving and to let her brother know that she was coming.

Jimmy was sitting on the top step. His legs on the second step were jiggling up and down in his little army boots.

Jimmy's body commotion had caused several of the supply items to fall from his lap. Frances said, "Jeez, Jimmy," as she alternately climbed the last few steps and picked up the fallen objects. She picked up one of her high-top tennis shoes. Jimmy had painted it completely black with a Magic Marker so the pair would match his army boots. There was also a little tin compass, which always said North unless someone shook it—then it said Northwest. The last thing was a long, narrow strip of paper that had a representation of the Mississippi River running down it. Jimmy had cut this out of a larger map of the United States in their family atlas. Frances wished that he would throw it away. It was hardly an aid to their minute explorations of the river.

While Frances put her shoes on, Jimmy stood in the back hallway, listing aloud the supplies as he stuck them in his baggy pockets. "Peanut butter and grahams, compass, map, twine, penlight, jackknife, a banana for me, and here is a banana for you."

Frances stood up, took the banana that Jimmy was handing her, and stuck it in the elastic of her shorts. "Here, Mom wants you to wear this," she said, while threading Jimmy's new belt through his belt loops.

"Nice." He hummed a note of pleasure, stuck his banana through his belt and patted it as though it was a pistol. "Ready, Eddy?" Jimmy asked Frances.

"You bet, pet." Frances stretched her brown arms over his little shoulders and walked him backward out of the back screen door.

On the stoop they both leaned down to pick up their walking sticks. Jimmy had smoothed them out by rubbing them against the concrete driveway. That was in the spring, and now the two sticks had become a part of their routine. Frances was fond of her stick; she liked its sanded softness. She thought, as she gripped the stick and walked with Jimmy out of the backyard, that the stick made being outside easier. It was not a superstition. Her stick was useful. She could test the depth of puddles before walking through them, turn night crawlers over on the sidewalk without getting the slime on her fingers. She could knock crab apples out of the trees, and she could knock any wise guy in the neighborhood if need be.

Jimmy cherished his stick as an object of fantasy. Frances couldn't keep up with its many identities: a sword, a staff, a laser gun. When Jimmy wanted to pretend sword fighting with her, she would resist, saying, "I don't want to break my stick."

They walked a short distance along the back fences of the neighboring yards and turned from the alley onto the sidewalk. They headed for the river, which was five straight blocks away. The sun was warm and persistent with promises to shine over everything by noon. Frances stood flat-footed for a moment, pulling up the heat of the sidewalk through her tennis shoes.

Outside, Jimmy forgot himself completely. Frances forgot herself occasionally. She was aware of certain precautions, like not looking into the sun too long.

"Crack, Jimmy, don't step on the crack!"

"Crack smack."

"You'll break somebody's back!"

"Not mine."

"Somebody's. Just play the game. Play it for me."

"Okay, crack shmack, crack smack," and he jumped on every crack he could see.

"Jimmy!" She grabbed him around the waist tightly with her chin between his shoulder blades. He giggled, then stopped. Frances breathed warm breaths through the shirt on his back. He made low growling sounds like a captured lion.

Frances held Jimmy in a grip that said, You can't get away. She might have held him forever, but he slumped down, making himself deadweight in her arms. He hummed a teasing little tune between his teeth. And while Frances became nervous about his tune, he slumped down just far enough to dangle his hands close to the inside of her knees. Then, when he had gained his position, he tickled her relentlessly there. They both fell to the grass boulevard next to the sidewalk and laughed until they ached. When they rolled away from each other onto their backs, she found banana smashed on the front of her shorts and shirt.

Frances scraped the mash disgustedly off of her clothes and wiped it onto the grass with her fingers. She saw that Jimmy's banana had also exploded at the top, and she caught him by the arm, as he rolled toward her, to save him from the mess.

"Watch out for the banana."

"Eyugh!" Jimmy feigned repulsion, and then, making his eyes wicked, he took the banana in his hands like a cake decorator and squeezed it onto her bare leg.

"God! You're such a goon. Why do I ever think we can be friends?"

Flat on her back, Frances draped her arm across her brow and looked at the sky. The sun was indeed getting higher, and she moved her arm over her eyes to block its glare. The weight of her arm against her eyelids brought the white lights back again, and she remembered the morning's early omen. "Let's go to the Connor wading pool instead," she said, without looking at him.

"No, I'm going to the bridge."

The day wasn't going her way, though she wasn't sure what her way would be. She was just feeling hot and listless.

"I don't want to go." She yanked the grass by her sides and looked at the sky again. Jimmy stood up to leave. There was no argument. She turned on her side a little to watch him, and as he walked away, he turned his black, bristly head ever so slightly and spoke the word that controlled her.

"Chicken."

She lay there with her face in the grass, saw a small black ant crawling with quivering effort up one of the narrow blades. After waiting for what she perceived as a stubborn enough amount of time, she stood up and followed him.

On the sidewalk ahead she could barely make out the figure of Jimmy with his stick by his side. She wasn't worried about catching up with him eventually. At least she knew she would along the river bank somewhere. She began to smell the river in the warm air as she walked forward. Her gradual anticipation of its sun-glinted surface took the place, step by step, of her former negative disposition. She forgot temporarily about the cracks in the sidewalk.

The river was the biggest thing Frances knew about. It frustrated her that Jimmy didn't understand how big it was. To him, it was a skinny thing cut out of the atlas, and she believed that he didn't think it had much to do with the rest of the country now that he had cut it out of there and kept it folded up in his pocket. They had argued about its size, but Jimmy still insisted that Lake Minnetonka was much bigger.

Once they crossed University Avenue, it was only a block to the river. As she waited there for traffic to pass, she studied a billboard posted on a building across the street. It was a picture of three men with various kinds of headgear and uniforms. The caption in the lower right-hand corner simply said, "Join the Army." She thought of Jimmy, whom she had lost sight of a few blocks back. Now she wasn't so sure she would catch up with him before he took off on his mission. What if she lost him? She pulled her stick up under her arm and broke into a run. She ran between cars to the other side of the street. Her legs were strong, and the spring in her calves excited the rest of her body.

When Frances came finally to the bluff, she felt small. The cityscape loomed at her from the other side of the river. In the foreground, along the opposite bank, there were many structures of industry—cranes, cables, electrical towers, black skeletal constructions that were menacing to Frances, even in the daytime.

Frances peered over the bluff and called down to the trails, but her voice was lost in the river, and Jimmy didn't answer. She suspected he'd taken the lower trails closest to the water where a bridge might be found. She descended steep stone steps and then made her way along the path beside the water. Next she chose a path that took her higher up to the middle ground. There she stopped and looked around her.

The bluffs overhead were built up with limestone walls to support the mill buildings on top. The numerous tunnels that pierced the upper walls, once used for drainage, were cracked and dry. A pair of pigeons fluttered out of one of these cavelike openings, and their racket startled her. She bent her head back to watch them. The sun behind them glared in her eyes so that her vision was shattered a moment with white specks. "Jimmy!" Where was he? She called again, her voice bouncing off the wall. She thought she heard something, but then it was lost. Then she was sure she had heard it. A small faint, "Hey!" He was above somewhere, but she couldn't see him. She looked higher up to the sound and spotted him. Her stomach jumped when she saw how high he was.

He was balanced against the sky on an old iron girder that stretched out from the mouth of one of the upper caves to the protruding rock of another bluff. The girder looked so narrow that Jimmy appeared to be suspended in air. As she looked at him, the sun blinded her again, and she couldn't bear it.

There wasn't time to take the trail back to the steps, so she began to climb the rocks at the foot of the bluff. Her ears were full of her own breathing, and with each breath she would call out to herself, "That's not a bridge. That's not a bridge. That's not a bridge." The closer she came to Jimmy's position, the more panicky she became, and her refrain turned to, "This is the bad thing. This is the bad thing." But then she caught herself and changed it to, "No, it's not. No, I won't let it be. No, I won't let you do it." She was losing her breath when she finally reached the upper trail. She ran along the upper trail until she was below the cave.

Jimmy was still teetering on the girder. His back was to her, and he was bowed slightly, looking down. She didn't call to him, afraid to startle him. Now she could see how he'd got there. He'd climbed down instead of up. There was even a sort of rock trail coming down from the high ground. A ledge jutted out from the wall in front of the archway of the cave. It was from this ledge that the girder was suspended.

It was necessary for Frances to climb the wall from below. It wasn't far up now, but it took time for her to search out the proper footholds. Normally, she would have been frightened of such a climb, but today she was frightened for Jimmy. Today she was sure the bad luck was his. Once, her footing slipped on a rock, but her hand grips were strong enough to hold her.

When she climbed over the ledge, Jimmy was watching her from his perch.

"Hey, good going, Franny. I've been waiting for you."

Frances gave him no reaction. She could see how rusty and decayed the girder was and understood how easily it could fall apart. She looked only briefly at the drop Jimmy was hanging over. He was above a small ravine full of rocks and other rusted beams that had fallen like this one would. Frances wanted to sound calm when she first spoke. She wanted not to be afraid. She thought perhaps she could change the bad luck if she wasn't afraid.

Her stick still hung from her belt loops. She knew what she should do. "Jimmy, I want you to come back here." She leaned out over the ravine. "I want you to hold on to this stick and cross back over here."

"No way, Ray. The idea is to cross this bridge."

Frances couldn't keep her voice level. "Jimmy, please."

He looked back at her, with challenge in his face. "And I say, Franny!" He began to bounce on the girder singing, "Franny, Franny, Franny." He was teasing. Across the short expanse she could see the dance in his eyes. Then there was a change. A curtain began to close over the dance, and she knew it was starting to happen. Jimmy knew what was happening too. A shred of a second before his eyes went blank, she could see the terrible fear, the kind that she had never, never seen on his face before.

She was on the girder before he began to stumble. When he did begin to lose his balance, she shouted with a deep voice, a voice not her own, "Hold on to the bridge."

Perhaps her words made him respond, or perhaps his own little body responded independently in that dawning moment before the seizure—that time between control and uncontrol. Something forced him to his knees, kept him from toppling over.

Frances straddled the girder and grabbed his belt. She stuck her stick through the belt and used it for a handle as she inched her way backward on the beam. She waited a little as he shuddered, and when he began to come to, she pulled him off the girder onto the ledge.

Groggy, but conscious now, Jimmy cried like a wounded soldier, all anguish and failure in something he didn't understand. He cried like it was a new thing to cry.

She laid her body across his and was quiet.

Jimmy said in small chokes, "I wet it, Franny, I wet my uniform." She felt the dampness too, but she kept herself from crying because she was the older one. She was the one who knew how these things could happen.

She nestled her face next to his and said, "That's okay, Jimmy, we can change it when we get home."

THE
GATE HOUSE

Long before the sisters moved into the gate house, when I was very small, I would jump up on the car seat when we passed it and shout, "Look at the ship!" My father corrected me several different times with no effect. So finally one day he turned the car into the driveway of the gate house and passed under the archway to show me the cemetery. He took me out of the car, and we walked along the paths between the graves. After our walk he carried me up to the gate house and introduced me to the old caretaker who lived there. When we returned to the car, it seems I was disappointed and would not look out of the window for the remainder of the drive. My father was sorry then that he hadn't let me carry on with my illusion a little longer.

I remember none of this story except for what my father has told me and the picture of a ship he bought me soon after. It hung on my bedroom wall for several years. This picture was meant to replace my lost idea of a ship. But the truth is it never made me happy. It was a picture of a ship alone in the half-light, rough sea all around it, and no land in sight. Because its beautiful sails strained forward in the wind, I wanted to know that it was going somewhere and would be there soon. Now I can see that ships are dreams, and there is no certainty they will take me where I need to go. There is only the possibility.

I've learned that life is not only a course set by choices, but that it is also subject to powers beyond choice. And none of us is exempt from this, as much as we would like to be. This is a disappointment, but it is also the beginning of a deeper life and deeper gifts, not the least being the gift of compassion. How we finally come to accept this is different for everyone, but one day we look back and we realize we do. I know for myself, though I wish I'd been wiser sooner, this acceptance only began when I met Clara and Connie.

Because of them I've come to love the gate house again. I can see that it does resemble a tall ship, the starboard side facing the graveyard and the port side facing the road. The archway attached to the house, which my father drove me through that first time, still remains the only entrance. Tall, pockmarked tombstones have settled unevenly into the ground, all leaning like plant life in one particular direction. I didn't notice this until I returned to our parish school across the street as a teacher. But I find myself studying the cemetery now.

When the sun rises, the gate house falls back into the immediate shade of our church. Both buildings support crosses. A stout stone cross atop our fatherly German church faces off the tall, mastlike cross attached to the highest point of the gate house. At sunset it is the gate house's cross that casts the longest shadow.

I remember Clara as having dark, round eyes like a dolphin. Her thick glasses pulled them out and magnified them—the way they might look under water. There was something else, an intangible quality about her whole being, that was like a dolphin's. She seemed prehistoric, belonging to a species that had survived many ages. Clara's body was substantial, and the few times circumstances pressed me against her, she felt to me like bread, not doughy, but firm like baked bread.

Connie was as small and fidgety as a squirrel. She would zip from one place to another in a room, usually for no good reason. She packed away odds and ends in her apron pocket, many books of matches, pens, bunches of crumpled Kleenex. It was always hard for her to find the right thing when she needed it, because there was so much clutter for her to sort through. Finding a pen that worked meant first grabbing two others that didn't. They looked too unalike to be sisters. Perhaps they were old lovers. It didn't matter. It mattered that they needed to be together.

I first knew them when I was eighteen, the summer between high school and college. I was waitressing as many hours as I could at O'Donnel's Tavern. It was a rite of passage for me to work at the tavern. An eighteen-year-old was old enough to drink in Wisconsin and so, too, old enough to serve drinks. Rusty O'Donnel, the owner and head barkeep, was a coleader with my father in the Cub Scouts. The autumn of my senior year our church held a Brat-fest in the parish parking lot to raise money for all the scouts. My father pulled O'Donnel over to the corn-roast booth, where I stood wrapped in an oversized, white institutional apron and huge asbestos mittens.

"Here's my best chef," he said, tipping my white paper hat over my eyes. "We would like two of your finest cobs." I kept the hat over my eyes and felt around for a couple of cobs, then held them out blindly in my big mitts. After my father had pulled my cap back up, I smiled at Rusty O'Donnel, who was a handsome man. He liked that I was funny, I could tell that.

"She starts college next year," my father said.

"Maybe she should work for me at the tavern next summer. She looks like a good worker."

I blushed and shrugged my shoulders to show them I was pleased. We all discussed the arrangements for a few minutes until it was settled. And that's how easy it was to get my first job. Everything used to be that easy.

O'Donnel called Clara "the big one" and Connie "the squirt." He had them on to cook the Friday fish frys, and the weekly job supplemented the little money they were able to make cleaning houses. Half of St. Agnes's parish and half of our neighborhood packed the frys. These were family dinners, the night when children's voices and mothers' voices mixed together with the gruffer voices, the regular voices. The wooden floor that groaned hollowly during the week lost its somberness to running feet on Friday. Families lined up in the bar waiting for a table to open. Mothers and fathers held their beers distractedly as they chatted with other parents. And the smallest children would scoop their hands into unattended mugs, bring the foam to their mouths, taste it, sneeze, laugh.

I learned how to turn my hips like a waitress, around tables, through crowds of people. Backward, I'd bump into the swinging kitchen door. Clara in the kitchen would say "Whoa, girl! You can't go faster than the food can be ready." Then she would pile an order on my tray, deliberately taking her time. When I became impatient and started grabbing things for myself, she would slap my wrists and narrow her eyes in mock fierceness. I tried hard to look like a good worker. If I knew Rusty or friends of my family were watching me, I would knit my brow and tap my pen against my tray as though I had a lot to think about. Usually I did. My head was full of the empty ketchup bottles that needed refilling, the highchair I'd forgotten to bring to the Kuzinskis' table.

Though Clara herself received little recognition, her beer-batter fish became famous around the city. It was a recipe no one else seemed to know, and it gave O'Donnel's a competitive advantage over the other fish frys in Milwaukee. Clara would soak the fish in baking soda and water to "freshen it up," and then she would get to work on her beer batter. She was smart enough to keep the recipe a secret, even from me, whom she was good to in every other way. I would try to study her process, but she would confuse me by sending me off to fetch some unneeded ingredient or by blocking my view of the bowl with her big body at some crucial moment. Clara's secret gave her a little power, if only to hold their jobs a few weeks past the time their drinking took over.

Connie made the coleslaw. It was an exhausting job grating cabbage after cabbage. Her dry, wiry hands were stained from the cabbage, and she complained that the job was "lousy." But I suspected that she enjoyed the rhythmic work since she only complained before the job and after. When she was at it, she worked frenetically, nonstop. She hooked into each cabbage with a claw grip, pressing all her weight into the head against the grater. She would reduce thirty-six heads to a mountain of slaw on the table, and not until she had grated a dozen onions to mix with the pile would she stop to take her cigarette break. With her hands raw, and onion tears condensed around her eyes, she would lean against the opposite counter, blowing smoke, studying the pile of gratings as though it was some devil she had slaughtered. When I made a point of complimenting her endurance, Clara chimed in over her shoulder as she dipped her fish, "Connie's a tough one, Connie knows how to hold up. Listen, darlin', Connie wouldn't be around if she didn't know how to hold up."

I learned about this "holding up" at the end of those Friday nights. At closing time O'Donnel would cajole his straggling customers to leave; then he would lock the doors and count his cash. After cleanup I was allowed one free beer and anything left in the kitchen to eat. I would join the "sisters" in their back booth, filled with their ashtrays, and their waning tumblers of Seagram and Seven. O'Donnel's wife, Marge, called the booth "Seagram's confessional."

Clara hadn't been married for long. Her husband drove a poultry truck from Occonomowoc to Chicago and back. He had met a woman on his run and made her pregnant; after this he stopped coming back.

She told me that Connie was pregnant once, but she miscarried after her husband pushed her over the coffee table. At the end of the night Connie would lift her glass, "Lord, bless us children every day, especially Friday, and if You still have time, wake me on Saturday." Her arm was bony and branchlike holding that glass in the air. I couldn't imagine her pregnant. Did she feel the infant squash in her stomach when she hit the table?

He beat her up after the bars were closed, so she started staying at Clara's apartment on Friday nights. She called Friday nights his mean nights.

"On his mean nights I would pack my nightie, some crackers, and some beer and go over to Clara's place above the library. It became so regular that he just started coming over there after the bars were closed. So Clara and I started going to the all-night Laundry-mat about midnight. We'd eat our crackers there and maybe sip some beer. We brought magazines. Sometimes I'd even wash Clara's hair in the utility sink. He never found us there, but it didn't matter; he just changed his mean nights around. It didn't have anything to do with Friday, more to do with just needing to beat me up once a week."

Connie would drag on her cigarette, thinking of these things as she talked, and with each piece of information revealed, she would blow the smoke far away from her face. She told her stories as though reading about someone else from the newspaper.

One night, however, she seemed upset. She pressed her little dry bangs down on her forehead, then pushed them back until they stood up like devil horns, then smoothed them flat again. "I don't think about those times anymore." She placed a new cigarette between her lips and pinched them together so that the unlit tip pointed upward. She fiddled with a match between her fingers, then her brow crossed, and her hand, detached as though it were not her own hand, moved to her mouth to take the cigarette away. At that moment I saw how her face could be different. The hardness was dissolved and replaced by a look of startled recognition, as if someone had just told her something she already knew, but that she had been hoping all along wasn't true.

"I've been having that dream again, Clara." She looked toward Clara, who looked back with expectation. "The one where I'm down at the park under the library in Occonomowoc. This time I'm fishing for minnows in the lagoon. I'm trying to scoop them up in a Dixie cup—you know, the way the kids do. It's getting dark out, and it seems that I'm supposed to be catching these minnows for dinner. But it's impossible, because my Dixie cup doesn't have a bottom. So I try catching them with my hands, but they are so slippery and hard to see in the murky water. When the darkness is almost down and everything around has lost its color, I have that dread again that someone is coming to get me. I can hear his footsteps shaking the ground around me."

Clara turned her dolphin eyes on Connie. "Am I in the dream?"

"No, you're not."

"How does it end?"

"I don't know. I just hear the footsteps, and I'm looking out over the water."

We three were quiet for a spell in the booth. Clara's breaths, close to my face, were slow, heavy, drunken. Connie flicked her cigarette and rubbed her eyes. My elbow had been resting in a small puddle of drink all the time Connie had been talking. I felt if I made any move at all she would stop talking. When she was through, I wiped my sticky arm with a cocktail napkin. It frightened me to hear Connie talk about her life as though it were an ordinary matter of fact. Although her dream didn't seem any more frightening than one of my own, I think I'd already come to expect that what people dreamed at night could often be scary, but this didn't mean it was real, that it was something to actually be afraid of.

I waited for a respectful amount of time, then asked, "How did you leave Occonomowoc? How did you come here?"

Connie began rambling. I couldn't understand her. I thought perhaps she had drunk too much and now the talk was over. I realized after a minute that she was talking about her house in Occonomowoc.

"I always wanted new furniture for my livin' room. The stuff we had was ugly. Not anything I picked. Somebody's old sofa, pillows they gave away at the bank, junky stuff, nothing that I ever picked. So I started savin'; I worked overtime at the cannery, keepin' that extra for my livin' room fund. I didn't tell Dwight—that's his name. I told Clara though, after a while. That fund made me feel better. Things got worse though. He got meaner, beat me harder. I got meaner too, stopped feelin'. I remember him smackin' me; I could hear the smacks, but I couldn't feel 'em. I don't think my face showed anything to him, but inside it was like my eyes were squintin' at him, and I was thinkin', Now I'm meaner than you. I drank more, off on my own, and I worked lots of hours, savin', thinkin' about the fund."

"That's when I was most scared about you," Clara said. "You stopped talkin' about it anymore."

"It was such tired shit; there wasn't nuthin' more to say. I'm glad you got scared. That last week Clara visited me at the cannery for lunch every day. I remember the first day she bought us each an ice-cream sandwich. We were lickin' away and Clara says, 'I got a fund too.' She'd been savin' it ever since her fella left her. But she didn't tell me about it. I still don't understand what the secret was, Clara."

"It was important. If I'd talked about it, I might have lost my purpose. You know, we talk about quittin' cigarettes every day; then we chew up two more packs before the next day."

"So, if you'd told me, I could have helped save more."

Clara reached over and rapped her knuckles on Connie's cigarette pack. With each word she rapped, "If I'd told you, you'd 'ave talked me into buyin' new living room curtains."

I could see that something sore was passing between the two of them, and I made awkward movements of leaving the table.

I never learned the details of their departure from Occonomowoc.

The summer was coming to a close; the neighborhood families continued to leave their kitchens because of the heat and crowded into O'Donnel's fish fry. The sisters had made friendly acquaintances and had grown to glory in their role as the cooks.

Odd uncles and divorced husbands came to visit the two at the kitchen window. Lighters flared in friendship; burly arms reached across the space to light Connie's or to light Clara's. Single men ordered two highballs with a wink to O'Donnel, and the second highball disappeared somewhere in the sisters' region. I had watched the drinks increase in number. O'Donnel watched across his bar as they teased one more fellow to bring a couple. He poured them out with concealed irritation, compromised between being a good manager and a good old boy at the same time.

Seagram's confessional overflowed after hours. In the beginning I liked sitting with them. They'd tease me and tug at my ponytail. They would introduce me to certain customers as "our college girl." What I didn't like was when they became drunk and emotional. Clara would stroke the back of my head, and Connie would pat my hand. They would say things like, "You're a good girl," and "You're going to be okay." Across the table they'd look at each other, nodding their heads in agreement. Once Clara looked at me, and her dolphin eyes welled with tears. Such a sad smile, I thought. Even her smile was like a dolphin's. She was looking at the whole world with that look, not just at me. After that I needed to convince myself that Clara couldn't see into the future.

O'Donnel lost patience one night. "I don't want you two hanging around here after hours anymore. Take your boyfriends somewhere else."

The last Friday I worked, Marge O'Donnel called me in early. "Your sister Annie? What's she, about seventeen? Bring her in; she can make some spending money. Those bitches are on a binge, no doubt about it. Ruthie Shulta was in here a bit ago, and she told me they've been sneakin' drinks out'a her and Ed's liquor cabinet. He had to start marking the bottles. Then yesterday was their day to clean over at the Shultas' house and they never showed, never called or nothin'."

We were failures as fish-fryers. Three more helpers and still the fish wouldn't have been on time for the customers. We lacked harmony. I tried to imitate the little I knew about the beer-batter recipe. Marge got half-through grating the cabbages and gave up. She pulled her nephew in from the bar to finish the job. Annie would have the potatoes fried before my fish was even a pale yellow. The food wasn't good. Customers made jokes about one more chance or they would switch to Weber's fry on State Street. Marge circulated around to most of the tables, berating the sisters when she could. O'Donnel draped his arm over the tap handles and shook his head to himself.

My college was small, isolated in the Wisconsin River valley. I settled into dormitory life easily. The other girls were like me. Though they came from different places, they had similar stories of home. We had nightgown sessions, all of us together with our knees touching. We determined out loud the details of our futures—our children, our husbands, our careers. Maggie Brandt was going to be an optometrist, like her father, and live somewhere near the ocean. Barb Cunningham was going to have three children before she was thirty. She would send them to Montessori schools and go to graduate school when the youngest was twelve. I was as dreamy as the rest of them. I decided whatever I would do it must allow me to travel.

Liz Bently said, "Ah, India or Thailand!"

I said I didn't think I was ready for the Third World.

"Well, what are you ready for?" she asked.

"Europe," I said. "It would be interesting to be in the place where we come from." She rolled her eyes at this. "Besides," I said, "there are so many trains there. I love riding trains. You can just sit by the window and watch the country go by; watch all sorts of people getting on and off."

"Just like watching a movie," Liz said. "Safe as that. Why not just get a job in a movie theater?" She hurt me with those words.

One Friday night, after a particularly satisfying and

giddy slumber party, I rolled away from the other girls to sleep and then dreamed about the sisters. We were together in a bus full of strangers. It seemed in the dream that I was their sister, and we were going somewhere together, but I didn't know where. It was black outside; the bus windows were covered with rain. The only light was the occasional glare of headlights from passing cars. The only sound was the rumble of the bus engine and the back-and-forth rhythm of its windshield wipers. I sat in a seat alone. Clara and Connie sat in the seat across the aisle, and they were as quiet as everyone else in the bus. I could see their faces only when they were illuminated by the passing headlights, and this illumination lasted only a moment at a time. Everyone was in the dark—no one made a sound—and when I finally opened my mouth to ask where we were going, I had no voice. It was a horrible feeling of being alone; we were all together on the bus, but no one seemed to acknowledge it. More than anything I wanted Clara and Connie to know I was there. I wanted Clara to reach over and touch my hand the way she used to in the tavern.

I awoke in my darkened dormitory, all around me the individual sleeping forms of the other girls. I still had no voice, no idea if I were to awaken one of the girls what I would ask her. I drew what comfort I could from the proximity of their bodies, the rhythm of their breathing.

Not far into my senior year, I was offered a position as sixth-grade teacher at St. Agnes School. It wasn't what I had aspired to. I had thought of my college education as preparation for the larger world, and I had set aside the offer as an option to fall back on if all else failed. But when I returned home in the spring for an interview with our pastor, our principal, and our parish board, I couldn't say that failure in my other pursuits had brought me there, only my failure, perhaps, to pursue anything. Liz Bently had been astute when she asked me, "What are you ready for?" The truth was I was afraid of the future, and I thought that being afraid was the same as not being ready.

On the second day of school, still steadying myself in my

new shoes as teacher, I found myself on the playground, heading off an argument between two of my tougher boys. I stood with both arms around the basketball they had been fighting over. Our discussion was about the advantages of sharing. It seemed I was getting through to them. But then I realized the small one, with the red hair and the slightly vicious overbite, had focused his attention on the sidewalk behind me. He was nudging his companion.

"Here come the cat ladies," he whispered.

I turned to see Clara and Connie on the other side of the cyclone fence. Connie, as wiry as ever, pulled an equally wiry white cat along by a leash. The cat was uncooperative, circling around Connie's ankles until it was tangled. At one point it pulled its head back against the leash with its small pink eyes squinted closed. Clara held her big, orange cat almost hidden in the fold of her great arms, the loop of her leash wrapped around her thick wrist. They made little progress along the walk. Connie spent time unraveling her charge. Finally she set it on the ground, positioning its paws in a straight line. Clara would walk ahead, then stop and wait for her sister, stroking her cat as she paused to smile at individual children on the playground.

I was uneasy about approaching them. They looked so odd, and some of the older children were laughing at them behind their hands. I called to Clara, who seemed to be smiling in my direction. I walked up to the fence, where some of the children were already congregating. Clara kept staring over my shoulder, but Connie recognized me.

"Clara, are ya blind? Look who's here! Lady, what are you doing at school?"

"I teach here."

Clara stroked the face of her cat with her thumb. "Isn't that sompthin', a teacher."

The recess bell was ringing. Children were sifting back into the school. "Don't go until you see where we live," Connie said.

"I really have to go in," I said.

"It's right over there." Clara pointed at the gate house across the street.

"There?"

"Yeah," Connie said. "Stop by for a Coke later."

I did walk across the road to the gate house that evening. I was curious about the sisters, but perhaps even more about the gate house. It had always been a kind of familiar monster across the road. A place I had thought I would only continue to wonder about. Once close to it, I found it a less threatening monster, more like a regular house when the shiplike lines were lost to my perspective. The landscape of graves was also out of my view behind some shrubbery that surrounded the yard. There was no front door, as the fence along the sidewalk came up too close to the border of the house. There appeared to be at least three possible entryways along the rear of the house, and I walked back and forth, at a loss as to which door I should knock on.

Before I came to any conclusion, Connie called from the deck above.

"Couldn't find the door, hey?" She smiled, waiting for me at the top of the stairs. Clara was shaded behind the screen door. I couldn't see her face, but in a shadowy way, her body smiled.

"Well, Connie, bring the girl in. Not much to see out there but rows of gonebys."

"Rows of gonebys? Oh, the graves." I laughed.

We passed through a dark entryway where we had to squeeze by Clara. First there was a smell of indoor cats and the stale, heavy air left by a thousand cigarettes.

"This is it," Connie said, leading us into the main room with a flourish of her arms.

The room was spacious, brilliantly illuminated by the early evening sun, which shone through the many floor-to-ceiling windows. From what I could see, there were three cats total. The largest cat, the one that Clara had been holding that afternoon, lay supine in a square of sunlight reflected on the floor. The cat that Connie had been leading earlier was now clawing at a large padded structure supposedly designed for that purpose. The third cat I only glimpsed as it scurried down a darkened hallway. The floor was largely bare, and our heels echoed against the wood as we crossed it. The whole space reminded me of a dance studio. It could easily have been converted into one, but care had been taken to huddle their furniture around little area rugs to form little rooms within the larger room.

"Well, sit down here in the living room, my lady." Connie pulled me down by my elbow into a plaid sofa. "That's new, and that, and this." She pointed to a coffee table, a lamp, and magazine stand. "Got all of this for less than half at a fire sale. A little smoke damage, but it'd get that way anyway just being with us." This was true, since smoke pervaded the room, little clouds of it poised in the low sunlight. With each object she showed I would say, "Oh" and "That's nice." At the same time saying in my head, "Cheap veneer on the coffee table, or The fabric on the couch is loud and passed out of style five years ago."

"How about some Cokes? Clara, get us some Cokes." Clara slid away on her heavy feet.

"Over there is the dining room,'" Connie waved toward a table with four chairs. "That's an old set, but we'll get a new one someday." She flickered about from one object to the next. "And that's my baby." She pointed to a modern-looking keyboard instrument.

"An organ?" I asked.

"Yeah, but it's a special kind. It has numbers on all the keys that you match to numbers in a book. You can play just about anything but never have to read music. Hey, I tell you what, I'll set up at the organ while you go see what is keeping Clara with the Cokes."

I was relieved to get out of Connie's new living room. I remembered the time Clara became angry with Connie—that business about spending their getaway money on new living room curtains. Her living room was all wrong—everything bought in a hurry. Standing in that room somehow made me feel her life was even more desperate than before.

I found Clara cutting up cheese. She said over her shoulder, "You see, we've quit drinking."

"Yes, I thought so." And since she brought it up, I risked, "How'd you do it?"

"Connie didn't want to die. I didn't want her to either."

"Wouldn't you have died too?"

"Maybe. You know, we drank together, but we drank different. I drank until I got too slow, passed out. Connie drank over the edge. She made herself stay awake to have another drink. She'd leave her body behind and just keep drinking."

"Did she really almost die?"

"Damn right. She was sick and yellow. I could have kept drinking fine save for looking at her in the morning. We were barely working; then we weren't working at all. I could handle that, but not for long, mind you. We had to turn around eventually. But Connie couldn't stand not working, so she made drinking her job—like it would get her somewhere."

"How are you now?"

"Good. This boat that we live in is the best place I ever lived. I'm getting close to sixty now; I enjoy the peace. We've got this place. We don't owe."

"How is Connie?"

Clara moved into the back hallway and lit a cigarette. "I think she must be fine, otherwise I couldn't be fine, or is it vice versa? She plays her organ. The furniture here is the best she ever had. She keeps herself busy."

"And you have your cats. How long have you had them?"

"Well, our two we've had since we came to Milwaukee. The shy one just came out of the cemetery one morning. Never made a sound, just sat on our steps and waited. Until we finally figured out to give her something. Strangest cat, doesn't seem to care about either of us. But she doesn't go away either."

Clara eased her shoulders into the corner of the foyer and lodged her foot in the crack of the screen door. She would squeak it open when it was time to flick a glowing ash out into the night. Once she kept the door open and stood in the air. "Did you see my garden down there?"

"No."

"It's right on the south side. I'm still pulling a lot of good stuff out of it. Maybe you'd like some squash."

"Sure."

Connie had started in on her organ music—"Greensleeves." Clara said, "He's been good to us you know."

"Who?"

"The owner of this place. He owns the cemetery, isn't that funny? Well, anyway, he was on the board of the treatment center me and Connie turned ourselves in to. When we got better, he took note of us and offered us this. Free rent, and we make enough with our house cleaning to take care of food and a lot else."

"Does it ever bother you, living in a cemetery?"

"No—bothers Connie though. She pulls the curtains over the windows that look out on the grounds."

That was my longest visit with the sisters. I wasn't comfortable in their house. I didn't like the smoke or the smell of cats. Sometimes I cut out articles about gardening or cats and took them to the two after morning mass, or I would stop by their fence on the way home if Clara was watering her garden. I maintained a certain social distance. This seemed appropriate. Did they understand this? They must have, since I don't remember them pulling on me. They had their life, and I had mine.

I already had three thousand dollars in a savings account for my summer trip to Europe. It fascinated Connie that I could go that far, to places where the language was foreign. I handed her my small French-English phrase book over their fence one day. She stood still for a change, with her head bent down in the sun, her cat winding its leash around her skinny legs. She read the first line, "How are you today? *Comment allez-vous aujourd'hui?* Huh! That's not so hard."

Even if I kept them at a distance, I liked to watch them. I realized that I was very fond of them, and in some strange way, I was invested in this new lease on life they had embarked on. I wanted them to succeed. I kept track of their rituals, their patterns. For example, early every morning

Clara poured a pile of peanuts on the grass outside the gate house. The squirrels and birds in the cemetery would congregate around the house. I felt a strange comfort in this ritual, as though I were a part of it. One day, I thought, I would be early enough on my way to school to catch a glimpse of her dress as she passed back into the house. But she was already gone every day, and I would find only the chattering animals, some of them still coming forward across the grounds.

I could hear Connie's organ practice waft over the playground at morning recess. She always seemed to be learning a new piece, and once she learned it, she didn't seem to improve much upon the playing of it. She would, instead, move on to a new piece, a new pattern of numbers to match to her keys.

They hung their laundry out on the deck at night, to keep the messiness of it in the dark, they said. In the early dusk one evening I left the classroom late, in time to catch them just finishing this task. They turned to each other as though they were just finishing a talk between themselves when Connie bent over, her arms curled out before her. I thought at first something was physically wrong, but the way Clara embraced her sister, I realized Connie was crying. I backed into the shadow of the school building and watched. Connie was hidden in Clara's arms with just a small part of her dark head protruding from a corner of Clara's shoulder. My strongest impression was the rhythmic movement of Clara's arm as she patted Connie's back. Over and over she patted her, until I could no longer see them in the resolute darkness, and I shuddered as I walked home with my first comprehension that pain could be constant and rhythmic like that, that the comforter needed to find the rhythm and know it, as Clara must know Connie's.

Clara died in her sleep on a Wednesday morning in the spring. I thought there was something wrong that morning when the animals and I once more intersected, and I saw that there was no food for them, although they continued to sniff and search around the yard. I knew there was something wrong when both of them missed mass, but I waited.

They said Connie didn't call anyone until Wednesday night. I imagine Connie trying to wake her over and over. I imagine the cats walking over her bed as though nothing were wrong. I imagine Connie starting for the phone again and again, but returning to her Clara, wanting nothing to be wrong. Why should Clara stop when there was still some left in the fund?

I heard the organ music on Wednesday afternoon. That I didn't imagine. Even after Clara was gone, Connie played it, and it wasn't difficult as long as the numbers were marked. People keep moving, don't they?

Even after they announced the news at Thursday morning mass, I couldn't go to Connie. I was not old enough, nor brave enough. I could not watch over her. All it seemed I could do was just watch her, furtively from the churchyard. Two dusky nights I watched that woman as she wandered over the deck's surface. She fiddled with unnecessary laundry, sometimes stopping to exclaim words to a billowing clean shirt or to ribbons of clean stockings. Sometimes she huddled over in that hurt way. But I couldn't go to her. I didn't know the rhythm, not yet.

HOMER

The earth around the potato gave in easily. It had rained the night before. The old man dug it out, wiped the mud off with a stroke of his thumb, and said to himself, "This is one I'll give to her." He rubbed it again with his thumb and wiped the skin back to expose a small, moist white spot. He'd show her how tender the skins were on new potatoes. He'd have to clean his fingernails though. Mud was caked under his thumbnail. The nail had grown long again. Over the years it had gotten thick and yellow, almost as thick as his big toenail. The others weren't so hard to cut, but the thumbnail—he'd just about given up on that. He'd work on it before he went out today.

He'd brought three blue enamel bowls out into the garden to fill with the vegetables he would pick. After he put the last potato on the top of the first bowl, he crawled over to his tomato plants. The tomatoes looked beautiful in a blue bowl. His wife, Jenny, had told him that, but he'd forgotten. Yes, she used to keep oranges in that color bowl, too, and banana peppers. Banana peppers and tomatoes together in a blue bowl; that would be perfect. He was sorry he hadn't planted

61

banana peppers this year. He decided the closest he could come in color would be wax beans. If he gave the girl one of the bowls along with the vegetables, would she think that was too much? When he was finished picking beans, he crawled back to the other bowls and to where his crutches were lying. In the garden he was as good as any man. Missing the lower half of his leg made no difference when he got around on his knees. And that's what he did in his garden.

He put the three bowls in a peach crate that sat on four low wheels. Then he hoisted himself up onto his crutches. He hooked a rope, which was attached to the crate, through his back belt loop and pulled the little homemade cart behind him as he crutched toward the house.

He washed his hands in the bathroom sink, swirling light brown water down the drain. He rubbed his thumb against the rust stains in the basin, but couldn't make a difference. He hopped a step back from the sink, one wet hand on his belt and the other arm draped over his crutch. "There's got to be some improvements around here," he muttered. He hopped back one more step and saw the whole of his bathroom in a way he hadn't seen it for years. He scolded himself, speaking loud and clear for the first time that day. "Now, what's the advantage of living under so many cobwebs? No wonder you never have company." He was seeing it through her eyes. He was thinking, What if *she* came to visit? He must have some better towels in the closet than those two he was using every day. He leaned toward the sink, looked into the open medicine cabinet: too many odd bottles with labels that had bled into single, dreary patches of color, bottles Jenny had bought years before, their purposes lost to him now. A small mountain of corroded razor blades on the first shelf, some so disintegrated they looked as though they were coated in toast crumbs. "What's all this?" he said. Jenny used to use his old blades for sewing and for scraping the knitty balls off of their sweaters. "And damn tooth powder over everything!" He removed fingernail clippers from the second shelf and blew the white powder off them.

He closed the medicine cabinet and set about trimming

his nails. With this task the old man was taking unusual care. He folded out the little blade that was hinged in between the clippers. "Rusty," he said. But it was good enough to scrape the dirt from underneath his nails. He needed better clippers for his thumbs. Those bigger toenail clippers might work. He wasn't sure, but he imagined one hanging over the girl's counter at the Stop 'N Shop. He usually stared up there when she had to turn away to wait on another customer. He imagined them hanging up there on cards, little clippers, and next to them big clippers.

He came out of his daydreaming and saw himself in the cabinet mirror. "Popeye," everyone called him. He looked at himself. He didn't have pop eyes, just gray, ordinary eyes. They were a blue blue when he was a boy. He confirmed this for himself. This confirmation of memory was an hourly struggle, now that there was no one left from his past. No one to say, "It's true, Homer, you had the bluest eyes as a youngster. You don't now, but you certainly did when you were younger."

Everyone called him Popeye because he wore a trainman's hat, because he smoked a corncob pipe, because his forearms were abnormally large from crutching for thirty years, and because he had an old man's voice. He was a character, and none of these characteristics would change. This he had determined a few years ago.

There were two people who called him by his true name: his friend Robert, who still worked with the railroad, and the girl at the Stop 'N Shop. He would give Robert some vegetables today, although he didn't believe Robert ever knew what to do with them. Robert ate out mostly. The girl, he was sure, knew about vegetables.

The kitchen of the old man's house appeared to him as forgotten as the bathroom had seemed a little while earlier. Years ago, in his parents' house, there was a copy of a painting that had hung on the wall as long as he had lived there. It had become so familiar to him that it grew invisible. He didn't remember it was there, until he saw the same print one day in a bank building. In the waiting room of the bank he stared at the painting and the title, *The Gleaners*, and searched his memory to know where he had seen it before. It came to him as he sat at the desk of one of the loan officers. At that moment he felt a panic-stricken sadness to realize how easily he'd almost lost an image from his childhood.

Homer stared hard at his kitchen. "Well, just a little bit here and there," he said, from where he stood in the doorway. He didn't need as many as four coffee cans for his tobacco spit. There were simply some things he needed to get rid of and some things he needed to add. There were too many newspapers and a fly swatter that wasn't good anymore. He could pack the jars of odd nails and hooks and hinges in the toolshed and make room for something nice on his windowsill. It wouldn't be too much to pot a geranium from the yard. There was so much he had let go since Jenny died. Everything but the garden.

Homer packed a large army-issue knapsack with the bowl and the vegetables and set out for the day. Robert's house was a block away, toward town. Robert always worked the third shift at the rail yard because it was the best pay and because he fancied working when most other people would want to be home. Lately, Homer had become more aware of his friend's habits. Almost every detail in Robert's life was drab and unconscious, except for his train set. Robert's train set was the largest, most magnificent collection in all of the Great Lakes states. It took up almost the entire first floor of Robert's house, and the tracks continued upstairs so the trains could travel from floor to floor. Homer was glad to see his friend's dusty old Dodge sedan parked beside the house. Robert's front yard was a short walkway in between two crabgrass patches the size of bath mats.

Homer pulled himself up the steps and crutched straight through the empty screened porch into the house. Robert had the thunder clouds going above his little train town. Tiny bolts of lightning leaped out of small puffs of gray smoke. Homer had asked once how they worked, but as usual Robert was noncommittal. Homer avoided crutching on the many miles of tracks winding over the living and din-

ing room floors. He hopped carefully around the houses of
the town, and he had to wait for one of the trains to pass in
front of him before he could proceed into the kitchen. Besides Robert's bedroom, this was the only room with furniture. The TV was blaring on the counter. It was always on,
even when Robert was away from the house. Homer had
heard the tinny voices coming through the windows. He
found Robert leaning into his open refrigerator, his dark
green work pants stretched across his round rear end.

"Looking for lunch, Robert?" he said.

Robert straightened up slowly and turned around just as
slowly. He was a middle-aged man with shoulders sloping
under his dark green work shirt. He always looked the same.
A little white V of T-shirt at his throat, with a few light brown
hairs curling over the neck. Homer looked at Robert's flat,
impassable glasses and smiled.

"Hi," Robert said in a soft monotone. In the fifteen years
that Homer had known him, Robert had used a voice neither
more nor less intense than this.

"Well, I brought you some things from the garden."

Robert pulled mustard, a plastic package of bologna,
and a little covered carton of margarine out of the refrigerator while Homer unpacked his bag. He came over
with these things to stand beside Homer at the table.

"What am I going to do with all that?" he said.

"Eat them, for God's sake!" said Homer.

"You know I don't cook."

"For potatoes you set the oven at 350. In forty-five minutes you take them out. Do you have hot pads?"

"Yeah, I have hot pads."

"You see, forty-five minutes for small potatoes and an
hour for the big ones. After they're cooked, it's no different
from eating them at a restaurant."

Robert spread mustard over his bologna sandwich and
didn't respond. This was the closest he came to being ornery.

"I see you added a couple grain elevators to the town
downstairs. Did you put some upstairs?"

"No," Robert said. "Upstairs it's not so agricultural; it's

more of a mining town, a steel mill town. I talked to a guy in
the yard. He's got a way to grind crude coal into little pieces.
I thought I could put a couple piles by the river up there and
build a couple barges."

"That would be nice," Homer said. Robert was quiet and
seemed to have forgotten about his sandwich. Homer tried to
look past the glare in his glasses. "What'cha thinking?" he
asked.

After a few moments Robert said, "I was thinking, if I
put barges in the river, I need to make the bridge into a
drawbridge."

"I guess that's true," Homer said. He could tell this was
one of those days when it was too hard to be with Robert.

On his way to the store, he tried to recall if he'd ever
talked about Robert to the girl. He knew he'd never mentioned her to him. Robert was more set in his ways than Homer, and Robert was some thirty years younger. The girl was
at least fifty years younger, but there was a knowing way
about her. There were people who knew more than they
could know from just their own life. Jenny had been like
that. He remembered the nights he had awakened with the
distinct sense she had left their bed. He would roll on his side
to be sure his wife was lying there asleep. He had never
found her gone. Still, on nights like those he believed she was
dreaming much farther back than the time he knew.

The Stop 'N Shop had been built ten years earlier. It was
across the tracks from the station where he had worked for
twenty years after his accident. He must have gone this route
ten thousand times. Homer had grown used to the way he
traveled down the street, a calloused swing from his armpits,
followed by the thump of his left leg on the pavement. He
had never learned to drive with his one leg, though he could
have. The year Jenny got sick, they had traded in their man-
ual transmission for an automatic. With each progressive
step of her illness she became more insistent that he renew
his license. One morning as they leaned over their coffee
cups, she had grabbed the cloth of his shirt cuff between her

fingers and said, "Homer, you've got to accept the fact that we're not going to be a couple forever!" He'd stood up to pour himself another cup of coffee and sat down again, tight-lipped, unable to look at her. She had started crying, as if surprised and hurt to hear her own words. He scraped his chair back, slammed out of the door. He forgot to pull his crutches into the car, so when he backed out he left them toppled over in the driveway. Of course he was too angry to learn to drive that day. He drove half of a block using his left leg, and then drove back into the driveway crushing one of his crutches on the way in. He threw the keys against the windshield; they slid down and clattered into one of the vents at the top of the hood. There he stood, wondering how he was going to fish them out. He was out of breath as if he'd been running. He realized if Jenny looked out of the window at that moment she would pity him.

That night Jenny had rubbed her hand in a circle over his lower stomach. They had whispered together, even though there was no one else in the house to hear. With the warm circle rubbed into his stomach, he had forgotten in the dark what was happening to her. Her voice was in his ear, as he had fallen deep down into sleep. "You were so beautiful; the bluest eyes I have ever seen. I wanted you more than anything, anything, anything. . . ."

The first day she went into the hospital, he had resolved he would learn in time to drive her home. But she had died two days later, and two days after that he had put the car up for sale for a ridiculously low price. It was bought that same day by an eager young man in the neighborhood. Homer cursed himself every time the boy drove by.

It was when Jenny died that Robert had proven himself a friend. He didn't come to the funeral, or send a note, but on the Saturday following the burial he had parked his car in Homer's driveway and come to where Homer was standing and looking over the spring mud of his garden. Robert said, "On Saturdays I do my errands. I figured if you had things to do in town, you could ride with me."

Homer could hardly make out Robert's uncomfortable

figure in the morning mist that had settled over his backyard. He had waved his hand, muttering, "I don't need
anything."

"What about seeds and manure?" Robert had said.

Robert's words had seemed unimportant to Homer. "I'll
get them soon enough," he said.

"Homer, you don't have a car."

Homer sighed and hoped it wouldn't require any energy
to make Robert go away. Robert had stood there for a very
long time and finally said, "Let's go to the car now." Homer
had gone with him like a sleepy child on his way to school.

In the car, Robert had given him a pad of paper and a
pencil, saying, "Make a list of what you need." Homer had
written down the words: seeds and manure. Gradually, Saturday after Saturday, Homer became more aware of the
things he needed, and Robert was always there at 10 A.M. to
fetch him.

There was an older nurse in the cancer ward. After it was
over, she had touched his arm as he stood by the elevator. "It
won't be more pain than you can bear," she said. "You'll feel
her gone only a little at a time."

It had finally hit him one day in the country. He had
driven with Robert to a large machinery auction. They
hadn't gone to buy the machinery, but to see what sort of
interesting odds and ends might turn up. The two of them
had ambled over muddy ground, stopping to look over skids
holding pipes, hooks, rusty brake drums. Auctioneers moved
through the crowd, stopping next to a tractor, or a skid of
goods. They used megaphones. Wherever they stopped, little
groups of men clustered around them. One auctioneer came
up to a skid where Homer was standing and let go his string
of names and prices. Homer couldn't understand a word of
his cacophonous mumbo jumbo. Crutching away, he was
made aware of how long it had been since he had been a
working man, once so familiar with most of those machines.

They hadn't come away with much. During the drive
home the sun was low and gold on the land. Through the car

window Homer watched the shadows getting longer and the farmhouses shining amber, the light hardly reaching their roofs. There were two chairs in the front yard of one of the houses. The farm seemed past its day, a clothesline had fallen, and the grass was growing up around the chairs. They were the common metal chairs with the shell-shaped backs Homer had seen everywhere all his life. They sat together at an angle that made him believe a man and wife would sit there after their dinner. Whoever it was who used to sit there did not sit there anymore, and this realization opened up in Homer and sent a full ache through his body. He buckled over and held on to his knee and the stump of his right leg. He hiccuped little gasps of air, trying to hold out, as if it were a wave of nausea that might pass. But it went on and ended in a long, long cry that he couldn't control. And after he had let go, there was a part of him that was left behind, perturbed: "That's an old man that's crying. Listen to that. Who's that crying?"

Robert pulled over to the side of the road and Homer stumbled out. Somehow he still had the idea he was going to be sick. He only cried. He stooped down and buried his hands in the gravel along the road.

After a while Robert came to stand beside him, close enough that Homer could feel the cloth of his work pants against the cloth of his shirt. And when they finally drove home, it was dark, and they didn't talk.

The girl's name was Elizabeth, cousin of the Virgin Mary. He'd researched it last week and found her story on the very first page of the gospel according to Luke. Homer, who hadn't looked through the Bible since Christmastime in his parents' house, had sat in the dusty, green brocade rocker of his own house, holding the first page of Luke between his fingers. He had turned the page back and forth, reading both sides several times. Now he repeated the story in his mind, adding a detail each time the rubber ends of his crutches pressed into the pavement.

At the store he looked for her behind the reflections in the glass door. When he got closer, he saw her hair and her brow bent over the cash register; her wrist was curved above an item on the counter. The bells rang when he pushed the door open, but she didn't look up, and if she had, it would have been with an expression no more surprised than Jenny used to have when he returned to the living room from the bathroom.

When she had finished with the woman she had been waiting on, she looked up. He put his pipe in his pocket and smiled at her.

"Hello."

"Hello," she said back.

He leaned his left thigh against the counter and let his crutches rest on either side of him. The straps of his pack had become twisted, so he struggled to pull his shoulders out of them. He moved his arms awkwardly and inside he was saying, "Jesus, hurry up before she tries to help you."

She made no move to help, and as he wrestled with his pack, he felt how very still she was. All this time he was looking down. He finally got his pack off and onto the counter. He busied himself with the ties on the flap of the knapsack. She placed her hand on the canvas of the sack, and he knew this was a way for her to say, "Don't fuss so much." But he couldn't stop, couldn't find anything to help him raise his eyes and look into her face.

The bells rang, and she moved away to the cash register to wait on a customer. He quickly set the tomatoes out on the counter. He pulled the blue bowl out and quickly filled it with tomatoes. He felt a rush of panic as he did this. He didn't want her to turn before he was finished, not just because he wanted it to be a surprise, but because there was something in the act and the way his hands looked that he didn't want seen. He sprinkled a handful of wax beans over the top, and when the bells on the door rang again, he looked up. She was looking at the bowl.

"Homer, the colors!" And she raised the bowl up to study the speckles in the enamel.

He looked at her chin and her neck and the way her arm traveled down into the loose sleeve of her smock. He didn't want to be gawking at her when she looked back at him, so he studied the many items hanging on cards above the counter. He saw the toenail clippers hanging next to the little clippers. He inspected his thumbnail, regarded the clippers again, and decided maybe it was better if he bought them when she wasn't working.

He went back into his pack, she put the bowl down, and he reached over with a gruff, "Here," and placed a potato in the palm of her hand.

"A potato," she said, then waited as if he had something to explain.

"Well, yes," he said. "It's a potato."

"It's just that a few weeks ago you told me that your specialty was potatoes, and I thought this might be one of them."

"Well, I don't know how special it is, but it's a good potato."

"Homer, you told me you had developed a special breed. I just want to know. Is this one of them?"

Homer looked at the potato and nodded.

She raised it up to her eye level. "I think the potato is a vegetable of great integrity," she said.

"Ha! Did you learn that in college?"

"No." She pursed her lips. "There was a lady, Mrs. Ruscuss, who lived next door to us until she died. She had a garden like yours, and I used to squat in that garden for hours with her. She used to tell me vegetable stories. My favorite vegetable story was about the potato. Mrs. Ruscuss was from Hungary, so she had a funny accent. She would say, 'You will neva eat a bodada wit out a hart. All bodadas have good harts. Dey're undaground vegetables und dey protect demselves, und dey take a long time to grow.'"

"Nonsense," Homer said.

"I listen to your old stories," Elizabeth said. "You could be polite enough to listen to mine." She turned around and began to stack cigarette packs into the rack behind the counter.

Homer said, "Aren't you going to tell me the rest?"

"Nope." She ripped open another carton of cigarettes.

"I have a friend Robert, who'd make a good potato," Homer said, trying to make her laugh.

"He's your friend you used to work with at the station."

"I didn't remember telling you."

"You were transferred to do scheduling after your accident. Robert works out in the yard, not physical work the way you used to work. He inspects cars, and tracks, and machinery. What you never did tell me was how you lost your leg."

Some schoolchildren came ringing through the door. Homer looked at the clock above the coolers. Three-thirty, already it was the beginning of the rush. He left her to tend to her business, and as he came back to the counter with a carton of half-and-half, he felt sad. He set the carton down to be checked out. Some more children rang through the door, followed by their mothers. Elizabeth answered a question of one of the mothers about the time of the next bread delivery. While her head was still turned in the direction of the ladies, she placed her hand on the carton of cream. Some of the children holding wrapped ice-cream bars waited impatiently behind him. She sighed a little for his sake, letting him know that she wasn't happy about the rush either, and she began to ring up his purchase.

A man in a suit with a newspaper under his arm pushed through the door. "Wehell, Popeye!" he said. He was a commuter who knew Homer from the station. Homer nodded and gave him a half smile. He leaned forward on his crutches as she totaled the machine. She turned to face him, and everything sounded quieter for a minute.

"Can't you just tell me just one more small thing about potatoes?" he asked her.

"They have long memories. Now, will you answer my question the next time?"

He shrugged and made a sound from the back of his throat. She looked at him for just a second before she waited on the children with the ice-cream bars. With only a small carton inside, he imagined his knapsack looked rather silly on his back. He hesitated a little on his way out the door. "What should I bring you next time? Should I bring you some zucchini?"

"Oh, Homer!" she said, unable to look up from the register. "You've brought me zucchini twice a week for six weeks now. I'll be leaving for school before I can finish even the half of what I have."

He stood by the door and waited for her to finish with the commuter's purchase. "What do you want then?" The commuter was walking toward him smiling. He tried to look past him at Elizabeth.

"Bring me some rhubarb," he heard her say. "But remember, I'm leaving soon."

"Allow me," said the commuter as he opened the door, making the bells tremble. "Popeye, I've missed you at the station. How long's it been? Five years?"

"It's been ten." Homer pulled his hat a little farther down over his eyes and crutched away from the man, who had already begun to thumb through his newspaper.

Six weeks' worth of zucchini, he thought, as he crutched along the walk. The season is getting on. Six weeks of zucchini and he'd known her now for ten weeks. Two months and two weeks, he thought. Homer needed to count like this—to keep his numbers straight—to tell one year from the next. Two more tomato plants this year. The pear tree is sixteen feet high, when last year it was only fifteen. And his life, like everyone's, he supposed, could be marked and measured. The day he began to work in the yard. The day he married Jenny. The day he lost his leg. The day he retired. The day Jenny died. And now, he had to admit, he was counting back to the day he met Elizabeth. Something had changed since Elizabeth. What that change was he hadn't talked to himself about. He'd responded to the change as he'd respond to an alarm clock in his sleep. Getting up in the dark, and moving about while still unconscious. Moving through a remembered ritual, and finally coming to in the dawn, at the breakfast table with food in his hands.

He'd talked to her about himself more than he had realized, and now she was asking about his leg.

He'd told her about it in his head.

What was there to say out loud? "The coupling slipped between two cars. I got caught. I don't know the details because I was unconscious." In his head he was able to tell her more. "It changed my life. In my dreams I walk down the sidewalk on two legs, and always in the end I'm walking to a sad place. When I wake up, I recognize the sad place is daytime and remember it's gone."

"Why does she want to know the details?" he muttered, for the first time feeling angry with her. And immediately after this outburst he corrected himself. It wasn't only the details she wanted. He'd bring her something good tomorrow. Then he heard her words. "Bring me some rhubarb." He was pretty sure the rhubarb was already past its time. But he hoped he might find a few young stalks. He hurried home.

In the garden he lifted the mammoth rhubarb leaves to find only tough, pithy stalks. It had been neglected for three years, and he couldn't find a single new plant. He went into the house, dejected, and sat on a kitchen chair with his elbows resting on his thighs. Then he stood up on his one leg and threw his hat down on the table. "Don't be such a miserable old cuss!" he said. He hopped over to the sink and picked up the coffee can in the corner. He cut off a plug from a square of tobacco on the counter, hopped back to his chair. He plopped down, set the can next to his foot, and chewed. He thought about the last time he had cut rhubarb.

That was the summer before Jenny had died. One day he'd cut the rhubarb in the habit of summers before, but then it came to him that she couldn't possibly have the energy for the canning this year. His hands were hesitant after that, but he had a compulsion to keep picking, a sense not to let good go to waste. By the time he was finished, he'd decided it would trouble Jenny if he brought any of it into the house. He left the basket in a far corner of the back porch, with the idea he could give it away to the neighbors.

The next morning Jenny, dressed in her nightgown and his wool socks, had gone out on the porch to feel the air. She came back into the kitchen, where Homer was drinking his coffee, dragging the basket behind her.

"Jenny, no!" he'd shouted angrily, because anger was the first to break out of all the feelings that swarmed between them in that minute. She pulled the basket over to the sink and started washing the mud off the stalks. He sighed. Then he came over to the sink. "Sit down now, you've washed enough." He finished washing the stalks and turned to find her chopping rhubarb at the table. He put his hand over her chopping hand. "Jenny, you don't have to." But she was stubborn about it. He remembered it being an awful tiresome job. The rhubarb was acidic and pungent and the sugar was sticky. There was steam everywhere, and it seemed they were never going to finish. There was always more sauce in the kettle, and then Jenny would come out of the pantry with a few more clean jars to fill.

But sitting there now in the kitchen, bent over his coffee can, he wanted to go on remembering that day. He had counted the jars when they were finally finished and then begun to take them to the pantry. Jenny had walked behind him, carrying two of the warm jars against the bib of her apron. In the pantry she had stood beside him. She reached up with the two jars. "Oh!"

"Oh, what?" Homer looked at her.

"This is the best part—bringing them in here and setting them on the shelves. It was always this time when I had the surest feeling I could take enough from the summer to last until winter."

Homer had chewed his tobacco out, and he was restless. He got up and dialed Robert's number. There was no answer, and he imagined the phone ringing next to the TV with its little people moving about on the screen. He hung up and went to the pantry. When he opened the door, the western sun shone through a little end window. The rhubarb glowed in the bottoms of the jars. He tried to detect the two she had set there herself, but they all looked the same, their tops covered with dust, because for three years he had left them untouched.

He brought two of the jars out and washed them. He set one of them on the table to give to the girl. He went on washing all of the jars, including the pepper relish and the stewed tomatoes she had canned in earlier years. He washed the pantry shelves before putting them back, and he went on to clean his kitchen, beginning to make the improvements he had decided to make that morning. He went to bed with a true, physical tiredness that he hadn't felt in a long time, and he dreamed back to being a boy, before Elizabeth, or Robert, or even Jenny had known him.

In the morning he was fervent in his washing and grooming. He waited with his cup of coffee for the time when the rush at the Stop 'N Shop would be over and Elizabeth would not be busy. When the time came, he packed the jar of sauce and set out. His scrubbed skin felt alive in the air.

His heart beat with a strong energy when he approached the store, and it felt as though he were marching up the incline of the parking lot. He came to the reflection in the door, and through the reflection he saw her solitary profile standing very still, with her chin lifted only slightly, as if she were listening for something and expected to hear it very shortly.

The beating of his heart had amplified to the sound of a marching band. His own voice rushed from some unexpected place, a shout: "I love . . ." He stopped. Both words startled him like pistol shots. He began to shake. Hunched over, he gripped the handles of his crutches, waiting for all the noise to pass. Did he really shout that out loud, or was it all in his head? He raised his eyes and looked through the door to see if she had heard, but she hadn't turned toward the door. She was as still as before, with only the slightest smile on her face. Homer looked around to see who else might have heard. There was no one. In his distress, he crutched away from the door to the side of the building. He stood facing a dark green dumpster.

After a while Homer went home. The shock of those two

words, whether they had been pronounced out loud or not, had been enough to undermine everything he had thought he had made himself ready for. He cut a plug of tobacco but didn't chew it, poured himself a cup of coffee and left it to get cold on the table. He sat down and stood up and sat down again. He took the Bible in his lap and searched for his name. He couldn't find his name or any clear reason for what was happening to him. He was an old man. He tried leaning back in his chair, like the old man he was this year, and last year, and the year before. He let his wrists hang limply over the arms of his chair, sighed, and put an attitude in his head about life being past. But he couldn't keep ahold of this attitude, because the girl's face would come to him smiling slightly, as if she'd just heard something and was about to tell him.

He got up and raised the window shade to let some of the afternoon light in. Out of the corner of his eye he saw Jenny pulling the other one up. He blinked and went on to dust the living room. That night he read through old letters, and he went to sleep with the words she had sent him across the ocean when he was a soldier. Words sent to him and meant to hold him for the long time before he could hear from her again.

He woke in the morning with the words, and they followed him into the kitchen and whispered to him all day as he cleaned his house. The next day he heard them too, but on the third day he was more alone in his work, except for sometimes when he would step back to appraise another pile of neglect he had found. Then he'd put his hands on his hips and say, "Look at this!" and he would feel her behind him, tying her apron strings, laughing in that low way she had.

While cleaning the shed, he found pruning clippers and was able, finally, to cut his long thumbnails. He marveled at the two pieces he'd removed, each the color and texture of seashells. The two little pieces had been on the ends of his thumbs for so long that he was reluctant to throw them away. He put them in his shirt pocket.

It was when he was potting the geranium that he felt

ready to go back to the Stop 'N Shop. Kneeling there, he dug his hands deeply under the plant to keep its roots safe. He pulled it gently out and tucked it into a clay pot. As an afterthought he poked his orphaned thumbnails into the soil of the pot. In the kitchen window the geranium's blossoms changed in color to a brighter, more precious red. And in turn the flower transformed the colors of the wall, and of the windowsill, and of all the objects nearest it, into new colors.

On Monday, Homer felt through the canvas of his sack to be sure the rhubarb sauce was still there. It was. He made it to the store just after the morning rush, and he did not pause at the door this time. The bells rang. The girl looked up, but she wasn't Elizabeth.

"Hello," she said, and she looked back down to what she had been tending to at the counter.

Homer said hello in a half voice that anyone might have in the morning, before they'd talked enough. He stood there and adjusted the pack strap which had fallen off his shoulder and waited for her to look up again.

She looked up with a quizzical expression, which cleared after a moment, and she said, "Oh, you must be Mr. Homer."

"Homer's my first name," he said.

"Yes, yes!" she said. "Elizabeth explained to me that you would be coming. She left a note for you."

He watched the girl as she rummaged in the shelf beneath the cash register. She was the same age as Elizabeth, but younger in her movements. He watched a flush come out on her cheek and neck. She was embarrassed because she wasn't finding the note. Homer tried not to think about Elizabeth being gone. Instead he concentrated on the certainty that the note would be there.

"Here it is!" The girl stood up blushing, handed him an envelope, and pushed the hair away from her face with both of her hands.

"Thank you." Then he cleared his throat and thanked her again more clearly. "And what's your name?"

"Barbara."

"No nickname?" he said.

"Sometimes," she said.

Outside, Homer held the envelope between two fingers, so he wouldn't crush it against his crutch grips. At the bottom of the hill, he stopped to put it in his pocket, changed his mind and opened it instead.

Dear Homer,

If you are reading this note I'm glad. It means you are back again. (Where have you been?) I didn't get to tell you how good your potatoes tasted—they tasted new like you said. I wanted to ask you about growing them. But since you didn't come, I looked them up in the encyclopedia. So you cut a little piece off the potato itself. As long as the piece has an eye it will work. Then I remembered Mrs. Ruscuss saying the eye is the part with the memory. Anyway, these are all considerations that I'll take back to college with me, and I'll see you again next summer.

Yours,

Elizabeth

It was written on blue paper, and when he was finished with it, he returned it to his pocket.

Homer went back up the incline and into the store. He loaded a shopping cart with flour, sugar, oil, eggs, and baking powder. When he finished with the purchase, he said, "Thank you. Barbara, I'll see you again."

He went to Robert's house. Crossed up the walk between the two small grass patches. Through the porch, and into the living room. He was careful around the little houses in the town. He waited for the train to pass before stepping over the tracks into the kitchen.

Robert was sitting at the table with a tiny bridge in one hand and a tiny bottle of glue in the other.

Homer set his bulging sack onto the table. He went directly over to the TV and turned it off. He reached in his shirt pocket behind Elizabeth's note and pulled out a single farmer's match. He struck the match against the stove, held it over the gas pilot. "Robert," he said, "you've never had my pancakes, and you've never had Jenny's special rhubarb sauce."

Still tired from the night shift, Robert took off his glasses and rubbed his eyes as if considering what had just been said.

HOUSE
OF
HEROES

I have three minutes to punch in at the Gateway Group Home, and the backdoor is locked. It shouldn't be. It's 10:57 P.M. and a school night, meaning most of the guys should be in bed. There are lights on downstairs. I rattle the doorknob a second time, and it flies open. Never put a refrigerator next to the door used by a lot of adolescents with violent behavior problems. It will always have a dent the size of a doorknob on its side.

Ajax is standing fifteen inches in front of me. It feels like fifteen, and I measure these things with Ajax, always calculating where he is. He jerks the sponge mop at me. *"Go around, woman!"* It's more than a bark, something akin to a roar; a bellow is the way I describe it, because it's big and dark and full of air. And as many times as I've been bellowed at by him, it's one thing I don't think I will ever get used to.

There's a brand-new fluorescent light in the kitchen, which I hate. It's a harsh, bright, tremulous light that would drive anyone crazy, let alone our guys. And right now, it's making Ajax's white T-shirt leap out at me from the darkness of his skin. Gripping the mop the way he is makes all the muscles in his right arm hard. He's standing in front of me with that impassive look, which isn't the least bit passive, which in fact is the lid he holds down on layers and layers of . . . *rage.*

There's a hollow stem inside me, the kind you find in percolators, leading up from my stomach to my throat. The adrenaline bubbles up, and I have to swallow.

I use a stock phrase to describe how I manage relating to young men with violent behavior problems. "I need to have a *porch on my personality,*" I tell people at parties or the parents of friends when they ask. "The porch stands between their reaction to me and my reaction to them," I explain. "For instance, if my little brother told me to 'Shut up, or I'll punch you,' I might just tell him to shut up himself. I know my brother. But if one of the guys is shaking a fist in my face, I have to be more careful." At this point the person at the party or the parent of my friend tries to look concerned. "You see, I use that little bit of space to guard myself. It helps me stay calm until I've had the time to think about what's really going on. There's always more going on with those guys than meets the eye." Sometimes when I go on about my job like this, I feel guilty. I wonder if I don't glamorize the work a little—make it sound dramatic so people will think that I'm interesting.

Nevertheless, standing here in front of Ajax is just another case in point. The minute he shouted, he opened my porch door. I imagine it's the kind of screened porch my grandmother used to have, cool and shady, yet with a view of the whole street. Ajax's shout is out there vibrating on the porch, but I'm still in the house, thinking about how I should respond. Should I just turn around and do what he's told me?

"Is that sort of like hello?" I say, trying to make my voice come out evenly.

But he's already turned away. The sound of metal scraping over the linoleum is just another reminder of his compulsiveness. He mops so often and furiously that the sponges wear down to nothing.

Things are not okay with Ajax. So I'm very careful about keeping my feet on the mat by the door.

"Would you mind punching me in then?" I use a matter-of-fact voice, not scared, not angry.

He walks his self-conscious, rocking walk over to the time clock, looks for a long time at the cards sticking out of the rack on the wall. He has trouble reading. Finally, he pulls out what I hope is my card and looks at it.

"Line it up on the 'in' space for the second day." I'm trying not to say it like he's dumb.

"I know!" another bellow. *Thunk.* He presses the lever down.

"I'll go around, then," and I go back out the door.

It's so cold. Rather than walking out to the sidewalk, I take the shorter trip over the frozen snow around the house; *scarda*, a college friend from Norway used to call it, one of the thousands of names they have for the different ways that snow can be. I don't know how to spell it. It's the kind you have to step lightly on lest you break through. So I'm stepping lightly. The pine trees in the yard seem almost shriveled from the cold. Through their boughs I see the bank sign, a block away, flashing 11:01 and then −17 degrees. The few cars driving past on the road trail huge plumes of exhaust. And from the sound of the wind rattling against the storm windows, I guess that the wind-chill factor must be about thirty below. This makes me feel sorry for myself, wondering why, when it's so damn hostile out, does it have to be hostile inside, too?

When I come in the front door, my eyelashes are frozen together, and I need to melt them with my fingers before I can see. The fabric of my jacket has absorbed the cold; now, like dry ice, it's putting a chill into the room. Art and Gail, the 3 to 11 counselors, sit at the dining room table writing the night's notes. They both shiver a little. Art looks up, but his expression indicates that he's still thinking about his notes. Gail doesn't even look up.

"Slightly Minnesota out there," says Art.

"Slightly," I say. And since it's the middle of February,

with as much winter ahead of us as behind us, that's all we need to say or can really bear to say.

I search their faces for what kind of day it's been, but it's useless; they only look tired. I can see that Gail is writing a lot in the behavior problem section of Trevor's notes.

The three of us are operating under a code of silence, since Ajax is within earshot. I can see him through the kitchen door kneeling on the floor, a bottle of 409 next to him and a rag wrapped around the tips of his fingers. He is rubbing away the scuff marks everyone has left and, using his fingertips the way he is, looks feminine. But he's rubbing hard, which makes his muscles pretty plain to see.

"Some problems?" I ask.

Art said, "Peter is having some problems being a dishwasher tonight. He called from the restaurant twice to say the other kitchen workers are teasing him. I told him just to tell his boss and come home before he gets in trouble."

"I was wondering about . . . ," I speak in an undertone and tilt my head toward the kitchen door.

"Yeah," Art murmurs. "But it wasn't so much his fault."

"Read this." Gail pushes over the note she's been writing.

> *Trevor was angry with Robert [Ajax's real name] for what he called "bossing him around." Trevor lost control, charged Robert, and hit him in the face repeatedly. Robert did not move or try to defend himself in any way. Trevor needed to be restrained.*

"Repeatedly?" I ask.

Gail nods, looking toward Art. Art puts his own fist up to his face and mimics what must have been Ajax's blank expression while Trevor was hitting him.

"Laura, what word would you use to describe the way Ajax was?" Gail asks.

I have a good vocabulary, and the other counselors are always asking me for better words to use in their notes. "Stoic," I say.

"Amazing self-control," Gail says. But we all realize that

Ajax's self-control is a mixed blessing, that this incident to-night is just one more thing to be stuffed under the lid he's trying so hard to keep in place. We've been watching that lid since he came, and it's beginning to rattle the way one does when the water starts to boil. When Ajax first came a year and a half ago, he seemed very quiet and adult, but even then, though he didn't talk much, the hard feelings would slip out. Sometimes it was just one word as he walked through the room; "Women!" he'd exclaim, like that explained it all.

My job here is a strange one. The description I found in the classifieds read: "Overnight counselor-in-residence for developmentally disabled teenagers with behavior problems." I didn't know exactly what that meant. But it went on to read: "Some meal preparation required; counselor is able to sleep during shift."

At the time it seemed that it might suit me, the sleeping part in particular. And I had a degree in psychology, even if I didn't consider it my main interest anymore. I'd kept my grade point up for four years, making myself ready for graduate school in clinical psych. But when the time had come to take my entrance exams, it seemed wrong. I realized I didn't look forward to being a psychologist.

So instead, I used my savings to buy a round-trip ticket to Europe. I loved riding the trains and reading. I read the classics mostly. Plays. Here I was traveling through all these ancient places, like Corsica and Athens, so far from home, and I was thinking about how Aeschylus and Sophocles and Euripides hadn't seen nearly as much of the world as I had, couldn't really know what Freud would come up with thousands of years later, and yet they wrote as if they knew everything.

How could they know so much? They had such a little time to work with, and they were under a lot of pressure, because every year the whole city would fill the amphitheater waiting for the new play that would show them how they were doing—what they as a community needed to do better. Maybe the pressure helped the playwrights to be profound. Maybe knowing the whole city was waiting pressed them to go very deep and to teach themselves about all those things like pride and betrayal and love. . . .

I would think about what I read, and there was something about riding the trains, the scenery speeding by my window like a long smear, that would put those thoughts into the perspective of time. If the great playwrights were able to show people certain truths about themselves thousands of years ago, why, I wondered, after all this time hadn't we wised up very much?

I met a Scottish woman on a train in Wales. She was in her fifties, a Katharine Hepburn type, brilliant eyes, ruddy skin, and not a humble bone in her body. "Ay yer takin' with heroes ar ye, lassie?" she had said when I told her about the great works I had been reading. She pronounced it *he-rose*, rolling the *r*. I told her that until this year I'd mostly thought of heroes as Superman types, guys who saved babies from burning buildings, saved the flag, things like that. It wasn't until now that I learned how troubled, even unlikable, they could be.

"Well, ye jest keep reading the classics," she told me. "They'll always be the best board to stand on, whatever you plan to do," she said. "I've a mind to send ye to my daughter where ye might lend her yer good influence." She was talking about her daughter who made films in Ireland. *Filems*, she pronounced it.

As it turned out, she followed through on the idea, and I spent the last three months of my trip in a film cooperative in Ireland, doing odd jobs to help out and learning how to manipulate subjects so they made sense in the frame of a camera. Things like, standing in a field, in a horse corral, me standing just outside the frame of the camera, but trying to keep the horse inside while someone filmed him. It wouldn't seem like much when you did it, but later when you ran the projector, you could see what the camera had captured. I loved it and flew home determined that's what I wanted to do.

It seemed like serendipity when I returned home to find a film cooperative had started up in St. Paul while I was away. I joined, wondering how I expected to support myself, and only a few weeks later I found the Gateway ad in the paper. Everything, at the time, miraculously fell into place, giving me this sense of destiny, you know, feeling sure this was what I was supposed to do. But that was five years ago, and lately the Gateway feels like the only steady thing I have.

I'm most likely to step back and think about how this job fits into the scheme of my life when I make the residents' lunches at night. Maybe it's the ritual of lining up six flat brown bags on the kitchen counter, then leaning on my elbow and writing each of their names on the bags in red Magic Marker. I used to write the names bigger, but one of the guys stopped taking his lunch to school because the other kids could see from the bag that he lived in a group home. I write the names as small as I can now. Some of the names have changed from year to year. But some, like Peter, have been here as long as I. Almost every night I blank out on one of their names, the same way my mother has been known to do when asked on the spot to list the seven children in our family.

"Who lives here again?" I've asked Art or any one of the many second-shift counselors that came before him and then burned out. Pulling his jacket on, getting ready to leave, he'll come look over my shoulder.

"Let's see, Jack, Trevor, Terry . . . that's three. Ajax . . . uhm . . ." Then we'll both laugh, rolling our eyes up to the ceiling, as if we can see them through the floor as they lie in their beds. Usually it's the one we should least forget. "Chip?" Art remembers. "You know, the little guy whose hockey stick is lodged in the TV screen right now."

But Art and Gail are gone, and tonight I have to remember all six names by myself. I'm on the sixth, but it's not coming readily. "Ajax! . . . right." As if he hasn't been here, when every muscle in my body has been keeping track of his whereabouts. I hear him running water in the basement laundry tub. Brushing his teeth. Running it and running it.

He washes up in the basement at night so he can take as long as he wants.

It's one of those things schizophrenics do; both he and Peter have habits like this. Peter, for instance, used reams and reams of toilet paper when he first came to Gateway; it wasn't unusual for him to clog the toilet twice a day. He was so small then, a twelve-year-old who looked about eight. I'd hear the elflike *dit-dit-dit* of his footsteps in the hallway, and I'd bound out of bed, following him to the bathroom. Outside the door I'd have to coach him. "Count the squares out, Peter. Five squares is all you need."

"Should I wet my pants instead?" He had a high voice then. "Should I run away and go to the bathroom at the gas station?" Sometimes he would just squeal in exasperation, and outside the door, I'd picture his sweet face all flushed, and his soft bangs, and his eyes glassy.

"If the john keeps overflowing, Peter, the living room ceiling is going to cave in." This was the wrong thing to say.

"Will we all fall through then, everyone but you, Laura?"

"It's just not necessary to use so much paper, Peter." He'd be a little quiet then, waiting for me to go away. But I wouldn't. Then he'd whimper, "It *is* necessary," and wail, "*Absolutely necessary.*"

"He has many, many of his own rules," the consulting psychologist on the staff at the time had said in a meeting about Peter. "He always feels anxious; it never ceases, and he doesn't know why." This is how it is for a schizophrenic. So he makes up reasons for why his life is like this: for Peter it's because it's raining outside, because he's walking on the wrong side of the steet, because the radio won't stop talking to him personally, because he lives in America instead of Russia. For Ajax, because he hasn't lifted enough weights yet, he doesn't live in the suburbs, because women won't have him.

They make up more rules to try to manage the reasons they've already made up, the reasons they feel so much pain—Ajax only goes to the movies, the Y, the stores in the suburbs; he only talks to women in his head, and he becomes compulsive about his ways, filling up his day with all these rules, trying to distract himself. He's alone.

So is Peter. "You can see he's already beginning to fail miserably in his relationships with others," the psychologist had said about Peter way back then. And I told myself to remember that—it wasn't because he hadn't wanted to like people. It's because if you keep failing, you give up; you don't trust others, and you don't trust yourself.

I think Peter's given up on friends, but Ajax still tries really hard to make people think that he's okay. When he started at the high school, he went out for football, swimming, and track all in a row, went to practices every single night and on weekends. He had something to come home and talk about, like he was part of the team. "We whipped them," he'd say when they won, or, "The coach was pretty pissed," when they lost. "We've got to get our asses in gear."

I went to one of his swimming meets because I'm a swimmer too, and it was something for us to have in common. He looked very sleek and strong in his suit, but he swam badly. He swam with his head out of the water and couldn't seem to coordinate his strokes. His coach was a woman, and I could imagine the time she had instructing him. He doesn't listen to people; he doesn't want to be told that he's doing something wrong. He didn't swim in the competition, just in an exhibition at the end. When he wasn't swimming, which was most of the time, he stood apart from the other guys with his arms stiff across his chest. I kept waving at him but realized he wouldn't see me without his contacts. So later I told him that I had been there, that he had looked very strong. This year he didn't go out for any sports.

The last thing that was written on the Xerox the psychologist handed out at that meeting about Peter was that we needed to realize how each day the schizophrenic wakes up is like starting all over again. But it's not the sort of cheery thing you think of when you read the bumper stickers that say, "Today is the first day of the rest of your life." It's a hair-tearing frustration for them because for some reason they can't use all the days they have lived before this one to help them. The way they learn about life doesn't take, in the way it does with other people. Like using bad paint—every day they paint the same wall with it; the wall dries, and you can hardly see where it's been painted. I don't know what to think about this. It's a hard thing to think about. Maybe the best way is to believe that if you stick with it, put that thin coat on anyway, every day, eventually it will look solid: I mean you keep talking to them, acting as if they will be able to hold on to some of what they need to understand and use it to get better.

I listen to Ajax *thump, thump, thump* up from the basement. I'm laying two slices of bread in front of each of the lunch bags. I don't turn around when he comes in, but I can hear the bitzy sounds playing out of the earphones of his Walkman. This is a way for Ajax to have solitude in a house full of people, and it's his way not to think too much.

All of a sudden there's a bang on the counter next to me. My elbows jerk a little. It's a can of frozen juice he's brought up from the freezer, along with a frozen block of butter and two loaves of frozen bread. This is another part of his daily routine, as is scrubbing the sink and sweeping the floor. Most nights after he brushes his teeth, he brings these things up to be defrosted for the next day. If he doesn't, I always wait until he goes to bed before I do it myself. It offends Ajax when people do things that he has decided are his own jobs.

Some nights Ajax might forget, and then some nights he might just decide not to bring the food up. And since it's a kind of favor to me when he does it, it's hard not to take it personally when he doesn't.

I'm still convinced that he doesn't want to talk tonight, but I say, "Thank you," and make a point of looking at him. I know this is the thing I should do, even though Ajax stares past me with a blank, sleepy expression. Then he leaves the room, and I can hear him slowly climbing the stairs.

No matter what, I feel that I should always keep a door

open for Ajax, even if it's only my porch door. To close him out wouldn't just be unkind; my instincts tell me it would be dangerous. I'm pretty sure that I stand for something in Ajax's eyes, and he stands for something in mine. I have to think that we're both probably wrong about whatever that is. But still, it's there. You know how it is when you meet someone who reminds you of someone else; even after you have known them a long time, it's hard to shake. Maybe it's just his name that reminds me of Sophocles's play about Ajax, makes me think of the kind of hero that Ajax was—all pumped up and strutting his stuff and being crazy. How crazy that Ajax was in the end.

"It's a love/hate thing," Gail said when I told her how I never know what to expect when he comes down to talk to me at night, "just like he feels for all the women here." But that didn't explain anything or make it simpler. The only ideas that seem right are these instinctive notions, like how I need to keep the door open. This makes him less scary to me, because I get a chance to know what he's thinking. And maybe this way, he gets to know me too, and can't as easily make things up about me. Although he still does it a lot anyway.

He's fairly regular now about coming down at night and talking to me while I cook. Once or twice a week he'll be here leaning against the counter, still wearing his earphones, which is nerve-racking, because he can't tell how loud he's talking, and he ends up shouting everything he has to say. Sometimes, but only when he's not touchy, I'll tell him that I wish he'd take them off when he's talking to me. But invariably he'll say in an even louder voice, "I can hear you fine!"

His conversation is disjointed the way you'd expect it to be when someone's thoughts play bumper cars with each other. He's hard to follow. "Say!" he'll say, then he'll put his chin in his hand and look down, smiling about something. I'll have no idea what it is, so I'll keep shredding the cheese or whatever I'm doing, waiting. "Ah, no." He'll straighten up, put his arms across his chest, act normal, manly. "Yep, went to Fire Explorers tonight."

"How was that?" I'll ask. His long-range goal in life is to be a fireman. Even he knows his chances of passing the civil service exam are nil. But he's determined. The Explorers is a teen group supervised by the fire department, sort of like 4-H is for farming.

"Good," he'll say, "real good." And there'll be that optimistic side of him that he has about 25 percent of the time. "Looks like I might be elected Junior Chief. I mean, if they vote for me," he says. I just go along with that as if that could happen—maybe it will. "And the women are great," he says. "Some incredible women." If they're in his group, I expect they're about fifteen or sixteen years old. He's seventeen, but he's always a couple years behind in his classes.

Then it gets a little more difficult. "Jennifer." He'll smile and roll his eyes up to the ceiling. "Jennifer Katz, wonder what's on her mind?" he'll say. "You know, she has these little loafers, you know, the real soft surburban kind. *Every single day* last fall"—he'll get excited—"she didn't wear socks in her loafers. Don't tell me she's not asking for it."

This is where I have to be careful. "What is she asking for?"

"You know." He'll roll his head, smiling, and then he'll stop abruptly, straighten himself up, get normal, manly. And I'll hear the little noises from his earphones like his thoughts scratching together. "No," he'll say, crossing his arms over his chest. "I don't know if she's loose or not. I saw her smoking a cigarette once. Not at Explorers—outside, near school. I was on the bus."

Maybe if it seems like a good time, if he's not too defensive, I'll say, "You know, Ajax, sometimes I don't wear socks in my loafers, and it doesn't mean anything. It's just a style."

"But it's the fall." He'll get excited again. "In the summer, yeah, but in the fall. I know what's going on."

If this same subject comes up a few more times, I'll say, "You know, Ajax, sometimes when you feel attracted to someone, it's just because you do, not because they're trying so hard to make you feel that way."

Most nights, it's just this on-and-off talk and quiet. Sometimes he even asks about me, as if he wants to start out the conversation politely. He'll say, "Say, so what did you do today—make movies, go swimming, the usual?" But he doesn't listen really hard. I'll stop talking, and the next thing he says has nothing to do with what I've just said. It's one of those bumper cars coming in and bumping the thought I had been following completely away. Yet there are certain things that I know he'll always ask. It'll be quiet for a while, and he'll say it softly. "Say, so what do you think of me—as a person, I mean?" Or he'll ask, "Say, do you ever see me married? I mean, do you ever see me as a fireman with a wife and kids?"

It's always hard to answer. "I think you're good-looking," I'll tell him, "a hard worker, you have a nice voice." And to the other question I'll say, "If that's what you want Ajax, I want it for you too."

Sometimes when it's quiet, and I'm cutting an onion or a carrot, and there's a gentle rhythm to that, it won't be until I look around that I realize he's already left and gone to bed. I'll feel very relieved then and realize that the whole time he'd been there it hadn't been peaceful at all. I had only been acting as if it were peaceful. "Soothing the beast," you might call it. Just acting very calm and gentle so he would feel that way too. I'll realize I'd even been willing the knife in my hand to look harmless. I don't like using them when he's around.

He isn't much taller than me, I know, because that's one of the things he does. It seems like at least once a week he steps up to me, close, and he says, "How tall are you anyway?"

"Five, five and a half," I always say. "What are you, about five, eight? That's taller than most of my brothers," I throw in so he doesn't get down about it. Otherwise, everything about him is powerful: the bass in his voice, the muscles, even the whiteness of his teeth. He has incredible teeth. He's beautiful really, but he doesn't think so, because as he puts it, he's *"not white."*

He was adopted by a large, white, liberal, Catholic family (like mine) and grew up in a small Minnesota town. He didn't realize at first that he wasn't the same color as his brothers and sisters, not even close to a single other person in his town.

Once a ditzy young woman interviewed for a counselor's position and had dinner with the whole group here so she could get to know them. She made what I would call the "ingenuous" mistake of asking him what his nationality was. He had just been getting up to take his plate out to the kitchen, and he leaned over, "got in her face," as they say here, using his voice as lethally as he knew how, "Indian, Mexican, black, Chinese," he boomed, "everything you can be that's *not white.*" He did this so eloquently that the guys and the counselors at the table applauded. That was the end of her.

He has thick, black, curly hair and his eyes are slightly oriental or Indian, you know, and the wide cheekbones. His color is mocha, with just a little yellow. Still, he has a hard time not thinking of himself as white. Who wouldn't if all your life all you saw was white, except in the mirror. Wouldn't that make you crazy? Nobody is sure what he is. His parents adopted him in the sixties when his father, who's a doctor, was volunteering in the California migrant worker movement. Maybe it was a way for the doctor to leave there and feel okay about leaving. His birth mother was Mexican, and she left him—that's all they were fairly certain of.

Ajax has a dry sense of humor, which isn't the case with most of the guys in the house. Peter has one too. That's the cut: both of them are MI, and the others are MR—mentally ill or mentally retarded. We hardly ever talk about them that way, even among ourselves, let alone to people outside. It's too clichéd—people conjure up this idea right away that we're not talking about people. They think everybody that's retarded is mongoloid, drools, and is always happy. They don't even want to think about the mentally ill. The MIs can have just as hard a time in school, because it's so difficult for them to concentrate. But there is this sophisticated humor; they're able to recognize certain ironies in their lives that I never hear from the others.

One night Ajax was resting his head against the hood of the stove while I stirred a pot of spaghetti sauce. "I have never been happy for a minute," he said.

"Not even for a minute?" I asked.

He looked out, then his cheeks dimpled, and he said, "Well, maybe for thirty seconds." Then, after thinking some more, he said, "No, maybe only as long as a puff on a cigarette."

"That would be about two or three then," I said.

"Two or three," he said. "That's about right."

The humor is a family trait. One of his older brothers (they're all older) is a comedian in the area, playing small dinner clubs and the like. He's very kind to Ajax when he comes to visit, and very funny. "I'm the one that nicknamed him," he told me one morning when he was waiting in the kitchen for Ajax to come down. "My parents adopted him around the time that Bobby Kennedy was assassinated— that was their reason for naming him Robert. But even as a little kid, he wanted to be someone else. He wanted us to call him Mr. Clean after that muscle-bound, bald-headed guy in the commercials—thought the guy had it made, the way he could vaporize and reappear in different ladies' kitchens. But my mother hated the name, so we came up with the compromise: Ajax."

"So you named him after a cleanser," I said. "Here, I've always thought it was after the Greek hero. But it makes sense, either way, I mean, considering his cleaning fetish."

"What about the hero?" he asked.

I'm always glad when people ask me about what I know, especially in situations like that where I'm standing in my apron and my aqua rubber gloves cleaning the oven. Most of the time I just have to let it be; you can't always be setting the record straight, telling people when they walk in to meet you, "Look, this isn't the only thing I do: clean ovens and pack lunches. I'm also a filmmaker and a deep thinker," and so on.

I liked this guy—maybe there was even a glimmer of an attraction. We were similar types. We both had our scruffy tennis shoes, peg-legged pants, oversized jackets, soft, faded, clean shirts. The warehouse-district look, the artsy, not-much-money look.

"Ajax was one of the heroes in the Iliad—in the same league with Achilles and Odysseus. After Achilles was stuck in the ankle and died, his mother had a contest for his armor. It was basically between Odysseus and Ajax. The rub was that though Ajax was the strongest . . ."

"Right," the comedian said. "I remember now—Ajax was the kind of all-star wrestler type."

"Right," I said, "but Odysseus was smarter and, so they said, had the favor of the gods."

"Ajax was the one that lost it, wasn't he?" the comedian said. "I mean not just the contest, his marbles. He's the one that rounded up all the livestock, the sheep, cows, dogs, and slaughtered them, thinking he was killing the enemy."

We could hear our Ajax upstairs, opening and closing his dresser drawers. Both his brother and I felt uncomfortable then, because we hadn't begun the story with any conclusions in mind. But the comparisons were sitting there now; they were hard to avoid.

The brother looked up at the ceiling and at his watch, as if he was getting a little impatient. Then he looked at me and said, "Does he scare you?"

"Sometimes," I said.

"My mother leaves when he visits. She still can't face him."

"What do you mean?" I asked.

"Since the assault—she was just so blown away."

"You mean the girl he pushed down the stairs at his high school?"

"No." He looked at me strangely. "Since his assault on her."

"Your mother?"

"Yes. Why don't you know this?"

"I just don't, I guess. I mean, Ajax told me that he'd pushed a girl who had teased him at school. And I read the psychologist's intake, notes on him that mentioned a sexual incident at home, but it wasn't specific. It left a creepy feeling, kind of in the back of my mind."

"Maybe they didn't make a big deal of it because he only went so far."

"How far?" I asked.

"I hate this," he said.

"I really would like to know," I said.

"He was fifteen. I really think he was too naive about what to do—he's like that—but it was an attempt. They were home alone; he'd been diving in the pool all afternoon. That was one of his compulsions at home, over and over—he would do that sometimes when he was mad or had something on his mind. My mother didn't even hear him come in. All of a sudden he was just there. He had his suit down, just enough, I guess, and he pinned her against the wall, pulled her skirt up, but, like I said, it only went that far."

I had started wiping the stove and the countertops when he began the story. I suppose it was my way of not looking upset. But in fact, since nothing needed wiping, I probably did look upset.

"He felt terrible after," his brother said. "It only lasted a few seconds, and then he ran away. My father and the sheriff didn't find him until the middle of the night, out in the field behind our house. He was still in his swimming suit, and he went with them, no trouble."

"Until the next time," I said. I was mad. Probably because I was afraid. I hate being afraid.

We heard Ajax on the stairs then. After they had left, I wished I had a chance to talk to his brother some more, instead of just getting mad like that, and then Ajax being there.

I used to get mad with my boyfriend in the same way,

not because he had done anything, but because I would be afraid, and he couldn't understand.

We lived in Selby-Dale, one of the worst neighborhoods in the city. I had a friend, down the street, who was raped in her apartment. It was hot, and she hadn't locked her windows. The guy just lifted the screen out, climbed in, and raped her. In her own bed.

For a while it seemed to be happening once a week. One assault in particular got a lot of coverage because the woman was a med student and the attack damaged her brain. She was coming back from the grocery store with breakfast things for the next morning, and the guy pulled her behind a garage and crushed her skull with a lead pipe. I suppose if you think of sparing her some pain, it was probably better that he crushed her skull before he raped her. But when you think of it in terms of sex, or of a man wanting to be with a woman, it doesn't make any sense at all, does it?

I needed to take the bus to the Gateway at night. Paul would wait with me at the bus stop. Some nights it would be more of a bother for him than others, because he'd already worked all day, and we'd have to leave in the middle of the news, so he would sigh heavily when he got up to get his coat and blink his eyes as if they were tired. I don't know what he would have answered if I just said, "You don't have to go tonight." I never did. I was mostly grateful. But one night when he was acting particularly bedraggled, I said, "I'm mad at all of you. I have to ask you to protect me from some other guy. It's not women I'm afraid of."

"I know," he said.

I said, "Why don't you stick to hurting each other, and leaving us out of it." I suppose that wasn't fair.

I've never really been hurt—not badly anyway, mostly scared. Once I was coming from the edit studio about 7 at night. It was dusky twilight, not a bad part of town. A man was heading toward me on the sidewalk, and I felt, you know, threatened. It was just a feeling. I kept walking, being ready, and when we were almost side by side, he grabbed my arm. He held it really tight between my elbow and my wrist. I had expected it, but I hadn't really expected it, because of all the times I have felt threatened and then nothing happens. His eyes weren't all there, and he had a scraggly beard, not necessarily dirty, but as if he didn't pay much attention to it. I looked around right away to see who else was near, but there was only someone—I couldn't tell if it was a man or a woman—a long way up the sidewalk. I was into my porch philosophy again because I froze, and I didn't say anything, just waited to see what he would do. I don't know how I looked, but he looked mean and dug his fingers into my arm. He just said very clearly, as if he'd told me the time and I hadn't really listened to him at first. "I could really hurt you." Then he walked on.

When I got home, I told Paul about it. Later when we were lying in the living room, watching TV, I asked him if he thought I was strong. He said yes. But I wanted to know how strong, because when I walked down the street alone, I'd always convinced myself I was—I'd always pumped myself up into believing that I could protect myself. I told him to try to pin me to see if I could get away. So we wrestled, and I really tried. Paul's not much taller than Ajax and not as muscular. But he was very much stronger than I. He got me over on my stomach and pulled my arms up behind me so I could hardly move, as hard as I tried. Whenever you struggle like that, your muscles quiver for hours after. He stopped, and he said he hated it; he wished we hadn't got into it. My arms were trembling all over. They wouldn't stop. And then I cried, because I felt so weak. I'd never realized how weak I was.

When I interviewed for this job, I remember sitting in the director's office with my short little resumé, and I had a feeling right off that it wasn't the psychology degree that would ace it for me. It was something less tangible. I told him that I was the oldest girl in a large family, that I'd been cooking the meals since I was twelve because my mom was a career woman, and I told him that I was used to the chaos of family life, all the little dramas that pop up, that I knew how to be calm in the face of them.

There are times it seems crazy to have a female on the night shift here, but most of the time it's the best thing. Like tonight—it's almost midnight and Peter hasn't come home. I have special protective feelings about Peter because he came here so young, and this is his only home. What would it be like if all the guys that grew up here didn't have any women around? The male staff hug the guys sometimes, kind of pounding them on the back while they're doing it. But it's Gail and I who do the main hugging. It's not creepy, except when the youngest, Chip, who is at that fairly curious stage, lingers a little too long. And it's awkward with Ajax too. Instead of coming and getting one, like the other guys, he'll stand at the end of the stairway once in a while and say, "I suppose I'm never going to get a hug." Then when you give him one, he'll kind of take over, basically pick you up off your feet. I've seen it with Gail, too, where you feel trapped and overpowered.

More than hugging, Ajax's way of being physical is to grip your hand or your arm and squeeze. It's not like the other guys never do this, but with them I always play a little. With Ajax, I let my arm go very limp. It's a way of not winning, but not playing either. I want him to feel silly and stop. Art says that Ajax just doesn't know his own strength. But I don't quite buy that. And I always feel a little hate toward Ajax, like a stone in my throat, when he does it.

Once I just said, "Take it easy, Ajax."

And he said, "Forget it then, I'm never talking to you again."

He's said this before, and when he does, I do my counselor thing and say, "That's up to you, Ajax, but I want you to understand that I don't feel that way. People have misunderstandings, and they can be worked out."

But he won't talk to me for a few days. I'll say "Hi" to him when he comes in, and he won't say "Hi" back. Sometimes I'll walk in the door and see him ducking up the stairway to avoid me. When he finally breaks the silence, it's usually like this: he comes in the kitchen in the morning, starts making his toast while I'm making eggs or something, then he says, "So, are you still mad at me?"

I'll say, "Ajax, remember, I haven't been been mad at you. You've been mad at me."

Once I was flipping pancakes on the grill and we went through this routine. He asked. I said the usual no, that I wasn't mad in the first place.

"Oh, ho!" he boomed. "Don't give me that. Women always hold grudges! I know how women are!"

Usually I just keep doing what I'm doing when I talk to him—it's a way of acting nonchalant. But that morning I set my spatula down and faced him. I said, "No you don't, Ajax, I'm afraid you don't know very much about women at all." It was still controlled, but that time it felt like I had walked right out on the edge of my porch, that time I got angry.

I've been making cheese enchiladas tonight. It's tomorrow's dinner. All they'll have to do is pop them in the oven. Some of these enchiladas have cheese and onions for the guys that like onions, and some of them have cheese and olives. As soon as I finish this, I'll make a banana cream pie, and that should put me in bed by 1 A.M. This is the dream part of my job, that I can sleep. As long as there aren't any problems, I can sleep and be rested the next day for the film work.

But Peter's not home, and now I wish I'd asked Art what the trouble was at work. I mean, I can guess. There's been a lot of pressure on him lately to be "normal." We just had a meeting with him the other day. He really wants to live on his own. We said that all he has to do is hold down his job for six months; then we could look at his plans to move on. He gets all flustered at these meetings. He's so long-boned now and thin, and he wears his hair long. He was sitting on the sofa, trying to be calm—keeping himself still by crossing his lanky legs at the knees and squeezing them together. He always wears big flannel shirts, buttoned up to the neck, and corduroys. And on the left side of his shirt there's usually one

of the cardboard badges that he makes himself. He was wearing his favorite at the meeting, the one with the three MX
missiles drawn on it.

He draws missiles all the time, pages and pages of them.
He even has some he made out of papier-mâché that are
about four feet tall in his closet. He also draws crocodiles,
and people he doesn't like being eaten by the crocodiles. And
he's into the Russians—he totally identifies with them or
wants to. Our current psychologist says this is his way of
identifying with someone that he feels is powerful, since he
feels so powerless.

We make rules about how he should behave. We say he
can wear his big, furry Russian hat around the house, but not
in public. We used to say he must always be normal. But that
was wrong. As soon as he stopped one weird thing, he would
only move on to another. When he was younger, he was as
crazy about rock stars as he is now about Russians. He
would draw pictures of Mick Jagger, and that's all he would
talk about. If someone happened to have pop music on the
radio, he would cover his ears and run out of the room.
"Wimp rock," he called it.

Then he had a short spell in between the rock stars and
the Russians, when he started drawing road maps. They
were good. He was a kind of genius in that department. I
would tell him I'd been to Chicago, because I'd know he'd be
interested, and he'd tell me exactly the roads I would have
taken. It seemed to me at the time that this was his own way
of knowing where things were. And it was a way to know
where he was. Drawing maps gave him confidence.

When he's not drawing, he spends a good deal of his time
sitting in a chair with a radio pressed to his ear. Sometimes
he wears earphones like Ajax. It wasn't until this year that I
learned he doesn't really listen to the music. I asked him
what the words to a certain Pink Floyd song were, and he
said he didn't know. "But you listen to it all the time," I said.

"But I don't hear it—just the sound—and then I think
about two white birds flying."

"Two birds?"

"But one wing, two birds with one wing."

I don't know. You have to be around them for a while; you almost stop noticing how weird they are. You start calling Peter Petrovitch just because he wants you to, and you let him take a shower at 3 in the morning (as long as he's quiet), so he can be the first one. Both Ajax and he want to be the first in. Peter always used to be, but when Ajax came, they had a regular competition. It would have been okay, except Peter was so noisy. He'd get up at 5:30 and start banging his drawers, dropping his shampoo. He's so gangly and uncoordinated. Ajax would hear him and leap up, grab his stuff and get in first. One night, probably when Peter finally realized that this was the way it was going to be, he threw himself on the shag carpeting in the upstairs hallway and moaned.

Most of our guys do various things to get attention, but not Peter. So when he does, I tend to respond. I got up and told him to come downstairs, and we made a deal: if he was really quiet and could get away with it, he could shower in the middle of the night. That way he would never have to feel desperate about it.

I wish Peter would call. The custard is almost thick enough. I usually don't make banana cream pie until the summer, but it's been so cold, I think everyone deserves a change.

Somebody's bed is creaking against the floorboards upstairs, "rock and rolling," as Art puts it. Masturbating, another thing you get used to. I went my whole first year not catching on, climbing up the stairs to see what the racket was about. I even began to think someone was trying to get my goat—making noises and then, when I came up the stairs, tricking me by pretending to be asleep. It wasn't until I walked in on someone . . .

I think that's Terry's corner of the house. He's Ajax's roommate. Sometimes, one of them will start, and in a little while you'll hear two or three other parts of the floor creaking—the kind of chain of events that occurs when a dog starts to howl in the neighborhood. Maybe I'm being disrespectful. It's just that I'm here by myself, quietly cooking, and it starts up. Sometimes it feels absurd, like I'm a cook in the galley of a ship, and the ship is rocking and groaning on the waves.

This is a private thing for them. Though Ajax has talked to me about it—not at first, but later, after he'd started going to sex education class. When he first began visiting me at night, he talked about wanting a girlfriend, but not necessarily sex. He'd be talking about Fire Explorers, getting excited, describing the number of valves in the fire truck's engine, how he and three other guys practiced manning the hose the other day, and he was the only one who didn't fall down. "I need this training!" he'll say. "Someday, I'm going to be out there, and people's lives are going to depend on me."

But then—and he always does this—he'll hear a certain song on his Walkman that brings back memories for him. I can't hear it, but he'll say the name out loud. "'Arc of the Diver,' Steve Winwood," he'll say. "Nineteen eighty, yeah." He'll get kind of gleeful. "I remember this. This was when I was *ten . . . years . . . old.* My brothers used to play it out the windows over the patio, and I'd listen to it. I'd practice diving to it."

When he talks about diving, I'm always reminded of the incident with his mother, but we've never talked about this. I'll ask him about the diving instead.

"You have to make the perfect entry," he'll say. I'll picture him on the board, and I can't imagine him ever making a perfect entry. "No splash, just . . ." He smiles and lowers one hand in a graceful motion. "Then you're in, completely in."

"Completely in? What do you mean?" He's used this expression before.

But he ignores the question, and it remains one of his private ideas. "There was another song, just before the diving one, that I used to listen to on my tape machine by myself. That was called 'While You See a Chance.' 'While you see a chance, take it . . .'" He'll close his eyes, singing and smiling, smiling and moving a little. I like Ajax when he's like this, when he forgets himself and acts silly.

"You must have been happy more than three seconds then," I'll say.

"Exactly three minutes and one second" is his answer. "If you play it ten times in a row, how many minutes is that?"

Then he thinks of a girl—there's usually a girl who goes with one of the songs. "Wendy Britter," he'll say. "I used to follow her home, until her dad got mad."

He's desperate to have a girlfriend. That's even how he puts it. "I'm *desperate!*" he booms, and raps his knuckles against the hood of the stove.

"That's kind of extreme," I'll say.

"You don't know." He crosses his arms over his chest.

He finds all the numbers for the cheerleaders and other girls in the upper echelon at his high school. They think he's weird, and they're not completely wrong.

"Nobody wants to go out with me! Lisa Daniels says she has a boyfriend. Stephanie Zimmerman told me she had to baby-sit, then I saw her at the mall with her daffy girl-friends." Some of the girls that he has called repeatedly sim-ply hand the phone to one of their friends, who pretends to Ajax that she is her friend's mother. He sent his three-hundred-dollar class ring to a girl he hardly knew in his hometown, and she sent it back with a puzzled note. Art has taken him aside on several occasions, trying to explain how he's coming on too strong. But this makes Ajax angry. He wants what he wants.

He wants a girlfriend, he wants to marry her, and he wants to have a baby with her. Boom, boom, boom, it's a cure-all.

"You need to take things slow, get to know each other first," I'll say to him, "or you'll scare them off. You'd scare me off."

Maybe that was the wrong thing to say because he began to consider me. "Say?" He'd be leaning against the counter, his arms across his chest, not looking at me. "If you were in my school, do you think we could?"

"Could what?"

"Be boyfriend and girlfriend?

"That depends."

"Depends on what?" He'll get hostile.

"Depends, on how we got to know each other."

"We just would."

"You have to start somewhere. I mean, if you saw me in the hallway, what would you say to me?"

Ajax turns to face me and kind of sways his shoulders like he's walking down the hall of his high school. "Hey, baby," he says.

"Nope," I say, "that wouldn't do it."

"Wouldn't do it!" he spits out his *t*'s like they're nails. "Hey!" he's louder than ever. "You're just being too sensitive. I hate it when women are sensitive."

I talked to our psychologist about how things were getting a little personal with Ajax. How should I handle it?

He said that it was good he was opening up. That these were important issues with him. That I could be open with him, at the same time guiding him in appropriate feelings toward me.

Two years ago there was another resident who didn't have appropriate feelings toward me. The first night that I met David, he was polite in that phony way kids get when they've been through the system time and again. He was tall and bony, and I guessed MI, because his eyes had that sleepy drugged look, and he kept wetting his lips, which is one of the side effects of Haldol. He shook my hand, which was not really a shake, but like a quick, dry pass over my palm. He said, "Oh, what are you making? Pea soup. That looks delicious. Well, it's good to meet you." The whole Eddie Haskell routine. Then he went out to have a cigarette with Jackie. Jackie came in a little while later and said, "Do you know what he said? He said, 'So, do you fuck her?' " Jackie kept his head down when he told me this.

I said, "He did, did he?" and I thanked him for telling me.

David is the only person who has ever punched me in the face. I'd always been afraid of being punched someday, the way you are afraid if you've never broken a bone, because it's a common thing, and you feel eventually your number is going to be up.

When it finally happened, I felt both relief and grief. Relief, because now I'd been hit and it wasn't so bad. Grief, because it still hurt—it was still a shock.

I learned to be on my guard with him, because that punch came right out of the blue. It was the morning. He was standing at the top of the stairs, and I was at the bottom. He'd just finished faking his fourth shower that week, and I said, "David, why don't you take a real one?" The next thing I knew, he'd thrown his bottle of shampoo at my head. He must have felt as long as he was in it this far, he should make the most of it, because he bounded down the stairs and punched me once in the eye and once in the cheek.

The psychologist said it was a matter of poor impulse control. But that was only the beginning.

I've wondered whether I could have handled the situation better with David if I had had more experience at the time. He was up and down for a while, and then he was mostly down—mostly hard to understand. He would visit me in the kitchen some nights the way Ajax does, the way a lot of the guys do. He had this thing with me, where he said, "You're an Earthling, and I'm a Martian." I just thought it was one of his ways of being playful, the way it was with Peter. He'd say, "You live in a house, have a car, and eat regular earth food. I live on Mars and don't eat and don't have a house or anything."

"Why don't you be an Earthling for a change?" I would say.

"No, it could never be that way," he'd say.

Some nights he wouldn't come down, but he'd shout from his room upstairs, *"Laura Wold!"* And he had this deep, baritone way of shouting *Wold* so that it sounded like a fog horn.

Insidious things began to happen—like my time card would be missing when I came in, or notes to the other counselors that I had left taped to the wall would disappear. When I'd ask him, he'd say, "Why do you always blame me?" I began to sleep on the couch downstairs because otherwise he would steal too much food from the kitchen at night. He didn't eat half of it. I would find a moldy package of hot dogs he had abandoned in the basement, or a cake on the counter that he had gouged into the middle of, not because he was hungry, it seemed, but because he wanted to have it, somehow stake his claim to it.

Things got worse. We'd find obscenities written on the walls, on our books, even on a jar of mayonnaise in the refrigerator, or a can of tomato sauce in the pantry.

After a long time of not coming down to visit, he did one night. He understood things were getting worse. He even said so. He said, "It's getting bad, Laura." I remember that I was boiling a big pot of water on the stove and that it made me nervous, because every once in a while he'd hold his hand over the steam.

"Tell me what you mean."

"I probably shouldn't," he said.

"Well, that's up to you."

"It's getting to be that time," he said after a few moments.

"What time?"

"You know," he said. *"Forced Vengeance* time."

Forced Vengeance was a movie that he'd seen not too long ago, about a man who goes on a killing rampage because of the wrong that has been done to him. He'd liked it and would talk about it now and then.

Then he seemed to get off the track, and he said, "How come I can't trust you?"

"I don't know," I said, "because I'm a trustworthy person, David."

"I don't know either," he said. "Maybe you'll be okay."

"I hope so," I said.

"But this is a bad one, Laura. This is the ultimate."

"Which is?" I said.

"You know, death."

"David?"

"It's my duty. People have tried to hurt me."

"Who's hurt you, David?"

But he wouldn't say.

I notified the psychologist about the conversation. He said that David had brought up similar issues with him in their recent sessions. He said it was good that David was bringing it out in the open. I told the director, and he said we'd need to watch and wait.

A week later it was a stifling hot summer night. The humidity in the air was like tapioca. Just moving seemed an effort, and sleeping was a kind of fitful delirium. Even sleeping on the sofa seemed too lumpy and hot, so I ended up putting my pillow on the living room floor. I would hear the guys get up to take showers, trying to keep cool, and a couple of times some of them went down to the laundry room to get more towels. I was in and out of sleep, not just because of the heat, but because I was a little sick with fear. At one point I could feel someone's footsteps on the floor close to where I was lying, and I felt trapped, the way you do when sleep has a hold of you and you can't break out of it, even though you feel sure there is something you have to do. I heard myself say, "David!" Then I opened my eyes, and he was standing there. It was so dark, but I could see it was his profile, tall, with narrow shoulders, and long arms.

"Do me a favor and turn the light on." I said this for two reasons: one, because I wanted the light on; and two, because sometimes when one of the guys is ready to have a fit, I ask them to do something completely normal and it steers them off course.

It didn't work. But at least it bought me enough time to get to my feet. "What time is it, anyway?" I'd gotten past him. I was almost to the light switch at the foot of the stairs when he got behind me and grabbed me around the neck. He was choking me. I guess that was better than stabbing me or hitting me with something.

When I started working here, I took a course called "Aggression Management." There are all kinds of steps you learn to follow in order to prevent something like this from escalating. So first I said, "David you don't want to be doing this." Then I said, "This hurts, I want you to stop." I wedged my hand underneath the arm that was against my throat to relieve the pressure. He was excited, and his breathing was irregular. He smelled like old cigarettes and perspiration. He would squeeze my neck really hard, then he'd let up, like he was building up his strength to go to it again. And then sure enough, the next time was harder. I wedged my hand in better and shouted, "Stop it! Stop choking me!"

Jackie was upstairs in his bed, behind his bedroom door. But I'd awakened him, and he shouted through his door, *"What's going on?"* Not like he had any idea, but like he was hot and tired and exasperated and wanted to go back to sleep.

But it was enough to break into David's craziness. He backed off. Then he slammed me on the back of the head with his fist and ran up the stairs to his room. I don't know why he did that. Except maybe it was like the last time, when he'd thrown the shampoo bottle—he'd gone this far; it made sense for him to get in his licks. Or maybe he thought it should be like the movies, where guys are always whopping people on the back of the head, and the people, of course, get knocked out, fall to the floor, and that is the end of the scene.

It was the end of the scene. I've wondered about how I went about things afterward. I mean, it was 4 in the morning, too early to call my supervisor. And I didn't call the police, because I had this idea that bringing them in when it was over would be like overreacting. I remember just thinking, He will not do this again, not to me.

I went into the kitchen and turned on all the lights. I put all the knives back in a corner of one of the cupboards. I took off the top of the pepper shaker, because my mother had once told me that's what I should do. It worked like Mace. Then I made banana bread with some overripe bananas I found on the counter. I remember that I was trembling all over, so that when I measured the baking soda out, it literally bounced off the spoon into the bowl. This made me kind of laugh/cry, and I thought about how this was just a little like being hysterical, but not the full-blown thing, which I was thankful for.

I decided to make pancake batter and homemade applesauce too, as long as I was up so early. And when Jackie came downstairs at 5:45, their places were all set, the juices all poured, and I was sitting at the table, writing in the notes about what had happened with David.

I loved Jackie so much that morning, because I needed him to be good, and he was. He said, "Howdy." His eyes are kind of close-set and his body round-shouldered and bearlike.

I said "Hi," and then he said "Howdy" again. He always says it two or more times. I'm not sure why.

I said, "Jackie, I need your help." He kind of jutted his lips out like, It better be good—but he always does this at first. I said, "David tried to hurt me a couple of hours ago. Now, I have to go up and wake the others, and I don't want him to hurt me again." I said, "I don't want you to do anything, or for David really to even see you. I just want you to be behind me in the hall."

Jackie is not a bright individual, but he understands things even if he's not able to explain them. He was quiet for a minute, looking down at the rug, like he was embarrassed or hurt or something, then he said, "Okay."

David was taken to a psyche lockup that afternoon, but it wasn't over. It was how I felt afterward that was the hardest. My landlady was old and close to deaf, and she'd usually be watering the lawn or sweeping the sidewalk when I came back to my apartment in the morning. She'd always ask me about my night. She thought it was a strange job to have and acted as though it was only a matter of time before I would get a new one. Invariably she'd say, "Did you get some sleep?"and, "Did they give you much trouble?"

And invariably I'd answer, "Yes," and "No."

But that morning, as she turned away to continue watering the lawn, I touched her arm, which was sticky from the heat, so that she would turn back to me and listen. I said loudly and clearly, "One of them tried to choke me last night." She looked at me puzzled, like she wasn't hearing me. It's nearly impossible when she's outside and you have to compete with the noise of traffic. I said it again, and then I pointed to the light brown bruises in the shapes of fingers that marked my neck. Maybe she's a little blind, too, because she just didn't get it.

She's an old Czech woman and a survivor of a concentration camp, which she has never talked about, except once when I asked, to say, "It's over. I lost my life and my soul there, but now I'm here, and I have a new life and a new soul." I didn't try to tell my story again. It was really nothing compared to that, was it?

I was so tired that I slept for a long time, and I didn't feel like going into the film co-op, or doing anything, really. The next day, while cleaning his room out, I found porno magazines in his drawers. The kind that favored the wide close-up shots of women's vulvas. Luscious and open and inviting images. Under the magazines I found some ripped snapshots of the staff and residents at Gateway. He'd torn off the part of the photos that I was in, so that all the scraps he'd saved were pictures of me. There were little pen marks on my face, and on the back of the pictures he'd written things like, "This is a fucking dead Earthling" and "Beware men, Laura is in you're penises," and some things I couldn't even understand, like, "No more danger." Was I dangerous? Why was I dangerous?

I showed them to my supervisor, and for a while they were in a cigar box on his desk where we kept pens, paperclips and odds and ends. But I was afraid they'd get lost, so I took them home and put them in an envelope to save for the hearing that was coming up. I wanted something to prove that it wasn't just poor impulse control, that it was part of his whole vision and needed to be taken seriously.

David called the group home from the hospital several times in the next couple of weeks. He seemed to want to talk to me especially, because he would call at 11:10 on the dot and ask for me. He was worried about what was going to happen to him. Sometimes he would say he was sorry, and he hoped I wasn't mad at him; sometimes he would remind me that I had been sarcastic, and sometimes it would be as if he'd forgotten the whole thing completely. I don't know why I felt I had to talk to him, as if I were concerned about being impolite. Maybe I just wanted to change my mind about him, have him change his mind about me.

The assistant county attorney rushed in just before the hearing. He hadn't looked at the case very well, because he didn't know my name and he didn't know David's. I brought my envelope of pictures up to the stand, but he forgot to ask about them. The psychiatrist hired by the county attorney said that David thought of me as his girlfriend—he was ambivalent, on the one hand saying he loved me, and on the other talking about how he had planned to kill me. Yes, he felt he was dangerous, which was the main issue of the hearing. The psychiatrist appointed by David's public defender thought David had some difficulty controlling his impulses, but that he wasn't a significant danger to society.

David, I could tell, was on a lot of medication. When another counselor and I first walked into the back of the courtroom, he turned and waved. It was a kind of geeky wave, the kind where he just held his hand up and fluttered his fingers. When I got up to the stand, he gave me another sort of tentative wave. He was sitting at a table across from me. His eyes were glazed over, and when I got to the choking part, he looked at the table with a far-off smile. That was because he was letting himself think of something else; Peter and Ajax space out like this too. I didn't feel sorry for him then, but I do a little now. At the time, I wanted the judge to recommend the harshest thing, which was to send him to a hospital for the violently mentally ill. Now I'm glad he just sent him upstate to a strict but not end-of-the-road place.

After the whole thing, I got depressed. I could only compare it to the way I'd felt once after a car accident. I'd been in the backseat, reading a story out loud to some of my college friends. We were all laughing while we drove through an underpass, hit a patch of water, and began to hydroplane. My girlfriend, who was driving, could do nothing to control the car. She turned the wheel back and forth, but we were in the air, and it didn't make any difference. I remember holding the magazine in one hand and reaching forward to lay my other hand on her shoulder, as if I could help her set us down again, put us back in control. We hit a concrete embankment at about fifty, and miraculously none of us was injured.

All night we were at a garage not far off the highway, trying to get the car repaired. We kept saying things to each other like, "Thank God it was a Volvo," and "I usually don't even wear seat belts." I remember the glare of the utility lights and the gray cement and an incredible sense of defeat. People always say brushes with death make our lives more precious to us. I think they can make them seem very small and worthless.

My feelings after the incident with David were like that night in the garage, only they lasted for a few months instead of a few hours. When you almost die of an accident or an illness, you get shaken up, you're reminded that these things happen, that you're vulnerable. But when you find out someone has wanted to kill you, probably still does, then you feel like you've been dreaming, that you've really been stupid not to understand such a thing.

I'd always believed that how you acted in life is what made all the difference—that being good somehow protected you. This was my worldview. But that changed the night David put his hands around my neck. It struck home that even I could be marked from the beginning simply because I was female. It didn't matter who I was; it only mattered what he thought I was. And so I couldn't trust my worldview anymore. But you know, you can't just instantly trade your worldview in for a new one. For a while, you don't trust enough to have one at all. That's depression, that's like not living.

I almost quit the film cooperative at the time, even when the others were really counting on me. We'd finally gotten a big grant, one that would fund a real film. We were on to bigger things. I'd even been the one to write the proposal that had brought in the grant. I had finally taken the old Scottish woman's advice—used the classics. The idea was to bring an ancient hero into the present and see how he handled himself. I'd done a lot of research, and I ended up picking the oldest hero from the oldest story back in ancient Sumer. It's not like this sort of thing hasn't been done a lot already. But I didn't think anyone had used this hero, Gilgamesh, before. I liked to think of him as the first hero. His story was passed on from campfire to campfire before writing was invented, way before we had even a few of the ideas that we have now. He was like a lot of other heroes, on a quest, killing monsters along the way, and ending up in the underworld, where he finally came to accept that he could not live forever, that all this time maybe he'd been expecting too much for himself. But because it was the first story, there's a special deep feeling, that this man was really only learning these truths for the very first time.

I had started to write a script, and we'd begun to cast people for parts when I got depressed—when I lost my worldview. My friend Hank and I were in charge of choosing the lead. These handsome men would come through, one after another, and I felt nothing about them.

Hank would say, "I like him, what do you think?"

"No," I would say, or, "He's not what I picture. He's not right. He isn't it. No, I don't know. Let me think about it. . . ."

After this had gone on just about forever, Hank said, "Perhaps we should start auditioning women. I don't think there's another male actor left in the region."

"Maybe I'm just beginning to think this whole hero idea sucks," I said.

"You're taking this project very personally."

"Isn't that what you're supposed to do? What's the point otherwise?"

And Hank, who's my friend, said, "That kid who hurt you, Laura, was crazy."

"It's bigger than that," I said.

"It just seems that way," he said, "because you're in the middle of it, because you're working in your own little house of heroes, because you're vulnerable to them everyday. It's that job of yours. Quit the damn place."

I started to cry before he even said it. "I can't quit my job," I said. "I'll never have another one like it, where I can come in at night and cook, and go to sleep, and have the time to do what I want during the day. It would change my whole life to quit that job!"

"You'd feel differently after you worked somewhere else for a while."

"I'd be kidding myself," I said, not really sure what I meant. "I mean, at the Gateway at least I don't have to pretend that things aren't crazy. All I have to do is look at one newspaper a month to see what a common thing craziness can be, and yet we all have to go around as if everything is fine. Peter only draws pictures of missiles. The guys on the hill are tossing around the real things. And group homes aren't the only places that women get hurt.

"At least at the Gateway I can talk to Peter. I can get through to him. If I'd just seen it coming, maybe I could have changed the thing with David."

Hank was looking at me and shaking his head.

I felt embarrassed. "I don't know what I'm saying. All I know is, I can't look at this Gilgamesh story anymore. Every woman who got married had to sleep with him first. He ran around like a crybaby because he found out he didn't have everlasting life. . . . You know what troubles me?" I said.

"What?" Hank was sitting back patiently, giving me all kinds of time.

"If you were to cast me in this epic, what part would I get to play?"

"Well, there's the high priestess part when she seduces Gilgamesh's brother out of the forest. And there's the goddess part—that's a big one." He's only half serious.

"Right," I say. "Gilgamesh hated her. He was so pissed at her for being powerful. He would have done away with her in a minute, if he had the chance. Why aren't there any parts that would be everyday parts? A part that would fit me?"

I wonder if, as you get older, you have closer and closer run-ins with danger. It seems that has happened with me. What's next? That's one of the reasons Ajax makes me so anxious, because he can seem like the next one.

Ajax has started going to a sex education group on Monday nights. It's one of those cases where a little knowledge might be too much. Their first group was about masturbation and fantasy: how it was okay; how this was a way to relieve their tension. Good, that's good, but now Ajax feels comfortable enough to tell me he has fantasies about me. "It's natural for you to fantasize about people you know," I say, hoping this is a cast of thousands for him. "You just have to remember that it's happening in your imagination and not in real life. You do that, don't you, Ajax?"

"Do you think I'm stupid?" he says. "It's just like when I tell you I love you, I only tell you in my head."

But he's had slips. Once, while I was packing the lunches, he came up from behind and pressed himself against me. I stiffened and said, "That's absolutely out of bounds, Ajax!" Then he just disappeared, slipped out of the room, like he'd never been there. And until I said something, I think, in his own way, he hadn't been there. He'd been in his head.

If things get too weird with him, what happens? Will I have to leave? Will he? Either way, it would be too bad. Too bad for him because we're finally getting to understand him better. He'd have to start all over again somewhere else. Too bad for me because this is my job, this is how I live.

I think I kid myself as much as Ajax. I tell myself, "He

just needs to know me a little better. He would never want to hurt me then."

While he's thinking, "She's going to want me someday. She has to, she just has to."

They found pieces of a woman's body two weeks ago. Terry, who stutters and loves to read the newspaper out loud, especially the gruesome stories, read it off the front page at breakfast. "It, it, it says here, 'A, a man—who was walking his dog—found the torso of a woman's body on a frozen swamp east of St. Paul . . .' What's a torso?" he asked. I reached over and ran my finger along his arm socket and then along his hip where his legs hook in. I didn't have to touch him, but it was a way of making it personal, so he could feel how it could be his body. "Oh," Terry said.

"Gross." Both Chip and Trevor started laughing.

"Don't laugh!" Terry said, knowing it would put him in my good graces.

Ajax jumped up excitedly to look over Terry's shoulder. "Man!" he said too loudly, because he had his earphones on. "The guy must have used a saw or something."

"Thanks a lot." Jackie sat back in his chair and threw his toast down. "Now I can't eat." But half a second later he leaned forward and put his spoon back into his oatmeal.

Peter wasn't even there. He was upstairs in his room with his pictures or his radio or both.

In the next few days they found some of the rest of her body. She was identified as a clerk in a grocery store who had never made it home after her shift. Never made it to her car, which was still parked in the parking lot. Gail was especially troubled by it because it had happened in Rosedale, where she lives. "You always think these things won't happen in the really cold weather," she said. She was keeping track of the story, and every night, when I came in, I'd ask her if they'd found him yet.

They finally picked him up. His wife suspected him because of the green shower curtain they had found around the body, the fact that theirs had disappeared. "He had a little daughter," Gail told me when I came in last night. She'd brought the article with his confession in it, but I still haven't read it.

It's 1:15 A.M., and I finally called Peter's restaurant to find out why he hasn't come home. I half-hoped that I would hear everything was fine, that he had just decided to stay on and finish his shift. But when the hostess answered, she was very flustered, saying they were having trouble with him, and that the manager would want to talk to me.

"You've got that right!" the manager said, when I told him I understood there had been some problems. "This kid can't seem to get through his head that he's fired. I mean out of here, caput, finished!"

"What happened?"

"I don't know where to start," he says. "First he has a fit, swearing at my cooks and throwing dishes. We tell him he has to leave, but he won't. He says, 'This is my job, I have to keep it, you can't take it away from me.' Something about how he has to keep it for six months, or he'll never get an apartment and be normal. I tell him maybe if he leaves right now without any other trouble, we can talk about it next week. *'Next week!'* he shrieks. And I say, 'Yeah.' But that's not good enough. He doesn't trust me, he says. So he goes back to the sink and starts washing dishes, only he's all upset and clumsy and not really doing the job. I say, 'Come on, we'll talk about it next week.' 'My crocodile, you will!' he says. Whatever is that supposed to mean?"

"Just an expression he has."

"Right," the manager says. "One of the least of his problems. Two of my bussers and one of my cooks escort him to the door. He's not a fighter. He left. But then he comes back in, says, please can he just go to work. I say no, and he needs to leave, or we'll have to call the cops. So it seems like he leaves, but apparently he hid in the back hall by the storeroom for a long time. He threw lit matches in the storeroom."

"Oh, no!" I'm surprised about this.

"It could have been a bad fire. If one of my cooks hadn't gone back there when he did, it could have gotten out of hand. We had five hundred people in this restaurant tonight. And still he's acting like we are in the wrong. He wouldn't give me your number. I'm glad you called because he had about thirty seconds before I called the police. I didn't want a lot of commotion with my customers still here. But it's the end of the night now."

"Can I talk to him?" I say.

"I can't lose my job!" Peter says when he gets on.

"Let's start from the beginning. What happened?"

"Org, that cook kind of guy, was here when I came in to work tonight."

"Org is not his real name, though," I say.

"Well, Lard Ass, then."

"Peter."

"Well, Don, then, or whatever. I suppose I'm in deep trouble now, and you want me to use real names."

"That's right," I say.

Then he starts to cry. "I'm in such deep trouble," he says.

"I know, sweetheart." And it sounds like something an older woman would say.

"Well, I came in tonight, and that Don guy was here. We don't get along really well. And some of the other cooks, and Ramone, who's a dishwasher, were there too. He and I have a lot in common. He's always been a cool, you know, sort of a communist and stuff, and on my side. So we're horsing around . . ."

"Were you talking about some of your sillier topics?"

"Well, Ramone seemed to like it. It wasn't super-unacceptable stuff. Just politics, just a little joking about crocodiles."

"And then what?"

"My dishwasher hat, you know, it has a cardboard band and then cloth. Well, the band had gotten all soggy and loose, and it was making me uncomfortable. So I got my Russian hat out of my backpack and wore that instead."

"Was it the visor hat or the big, furry one?"

"Big furry," he says.

"I bet that wasn't such a good idea."

"No, it wasn't. Ramone didn't like it. He said I was being too weird. The cook told him I was a mental. Then it was like Ramone was on their side. Then they were saying, 'You re-tard! You faggot!'"

While I'm on the phone, Ajax has come down and is leaning against the doorjamb, waiting for me to get off. He doesn't like it when I'm on the phone. "It's going to be a few minutes," I say to him. He rolls back around the doorjamb and is gone.

"Tell me about the fire," I say to Peter.

"They say I started a fire in the storeroom."

"Why do they say that?"

"Because I was back there, and then there was a fire."

"What about lighting matches?"

"I was in the back hallway. They thought they'd kicked me out, but I came back. I was smoking a cigarette, and I started lighting matches and throwing them. They say I started the fire, but I wasn't trying to. I was just throwing matches. Must have been one of the cartons of trash caught on fire."

"How do you know that?"

"Because there was a little ball of fire in it."

"This is very serious, Peter."

"What are my consequences going to be?" He meant at the Gateway, that he was going to be in trouble with us too. "Will I be able to take a shower when I get home, even if it's late?"

"Yes," I say.

"The water pressure wasn't very good yesterday. Do you think it's fixed yet, Laura?"

"No, I don't, Peter, and I think you're starting to worry about the wrong things here. There were five hundred people in that restaurant tonight."

"Now I'm kicked out," he says.

"I'm afraid so, Peter. Now you need to try to be very calm and come home."

I talk the manager into calling Peter a cab. While I wait for him, I read the newspaper article Gail had left me. They had recorded the statement of the man who had killed and dismembered the girl in Rosedale. He never used the words *I* or *she*.

> Some sexual advances were made. The advances were rejected. Some hitting took place. This went on for a while. The sexual advances were then accepted. Emergency medical services were not called, then death occurred.

I watch a few minutes of an old John Wayne Western on television. I play Predict the Dialogue. An old pastime from college. John Wayne is the easiest. You just try to guess the exact thing he is going to say and then say it at the same time he does. "Why, thankya, ma'am," you say along with him, or "I oughta . . . ," or "Maybe this town isn't big enough. . . ." But you have to do it just exactly with the same sway he does.

"Who are you talking to?" Ajax is down again.

"Why, I'm talk'n to John Wayne." I do my best imitation. I don't care if he gets it or not. And I realize I'm angry at John Wayne. I'm angry at Ajax. And I'm angry at those dead, gray, remorseless words I just finished reading in the newspaper. What would it have taken for him to see her as human, for him to see himself as the same?

I turn the television off and get off the couch, because I don't want him to sit next to me. I go in the kitchen, wrap the pie, and put it in the refrigerator.

"You're in a bad mood," he says. He sets himself up against the counter, like he's planning on having a long conversation.

"I'm tired," I say, "and Peter is in trouble, and I have to wait for him to come home." It's not the whole truth.

"You worry too much."

I might as well play Predict the Dialogue with Ajax now.

"You're too sensitive." I'm hearing him say it before it's even said.

"It takes all kinds." I have my own predictable response.

"It's better to be strong. I'd like to see you get hit in the face six times and not flinch."

"I was sorry to hear that Trevor hit you, Ajax. I was hoping you'd want to talk about it."

"There's nothing to talk about!" he booms, setting up a rattle in the silent house and reminding me of how late it has gotten.

I go around with the sponge, wiping off the counter, the fridge, anywhere I can. All I hear is the scratching sounds coming out of his earphones. He's stonewalling me. I can't predict what he'll say next, or whether he'll say anything at all. Maybe he'll say, "We're never going to make it, are we?" like he said last week, and about two weeks before. I can't say, "Yes, we will," because I know he's still talking about being boyfriend and girlfriend. And I can't say no, because we should at least be able to understand each other, because it's when we don't that it gets so dangerous.

He's giggling a little. I imagine it's about something he hears on his radio, or it's about something he's thinking. But he says, "Laura World, I'm giving you a new name." He's teasing me. But I'm behind my door, and there's a porch in front of me and I don't react.

"Laura World." He sets it on the porch, and I'm looking at it. I'm quiet, and I have the time to think about what he means. Is that what I stand for to him? The world? Coming into this house every day, bringing it in with me, as if it's a secret I'm keeping from him. That's a lot of responsibility, I think. He's the hero and I'm the world. And he thinks that he's locked outside and has to get in, be completely in. And I decide right here and now that just because I'm a woman doesn't mean I have to be the world to him. And I decide that everyone is a hero, including me. And then, I'm ready to say something back.

I say, "My name is Laura Wold. I'll never answer to the other."

"Yeah," he says. "What if I call you that tomorrow?"

"I'll tell you my real name again," I say.

"And the day after?"

"I'll tell you again."

"And after that?"

"Every day after," I say, "until you get it right."

ACCIDENTS

It was the third Saturday in October, and all the leaves in Minneapolis had been brought down in a storm two nights before. Every weather report was saying clear skies through the weekend, and Friday's sun had already baked the dampness away. This was the day to rake. Anyone could have started the day the leaves began to drop, but being experienced home owners, we knew it was the big fall one waited for. It seemed the whole neighborhood was out in their yards, and if you listened, you could hear a unison of strokes as the leaves were slowly pushed down toward the street.

I say pushed down, because our street actually furrows down the middle of a hill, and the lawns on each side of it, including our own, slope up and away from it. This means that there are many steps to shovel in the winter and grass mowing is an almost perpendicular task, some of us using ropes to pull our mowers up the incline. Despite these disadvantages, we enjoy this hamletlike quality and a satisfying view of Minnehaha Creek curling through the park at the end of our road.

I had just rolled a pile of leaves onto the sidewalk when I heard my nine-year-old, Neil, calling me. His voice was faint in the distance. I watched him gliding his bike over the soft grass of the park, his sandy hair lifting into wings on each side of his head.

All my children are beautiful, but Neil has a physical grace and confidence that has caused even some of the other fathers in the neighborhood to comment. "A natural athlete," someone will say. Or watching him descend the wooded hill behind our houses, one foot following another, no concern for weight, or gravity, or loose ground, I remember Dave Ferber from next door, turning away from our conversation, removing the pipe from his mouth, saying, "He's really something, isn't he?"

Something. None of us can name it, but we watch him with a mixture of joy and humility and loss. It's as though the bike under his body, or the tree he climbs, or the water accepting his dive have never been things separate from himself—no more troublesome to him than the opening and closing of his eyes. He intimidates us, his ease and certainty reproaching our own daily fears. And yet we root him on, paradoxically: though his is an impossible magic that cannot last, we persist in believing that it should last and should have lasted in us.

When I waved to Neil now, as he rode from the park, it seemed to prod him into leaning forward and riding faster. He went over the curb and across the road with barely a glance for traffic. "That was careless," I would tell him. But as I watched him come up the sidewalk toward me, I could see he wasn't riding easily at all. He pumped awkwardly up the incline, his feet straining on the pedals each time they revolved. His tires clattered through the leaves on the walk, and he was winded. I could see that the cuffs of his sweat-shirt were wet.

"Hey!" I shouted, "slow down!"

"Dad!" he was calling. "There's a guy!"

"What?"

"There's a guy in the creek." He was gulping.

"What are you saying?"

"It's like he's stuck under the bridge. He's not moving."

He led me on his bike back to the park. I didn't call out to anyone to follow us. I think, like many others, I resist being alarmed until there's no other choice.

He was fifty years old, perhaps a little older. Everything that would have been ordinary on a living person looked extraordinary now. His Adidas were still laced and tied in the bows he had made. His wristwatch had dark green weeds tangled around the band. He was on his side, his neck twisted, and his face turned into the ground. Somehow the current had begun to pull his sweater off. One of his arms was half out of its sleeve, and this gave him the appearance of a small boy tangled in his undressing. His back was naked except for streaks of mud like brush strokes across his white skin.

I climbed down to the concrete foundation of the bridge, which was slimy from the recent high water, and then stepped into the mud and stones where he lay. I touched him in that place just below the neck and between the shoulders that commonly collects life's tensions. His flesh was cold and spongy from being in the water so long.

Neil stood on the bank above, his hands held out tensely at his sides, as if waiting for directions from me.

"I have to call the police, Neil," I said, as I climbed back up the bank. And he turned to follow.

"No, you should stay." I put my hand on his shoulder, and for the first time since he had come to get me, I looked directly into his face. His mouth was agape. I could see his top teeth. There was a knit in his forehead. "I'll send one of the neighbors to wait with you. Right away," I assured him. And then his face became smooth in the way all my children's faces look, even the youngest, when they surrender to do what I ask.

I regretted leaving him before I had even gone. But it felt wrong to leave the body alone. What seemed most important was to set into motion all that needed to be done: the police could begin to find an explanation; the man's family would know; a rescue squad would come to carry him out of the creek. It was as though a hole had been ripped in the day and I had to mend it.

The neighbors, one by one or in groups, were gathering by the bridge. Each one that heard the news would tell some-one else. Like playing hot potato, they could barely hold what they knew before they needed to pass it on. It seemed a while before the police came, and during the wait, questions circulated through the gathering about the man. Everyone wanted to know as much as they could—a way, I think, of being responsible about something that you can otherwise do nothing about.

The younger children were turned away. My eleven-year-old, Brian, arrived on the scene with two of his friends and their bicycles. "How'd you know he was dead?" he asked me, still perched on his mountain bike and flicking his hair out of his eyes with a flip of his head, a new habit that I found par-ticularly annoying. "You touched him?" he said, scrunching his face at his friends. His friends also scrunched up their faces, but more politely, probably in deference to me. They were all wearing T-shirts with the word *Buckers* written on the front in black marker.

They walked over to where Neil was standing with one of his friends. They were out of earshot, but I could see Brian nudging Neil, and then some general jostling amongst them and smiling. Neil smiled slowly and blushed, stretching the sleeves of his sweatshirt over his fingers as he held his arms out at his sides. He seemed to be glad to have this sudden admiration and relief from the tension, but there was also a restraint, as if he were aware these were probably not the right emotions for him to be having.

A woman nearby, still holding a garden shovel in one hand and both of her muddy work gloves in the other, tilted her head in my direction and said to her friend, "Ask him about it."

Then the police arrived, and I felt relieved that she

didn't have a chance. People, one after another, pointed out the location of the body. One of the officers, who had been talking over his hand-held radio, probably notifying the ambulance, started to slip on the round stones of the creek bed as he climbed down. There were little gasps and some "Watch its!" from the crowd above him.

One officer put his finger to the man's neck, checking his pulse, and the other unbuttoned his back pants pocket and pulled out a wallet. They looked at his identification; then they conferred with each other.

"Who was it that called us?" the officer with the wallet stood and asked.

Neil looked over at me. But it was Brian who shouted that I had.

The officer climbed up the bank with his notebook. He was slight with blond hair parted at the side.

"It was really my son." I motioned to Neil.

Neil was wearing what Claire calls his stranger's face, a passive, almost dull expression he tends to hide behind when he encounters someone new.

"What time would you say you found him, Neil?" the officer asked.

"'Bout an hour." Neil's face was red. "I think he drowned."

"It's okay," I said to Neil. He seemed guilty, as though the police believed he was somehow at fault.

After the ambulance had come, the other officer joined us. "You get all their information?" he said to his partner, giving us only a cursory glance, and I had the impression that without knowing what we had said, he already considered it insignificant.

"Do you know anything about him?" I asked.

The larger officer had hair even darker than mine, a black mustache, and heavy black eyebrows. He looked down at his notebook and almost imperceptibly turned his body toward his partner. In this way it seemed that he was slightly conferring with him. He pushed the brim of his cap up with his pen.

"He fits the description," he said, "of someone missing in St. Louis Park."

Maybe he was making this allowance to me because I had gone to the trouble of calling.

"We thought it was crazy," his partner said.

"His wife made the report," the dark officer said. "The culvert in front of their house clogged up during the storm Thursday night. There were so many leaves—they probably got thick and created a sort of dam. The driveway was flooding, so her husband went out with a pitchfork to work on the jam. It was rushing hard through the culvert when she went out—she thinks it carried him right through."

As I tried to imagine this, Claire came home.

"There's Mom!" Neil shouted, even though he was right next to us.

The larger officer turned in the direction of our house. The walkie-talkie resting on his hip was spitting static and the in-and-out announcements of the dispatcher. "You live right on the corner," he said.

Claire was helping little Maggie out of the car. She'd bought three large pumpkins at the farmer's market, one for each of the children, and she was setting them on the edge of the driveway. Claire's movements are deft and graceful, no matter what she does. She has the kind of blond, straight hair that all the girls wanted when we were teenagers. She wears it to her shoulders now, and as she leaned down to take Maggie's hand, it was falling around her face. We were all watching her, as if pulled out of the context of time, as if we had the leisure to do so.

"Don't call her right now," I said to Neil.

It must have been painful for him to watch her unload groceries from the car, unaware that we were standing there with the police in the middle of a tragedy. I was already saying in my mind the things I would tell her: "He must have slipped in the mud," I would say; or, "When he had finally freed the blockage, an enormous rush of water knocked him down and carried him through the tunnels. . . . Like a damn piece of wood," I would tell her.

"He looked a lot like Mr. Ferber." Brian was comparing our neighbor to the man in the creek.

We were eating pizza on paper plates in the middle of the living room floor. Claire had put a bed sheet over the carpeting to serve as a sort of picnic blanket. I was setting up *Karate Kid* on the VCR.

"I don't know about that," I said to Brian.

Maggie had fallen in love with her pumpkin and insisted that it be by her side all day. Claire or one of the boys or I would lug it around for her. Brian had drawn a face on it with a black felt-tip. And now Maggie was holding a piece of pizza up to its mouth and telling it to eat.

Neil was cross-legged on the floor, chewing his pizza seriously.

"Neil, didn't he look a lot like Mr. Ferber?" Brian asked.

Neil had a little tomato sauce on the corners of his mouth. He was trying to bite through a slice, but the cheese slid off in one piece and was dangling down his chin.

"Good job!" Brian laughed.

Neil leaned over his plate and let the cheese drop from his mouth while he giggled.

Brian was bent forward, laughing with Neil. "Did you see that guy's arm?" Brian was primed, he wanted to really make Neil laugh. "It was all twisted around, like it was on backwards, like a GI Joe doll's or something."

Neil put his hand over his mouth, holding in a laugh.

Little Maggie got caught up in the enthusiasm, naturally thought it had something to do with her. Laughing, she lifted her piece of pizza in the air.

Claire, staring at the three of them, an initial stage of disbelief on her face, said, "Now, that's enough!"

Brian was cackling, unrestrained. "God," he said, "was that strange or what . . . ?"

I was on my knees at the edge of the sheet. I reached over and slapped him on the mouth.

He was kneeling too, sitting back on his heels. He lowered his head immediately, his blond hair falling around his face.

Neil lowered his face and looked like he might start crying, as if I had hit him too.

"Bruce?" Claire said.

She thought I was overreacting, so I gave her a grave look, something to compare the slap to.

Maggie hadn't caught up with the present mood and was still laughing, playing some animated game with her pizza.

"Don't you get it, fella?" I said. Brian had his chin tucked into his chest. "That man was dead. He *could* have been Mr. Ferber. Would that have been funny?"

Maggie was finally aware of the change of tone. She had grown quiet and was looking at us wide-eyed.

Claire reached over and put a hand on Brian's neck.

I couldn't look at Neil.

On Sunday, there was something written about the accident in the paper. It wasn't a separate article, but included under the heading "NEAR-FLOODING CONDITIONS IN TWIN CITIES AREA CAUSE FOUR FATALITIES." Two of the accidents were due to cars hydroplaning, and one was a car going over a flooded bridge. "Robert Enders," it was written, "was swept into a city drainage canal and carried seven miles, where he was later discovered by a boy in the west Minnehaha Creek."

Finding it in the paper made the event into something tiny and unreal, as if seeing it through the wrong end of a telescope. What we had found the day before had been reduced to a minor article, cluttered in with reports of fires and plane crashes. It was humbling, reminding me that tragedy is as random and even secret as the death of stars, how a life can dissolve and drift into particles, with so few even witnessing it. I was comforted knowing there would be others who saw the article, and that each of them would feel their own brief but particular grief about it.

But Neil didn't recover as easily. "He's afraid of everything lately," Claire told me one day as we were pressing putty into the cracks of the sun room windows. We had a view of the boys and some of their friends as they played football in the yard. "I dread taking him in the car with me. He slams his foot down on the floor every time I approach a traffic light. Yesterday, he had all three of us testing our shoulder straps, even Maggie, sitting there in the driveway, lunging forward to see if they would catch us."

I watched Neil resting the ball against his chest, looking for an open throw. The other boys were closing in on him, but he took his time, made a smooth pass to one of his friends, his arm cleanly following through and dropping to his side.

"But look at him," I said to Claire.

"You only see what you want to," she said, and proceeded to scrape some of the old glaze off the glass of the window, making an impatient scratching sound.

Claire is very opposed to greasy food, but every few months we have what is traditionally called "grease day." It's my own tradition, and the only time, really, when the kids and I get together to live out what I like to imagine might have been my life-style without Claire. On a Saturday morning in mid-November I put a pot of oil on the stove and fried doughnuts into the afternoon. Claire had conveniently found some shopping to do. The boys stood at the kitchen table press-cutting the rings out of the dough, and Maggie sat on a stool with a dish towel wrapped around her. We'd given her a paper bag full of sugar, and once a batch was cool, I would drop them into her bag and let her shake it up. She was very happy about this.

By three in the afternoon we were finished with the doughnuts, and I started to fry potatoes and fish and onion rings. The boys had set the table with paper plates, napkins, catsup, and large tumblers of Coke. I was pulling the fry basket full of fish out of the oil. I hadn't let it drip long enough, and when I swung it out of the pan, oil trickled from the basket into a puddle by the flame. The puddle immediately ignited, and the size of the flame was enough to start the side of the pan on fire and eventually the whole pan. Then the mitt I had been holding the fry basket with caught on fire, and though I was quick to throw it off, I could feel that it had burned my wrist. The smoke detector was screaming, and this made Maggie hysterical. I was grimacing in pain, at the same time yelling to Brian to find the baking soda. All I could think was Don't use water, use baking soda. Once Brian had found the Arm & Hammer, I sprinkled it around the pan—which helped—but the pan itself kept raging. The kitchen was full of smoke. I shouted at the kids to get out. I could barely see them. Then miraculously the flame in the pan disappeared. Neil had found the pan cover and smothered it.

We needed to open all the windows in the kitchen and close its doors. I deactivated the fire alarm, which wouldn't quit buzzing. We moved the food into the sun room, and when Claire came home, we were all sitting there. Maggie was still crying, as if she'd come to the circular notion that she needed to cry because she was crying, and so on.

Claire took Maggie into her lap, and this helped reduce her sobbing to a soft gurgling lament. Brian and I had stacked the fried food on our plates. We held the plates in our laps, but neither of us had the additional presence of mind to start eating. My hand hurt, and I had wrapped a wet rag around it. We had put food on Neil's plate, but so far he hadn't taken it. He sat in a chair noticeably off in the corner, his arms folded on his chest.

I explained to Claire how Neil had saved the day.

"Well, you should be proud of yourself!" Claire exclaimed, still rocking Maggie.

"A fireman showed us what to do in Boy Scouts," Brian interjected.

"So you know what to do, too," Claire said to Brian. Claire looked over at Neil. He looked back at her.

"I hate this house," he said.

"Honey, why do you say that?"

"Nobody knows nothing."

Claire looked at me. But I was quiet, waiting for the inevitable.

"Accidents happen," she said. "We're all right now."

"No, he was stupid." Neil stood up. "With a stupid burned hand." Then he walked out of the room.

I was watching the circle of grease widen on my plate, telling myself this was a natural reaction for him, not to take it too seriously.

"You need to talk to him," Claire said.

A few days later I'd brought engineering specifications home from my office and was going over them at the kitchen table. Claire was home from her teaching job. "Bruce?" she said from the kitchen door. I looked up to find her with a bundle of sheets in her arms. I could smell the urine. It was incongruous against her clean, pressed blouse. And immediately, before she even told me what it was about, I wanted to retreat into the clear white lines on my blueprints, convince myself that the assembly of a thermostat, something I knew about, could outweigh anything that might try to confound us in our home life. But I could smell my own boyhood, and I knew, in the way that a memorable smell is like a book you once read, which you forgot you read, but which you will always know deeply, that the sheets were Neil's and that it meant his life was complicated now.

When I was eight years old, I used to make up reasons why I couldn't contain myself at night. Because I was allergic to canned pineapple-grapefruit juice, I told myself, which I didn't like, but which always seemed to be on sale and restocked in our cellar before we'd even gone through the last crate; or because my older brother, my nemesis, must be dipping my fingers in a cup of warm water at night. So I would sleep with my hands tucked under my body.

But the problem persisted, and it became clear that sleep was the culprit. It seemed I was defenseless against it. I fell into it at night, like Alice down her rabbit hole, and I knew that I dreamed, but I could never remember what. I'd awaken in the morning feeling as if I'd been through a horrible struggle, like a hero after his journey, and I'd find the bed wet, and I'd feel that if I was a hero, I was a hero fighting a losing battle.

"What do you want me to do?" I tossed my pencil down, feeling exasperated and humiliated, as if the sheets Claire was holding in front of me were my own.

"I have no problem with talking to him myself—put my degree in developmental psychology to use."

"You could," I said, leaning back in my chair, determined that if she was going to look at me like I was a jerk, I might as well act like one.

"But I don't have something to share from my own experience—something that might be an enormous relief to him."

She was talking about more than Neil's bed-wetting. She was talking about why I hadn't talked to him after the fire. And this brought to the surface something that had been nagging at me all along. I believed if Neil had taken her to the body, instead of taking me, she would have found a way to protect him.

After dinner, while Brian took his shower, Neil and I sat on the foot of the stairway. His hair was still damp from his own shower and smelled like shampoo. He was wearing pajama bottoms but no shirt, and even though he said that he wasn't cold, I made him wrap his towel around his shoulders. "Your mom says you've been having some accidents at night." I had already told myself I wasn't going to start the conversation this way.

"It won't happen again." He tucked his chin in.

"Did you know that I used to have the same problem?"

"Yes," he said stoically.

Great, I thought, Claire had already told him—now what was the part I was supposed to tell him?

"Well, I don't anymore," I said.

He was quiet.

"But when I did, I used to tell myself not to, and I still did."

He didn't respond, and I imagined he was determined that wasn't going to be the way it was for him.

"It's nothing to be ashamed of, Neil, even if it happens many more times."

Then I took him down to the basement and showed him how to run the washer. "We don't mind doing the sheets for you," I told him. "But sometimes I used to feel better when I could do them myself."

Neil continued to wet the bed regularly. Brian was un-characteristically kind about it. Except for some nights when there was an unresolved animosity between them and I would overhear his: "And you better not stink the room up again." The best, last shot he could give Neil—leaving him with something he had no answer for. I'd stop Claire from interceding, and I'd stop myself, knowing it was only a way of making Neil feel weaker. But Brian's words would put me on edge. I felt as invested in Neil's making it to the morning as he was himself.

He'd become even more concerned about house fires now that winter was setting in. Sometimes we would hear him on the stairs in the middle of the night, and we'd figure that he was checking to see if we'd really unplugged the Christmas tree lights as we had promised. One night he came into our room and said to Claire, "Feel my heart. Does it sound right?" He'd been lying in his bed imagining that it was off, that it might be beginning to fail.

His concerns were relentless. And if that wasn't bad enough, some days he would have spells of arrogance when he let us know that no one but he had enough sense to make it to the next day. One evening I walked into a scene between him and Claire in the kitchen. "I like my garbage disposal!" she was shouting. "I intend to use my garbage disposal! If . . . If . . . You. . . ." She'd run out of her usual poise.

Claire thought it was worth talking to a psychologist about, but I wanted to believe that what was happening to him was still containable. Bringing someone else into it might make what was wrong even more solid and hard to shake.

One night, after she had put her book down, put out the light, Claire turned on her side and began to rub the back of my neck. Though her hands were a comfort, lying there in the dark bedroom, there was also a feeling of being pulled into some bleak outer region. Lying still, trying to discern what it was, I remembered how I had touched the body of the man in the creek. The preciousness of her touch then was as much a source of anguish as it was of tenderness. I was struck down, as we all are at times, with the realization of how fleeting a simple happiness can be. How, when looked at from the distant perspective, like from the god's eye above, looking over our tiny lives and the eternity that surrounds each one, how then each happiness would not appear as even a spark of light.

As Claire rubbed my neck, I didn't know what to say. But after I'd let my thoughts stray for a while, I turned over, and I told her about the first wake that I'd ever been to. It was for a boy a year younger than myself. His name was Jeff Thorn, and he had fallen through the ice of a pond near our house. He'd been in my Boy Scout troop.

"What on earth brought that to mind?" she asked, continuing to massage my neck.

I told her that I'd been thinking about the accident, and how any thought of death always brought back that first experience in a funeral parlor. I'd been told to wear my scout uniform, and when it was my turn to stand by the casket, my knee socks had fallen down. I wanted more than anything to pull them up, but I knew it wouldn't be right. I remembered the curve of his head under his blond brush haircut, and most remarkably that his lips were nearly blue, giving me the impression that he was still cold.

Whenever I saw his brother in school, or his parents in church, even after some years had passed, I would always wonder how they thought about him. He had been with two of his cousins when he had fallen through. One cousin was saved by the other. But Jeff wasn't grabbed in time and was pulled by the current under the ice. That was the cruelest part to accept—that he was floating just under the surface, but unable to be reached.

The next morning Brian and I were sitting in our pajamas at the kitchen table, a bowl of cereal in front of each of us. Before he had even poured his cereal, he had dug a small booklet of paper and ink tattoos out of the box. Super hero tattoos. He licked his arm and pressed one of the small squares against his wetted skin. When he peeled the paper off his arm, I could see that the image had transferred perfectly. I went back to reading my paper, only to be intermitently interrupted by, "Look, Dad," showing how now he had put one on his chest, now on the palm of his hand. Brian's at that age that vacillates between being very cool and not cool at all. And if he irritates me, I have to remind myself that it's because we're a lot alike.

Neil had taken Maggie, in her snowsuit, out on the patio, and we could watch the two of them playing through the pair of atrium doors that faced us. Though the patio had been shoveled the day before, another dusting had accumulated overnight. The sun was out, which made the few snowflakes in the air glisten around them. It was a happy sight.

They were playing Follow the Footprints. Neil was the leader, and he was taking carefully small steps so that Maggie could follow him. Maggie can be tyrannical when it comes to play, and whenever it appeared that Neil might stop, she would grab his legs and whine. As she did this for the third time, Neil picked her up around the waist and began to spin. Her face appeared as only a small circle in the centrifugal splay of her pink snowsuit. Neil's head was back, and his eyes were closed. Maggie, startled at first, leaned her head against him and smiled, a peaceful, satisfied smile. It was a matter of trust, I thought. That was how he was. And for the first time in months I felt easy about him.

We were invited to a party on New Year's Eve. We had

arranged for a baby-sitter, really a chaperone for Brian, since he was having his own sort of New Year's Eve sleep-over with some of his friends. I'd bought some nonalcoholic sparkling wine for them to open at midnight, and I could hear them making bets in the basement about who was going to be able to pop the cork. Maggie was already asleep, and Neil was in his room. Claire was dressing. There had been weather reports all evening about a blizzard on its way, and the travel advisories cautioned anyone who had plans to drive out of town, but we were only a mile from our party. I needed to pick up the baby-sitter. When I went to warm up the car, it seemed oddly settled in the snow; all four tires were flat.

I bumped down the basement stairs. Brian was crouched by the fireplace with two of his friends. He had a pack of cigarettes in his hand. "That's out!" I grabbed them from him. He shook his hair back, looked up at me startled. "Now why don't you tell me about the car?" As soon as the words were out of my mouth and traveling the short space between us, I knew it wasn't his doing. "Never mind. No smoking!" I said. "We're going to be home tonight."

I found Claire in the bathroom, surrounded by her makeup and the aura of perfume. I put my hand on her elbow and nearly shouted, as if there were some noise I needed to compete with, "Cancel the baby-sitter."

"What's wrong?" she asked.

"Neil," I said. "We're going for a walk."

"There's a blizzard out there!" I heard her say.

But I was already out the door. Neil had heard everything. He'd come out into the hallway. He stood with his legs set apart, like this was a showdown.

"There's a blizzard out there," he said.

"Good," I said. "You can protect me."

Outside, the snow was blowing and drifting more than it was falling. We could barely see the street. Our Christmas lights outside were lit; they were wound around the long stairway railing that led to the sidewalk below. I could hear them clinking in the wind as we made our way down the steps. The sound was like a charm. The blowing snow was painful against the face, and we had to keep our eyes narrow. Neil was wearing the hood up on his jacket, so he wasn't much more than a small dark form moving alongside me.

"We'll walk along the parkway," I said. The wind was shrill, and we could hear the old bodies of the nearest trees groaning against it. Everything was white, except for the silhouette of the creek as we approached it. The bridge was white, except for the dark arch underneath it.

"That's where you found the man," I said, knowing that he was already thinking of this.

"Yeah." I could barely hear his answer over the wind.

Now I was doubtful what business I had bringing him out here. Before, in the house, I had been so sure that out here was part of the whole explanation that I somehow needed to give him. But I didn't know what I wanted to say, and his silence, the fact that he didn't object, was a reproach to me. He thought I was a fool, and this was simply a time for him to gather more proof of that.

"I want to talk to you," I shouted over the blowing.

But he didn't answer me. He had his hands deep in his jacket pockets and looked like all he could be concerned with was resisting the cold. We were walking along the creek path in the direction of Lake Harriet, and for some reason, maybe because the path was on lower ground now, the wind had died down.

In the quiet, Neil suddenly appeared so small against the great white background. I slowed my pace, because I realized he'd been walking double time to keep up with me. He was just a little boy, yet I had wanted somehow for him to get through these things and still seem powerful. Now I could see he was just terribly alone.

"I'm sorry I left you that day," I was shouting, still not accustomed to the new quiet. We could hear our boots crunching in the snow. I was getting used to the cold now—it wasn't as painful, but it made me more aware of how he wasn't talking. "Neil?" I finally said.

"We could have saved him." He said it so quietly, I wasn't positive that this is what he said.

We kept walking. It must have been clear to him, as it was to me now, that we would end up at Lake Harriet. I understood what he said. Even I had believed the man might have survived until I had actually touched him.

"No," I said. "I touched him. I felt for his pulse. Honey, we couldn't."

"But I touched him too!" He had turned around, was walking backward; his hood had fallen away from his small face.

His sleeves had been wet when he had come to get me. I should have known that with his easy confidence he would have barely hesitated to go down there.

"He was just hurt!" Neil was shouting, facing me. We were reaching the end of the path. The lake was a great open expanse behind him. "We could have done mouth to mouth, something, right away!"

"No, Neil." I continued to walk forward slowly, while he slowly walked backward. "It was right for you to want to do something about it. It's just that we couldn't."

And then we were on the shore of the lake, and he was weeping. I picked him up and walked out onto the ice. He didn't wrap his legs around me but let them dangle, making himself heavy—one last gesture to deny the way things are.

I told him the ice was safe, that it was January now. But even in some Januaries, I told him, people have been known to fall through the ice. "If I fell through the ice, right now," he cried, "you could save me."

"I would try," I told him. And saying this made me start to cry. He wrapped his legs around me. This was the first time we had ever cried together. And we stood there for a long time, under a clouded night sky without stars, and looked back at our footprints in the snow, letting in the gentleness that follows a subsided blizzard and the time it takes to go on.

THE
MEADOW BELL

Lakeund Kramer was watching Jimmy, who sat in a patch of shade on the front lawn, just beyond the driveway to the farm. It was August. The boy was sitting Indian style, bare-armed and bare-legged, with oversized blue thongs on his feet.

Lakeund couldn't at first make out what Jimmy was playing. He had gathered mushrooms, that's what he had done—the soft gray and beige variety. There was a pile of various sizes in his lap, and he was arranging them into some kind of scene in the grass—a farm, where the smallest mushrooms were the people and the animals.

After a minute, Jimmy looked over as if Lakeund had called him. His face was too far away to really see, but Lakeund saw it in his mind, and this impression was as strong as if he were staring at a clear photograph. He was an open-faced little boy with round eyes and a blond down on his skin that make Lakeund want to touch him. He walked down the driveway closer to where the boy sat. He'd thought that Jimmy was smiling, but now he could see that he was not. He was simply looking, taking Lakeund in, or perhaps he was taking in the yard, or the trees, or maybe the whole afternoon. Lakeund didn't know. He was close enough to see that Jimmy was wearing his thongs on the wrong feet and how they curved out in an awkward way. It was very quiet in the yard, but after a moment a car could be heard coming up the road.

Jimmy jerked his arm up suddenly, the way children will do when they want to surprise someone. He was holding one of the mushrooms, a remarkably slender one with a small top. He was very pleased with this mushroom, and this made Lakeund smile. "You're right, honey," he said. "It looks just like a little man."

It was their neighbors, Roman Kohl and Harley Brandt, they had heard approaching. Lakeund watched them pull off the road, with a flash of sun on their windshield and so much dust that at first he hadn't recognized their truck. At first he had believed it might be someone special, and he had quickly stripped off the white smock he had worn all day to make cheese. He had gathered it into a bundle and hid it deep underneath the boughs of the pine tree that shaded the cheese house. Looking up from behind the tree's boughs, he put one finger to his lips to show Jimmy this was a secret they shared.

Now Harley and Roman had him surrounded in the driveway with their usual conversation. Their words passed over Lakeund's head like the honks of geese—the high migrators that one cannot even see. Roman shifted his belly from side to side, first leaning his hand on one hip, and then leaning his hand on the other. Harley kicked up little poofs of dust with his shoe. Though they had lived on the same road as Lakeund the length of their lives, they were not his friends. Roman and Harley had always had ideas in common. They had been planning and scheming and failing since they were little boys. And they never stopped trying to draw others into their partnership. Lakeund had little time for them. When they directed the conversation at him, Lakeund would nod or smile or comment on some small piece of information he had been able to pull out of the blur of their voices.

"The big lake . . ." Roman was saying.

This brought Lakeund back to the discussion. "You're talking about Michigan? You're talking about fishing?" Lakeund focused first on the bulb of Roman's rosy nose and then on the insignia of Harley's visor cap, which said: A-1 SPARK PLUG.

"Yeah! Where you been?" Harley said. "After a few stops tonight, we're driving on to Green Bay. We'll sleep in the truck tonight, and in the morning we'll do some big lake fishing. You had a good time of it last time you came along."

Lakeund knew this was true. But he said, "No, the last time I caught hell from the family."

"That's because you never told them where you were going," Roman said.

"No," Lakeund said. "Too much work." And he thought about how successful his business was, and how the two of them should know it hadn't gotten that way from goofing around.

"Well, come to Peter's for a beer anyway."

"Not tonight," Lakeund said. "Eileen will be expecting to go to a fish fry." He felt for the cloth of his pockets as the two of them shrugged their shoulders and got back into the truck.

Jimmy jumped to his feet as he heard them start the engine, and Lakeund's hands came out of his pockets as he watched the boy run alongside the truck, almost tripping over his thongs. There was something in the boy's excitement that made Lakeund begin to run too. Suddenly he wanted to go with them, not for the beer, but just to be away, to be somewhere else. And they must have seen him in their mirrors, because they stopped in a cloud of dust. Lakeund dropped the tailgate and hopped on.

But Jimmy was left behind. Lakeund could almost feel the dust left around the boy as they drove away, how it sprinkled down on the skin of his shoulders and into the short hairs on his head. He held a large blue thong in each of his hands and waved them in the air.

Lakeund waved back. But he couldn't be sure if Jimmy was meaning to wave goodbye or if he was just simply waving the dust away. "Tell your mother I'm over at the Meadow Bell!" he shouted. "Tell her only for a beer. I'll be back soon."

The boy stopped waving and seemed to listen as he held each thong out to his side, looking like a little airplane at the end of a runway, still as could be.

The family got another dreamer when Jimmy was born. Of all his children, this was the one he most wanted his sister, Lucy, to know. And yet this was the only one she didn't know—the one that had come well after they had lost touch.

Lakeund let his legs hang over the open tailgate as they drove away from the farm. He felt a familiar sensation in the weight of his dangling feet as the road passed beneath them. When he was a child he used to consider the danger of this. He remembered that Lucy had made a game of the danger and dared Lakeund to try anything she thought he was most afraid to do. Once they had gained speed on their way into town, she'd move a feed bag to block their dad's rear view of them. Then she would start in with the dares. "Do one foot!" she would say, and show him how to lower a leg closer and closer to the road, until the toe of his shoe was tip-tapping against the pavement.

He had eventually taken on every dare except one. It was the one where she would hang backward off the tailgate while he held on to her knees. From the position he held her, he could never see how close to the road she dangled. But she would pull herself back up laughing, saying her hair had dragged over it. And once she let the tips of her fingers scrape along the blacktop. When she had come back up, she showed him how her nails had ground down. There were bright beads of blood where the ends of her nails used to be. And they both had looked at her fingers like they'd been changed into something they'd never seen before.

The road kept coming out from under Roman's truck,

putting a distance between Lakeund and his farm. The farm was a scene now, and whenever it looked that way, whenever there was this distance, the place became a memory, an idea, rather than something he belonged to. The farm was a photograph he wanted to send to Lucy. It wasn't as small as it had been when she left. There were two new silos, the cheese house, the extension on the milking barn. There was Bernard's new house and the house Lakeund had restored for his own family. If ever she came home from either direction, she would see the signs that said: KRAMER FARMSTEAD CHEESE— THREE MILES. And yet imagining what she would think when she saw them was partly disappointing to Lakeund. She would never look at them, he knew, without being reminded that the farm had not been her choice of life, and why.

The Meadow Bell was a roadside bar. It was close to the road with only a small patch of gravel in front. There was room for five cars; any others had to park in the weeds and grass up against the barbed-wire fence that bordered the meadow. Cows grazed in this field all day until evening, and after they were gone, there was still the scent of them in the air.

A large copper bell hung from a post in front. It had hung there before Peter Kohl had bought the place and named it for the bell. Peter Kohl was Roman's older brother. He had painted the post light blue like the building, and one year he had paid a man from the city to paint the copper with an American eagle.

Some nights when a farmer would get drunk, he would ring the bell before he went home. A statement was made. It was just a vibration in the air, and yet it was a unique vibration, something he alone could understand the meaning of. And perhaps hearing the sound resonate over the meadow helped each man feel finished for the night. He walked away feeling he had rung the bell well—that this time he had sounded a clear, good song from it.

It was cool and dark and musty inside the bar. It was a cinder-block building with a cement floor. There were no windows to speak of, only some places close to the roofline where the blocks had been left out and double panes of glass put there instead. This way, it seemed to Lakeund, the light never touched the room itself but hung in dim, smoky beams overhead. A rectangular plastic lamp that said SCHMIDT hung low over the pool table so that the light was limited there too. It only shone on the blue jeans of the two young men who circled the table.

As they walked in, Roman stopped in front of Lakeund and Harley. He put his hand to his brow, as if to look past some glare, but there was only the dimly lit bar ahead of him. There was one customer on a corner stool at the bar, a city man wearing a fine suit.

"Peter, where are you?" Roman called. The city man looked into his drink, as if each ice cube needed consideration. With the stranger there, Roman moved ahead more hesitantly, like a dog in a new yard. He smoothed each of his hands over the sides of his belt. It used to be Roman's habit, Lakeund remembered, to hitch his pants up across his belly, especially when he was about to meet someone new. Now there was only this small gesture left from the old habit.

"Pete?" Roman said softly as he peered over the bar.

"Yeah!" the voice came from down below.

Lakeund and Harley moved in closer. "What'cha doing down there?" Harley asked.

"Looking for a thumbtack."

"He was going to show me a trick." The city man looked directly at the two of them.

"Oooh! The dollar trick," Harley said.

The ceiling above the bar was papered with dollar bills. Peter had a way of tossing a bill pierced by a tack so it would stick. Since the locals had watched the trick many times, they already knew Peter could do it. But a stranger would give up a dollar or two just to see something he had never seen before.

"Ha! Got one." Peter came up from the bar. He was wearing his usual white shirt. Lakeund always noticed the little plastic case of pens that Peter kept hooked in his shirt pocket, and he thought of Peter setting it on his dresser every night. It never seemed to Lakeund like something a bartender should wear.

"It's been a while, Lakeund. Was beginning to think you and your brother never left your land anymore."

"Looks like I came in time to see the old trick," Lakeund said.

Peter set the tack on the Formica bar and brought some beers and glasses out. The stranger picked up the tack and rolled it between his thumb and forefinger. "Now, how is it we bet on this?"

Roman and Harley moved up to their beers, and Lakeund came around to the stool to the left of the stranger. He noticed the man had thin black socks. He could almost see the man's skin through them.

"Those are the winnings." Harley pointed at the ceiling. "A dollar a crack. If he misses, you get the quarter."

Peter picked up a dollar from the man's change on the bar. "Okay?" he said.

"Okay," the man said.

Peter stubbed his cigarette out, took a quarter from his pocket, and pressed the quarter against the back of the thumbtack into the dollar. They could all see the point coming through George Washington's chin on the other side. He walked away, looking up for a clear spot on the ceiling. He folded the dollar around the back of the quarter. "That's the secret!" Harley bounced a little on his feet. The city man sipped his drink. Peter made an underhanded toss. It went up, the quarter came loose, clinked against the bar. And the dollar, creased in the middle by the tack, came down with a slight flutter like a bird that's been shot. They all watched it fall. Peter scrambled under the bar to retrieve the quarter. When he found it, he set it before the man. "I'll bet you a night of free drinks I don't miss again," he said.

"That's a bargain," the man said. "Go ahead."

He found his spot again. Everyone was quiet when he made the toss, but once again it fluttered down. The quarter clinked down on the floor, and it seemed that everyone was listening to the thin sound of it rolling away. Peter didn't look for the quarter this time. He brought the dollar back to the man.

"Bad tack." Roman rolled it between his chunky fingers.

"Must be," Harley said.

Lakeund decided to look at his beer for a while. Everyone but the stranger seemed crestfallen about Peter's miss. Now everyone had been put in the spirit of being alone. Even Harley looked drawn into himself.

Lakeund wanted to say something to make it easier. He wrapped his hands around his beer bottle, as if the cold against the soft center of his palms might shock some words out of him. He always stalled at these times, working up the courage to open his mouth. But the words never came soon enough. He would be almost ready and then realize the opportunity had already passed.

His hands became cold and damp around the bottle. They had felt the same way in the cheese house this afternoon. He'd been leaning over the vat, pressing the curds together with his gloved hands, when he began to feel a numbness in his fingers. He told himself it was impossible to freeze his fingers doing the work. But finally he had needed to tuck his hands in the hollows of his armpits.

Now he remembered his gloves still hung over the wood of the back fence. He had only gone outside to rest. Eileen had come from the front shop where she sold cheese, then out through the back room looking for him. He hadn't heard her coming. She slipped her cool hands around him from behind, caused him to shudder a little.

"Did you lose something?" she said.

"What?" He hadn't turned his body to look at her but looked out at the slope of the nearest field, where the first group of cows came walking toward home.

"Bernard said you came out to find something."

"Dry gloves."

She went to feel his hands, but he stretched them away from her reach. "Don't worry about it," he said. "Can't I take a little break?"

"I didn't say anything!" But he knew she was feeling anxious about him, and it made him angry. He set his teeth a little and remembered his mother's expression: "Why don't you go out and come back in again?" He turned to face Eileen finally. It wasn't so hard. She was holding a neutral expression.

"The weeks get pretty long in the summer, don't they?"

"Yeah, they do." Her expression softened, grew a little less guarded.

He had tried to make peace with her. He talked her into closing the shop earlier tonight, so they could make it to a fish fry, even though it was Friday, and there were so many city people driving north past the farm. Fridays they always sold the most off the road.

She would be looking for him soon to go to the fish fry. He should be home in an hour, but he already dreaded that he wouldn't make it, that she would come back out again and those sad gloves would be there.

"I'd like to see you do that trick again sometime using a sharp tack." The stranger looked up at the old bills on the ceiling and said this as if to the whole group rather than to Peter alone.

"And you'd be sure to see it work too," Roman said.

Harley smiled at Lakeund. Now everyone was feeling better. "If I'm going to be serving you free for the rest of the night, the least I could get is your name." Peter wiped the bar in front of the stranger and put a dry coaster in place of his empty glass.

His name was Bob Lowell. He watched Peter rummage in the refrigerator for another piece of lime to garnish his second gin and tonic. A young man and a woman with long smooth hair came in the door, bringing a square of sunlight across the floor. Then the door slammed shut behind them, and it was dark again in the room.

The man came up to the space at the bar between Lowell and Roman Kohl. He ordered a beer for himself and a whiskey sweet for the girl. She sat down at a small table against the far wall and leaned her back against the cinder blocks. She pushed the sides of her hair behind her ears with each of her thumbs.

The shy one on Lowell's left, the farmer, grew even more still when the girl entered. He was looking steadily at his empty beer bottle as though it was the most important thing at the moment. But Lowell had an idea that he was really watching the girl. He suspected the farmer was one of those taciturn fellows who paid attention to everything but never let on.

He liked this Wisconsin bar. This was exactly the place he had hoped to run across when he had chosen to drive rather than fly from Minneapolis. It was an opportunity to get a sense of the area.

Lowell was an engineer, a designer of small airports. It was his intuition about human personality, however, that he held in his own highest esteem. And this quality more than anything else, he felt, made his success as a designer. Airports, after all, were designed for people. He always impressed this upon his clients. The shape of a door handle, a particular grouping of chairs, precisely where the sun would enter a terminal's window at lunchtime, or sunset—these were things that concerned him: they had to do with realizing people's needs.

The girl lit a cigarette, exhaled, took it in again, and blew it out. She surrounded herself with smoke and that defensive look that women seemed to need when alone in bars. Then the young man walked back and sat down in her smoke.

Roman and the nervous man, who had introduced himself as Harley, were shaking dice together in a plastic cup. They would spill the dice onto the bar, count the roll, then quickly fill the cup up again for another shake.

One of the pool players brought an empty pitcher up to the bar to be filled. The beer gurgled out of Peter's tap down the inside of the pitcher. There was a smell of old perspiration from the young man's clothes.

The farmer's hands circled his empty beer bottle. Lowell

noticed that they looked very white, as if they had been under water for a long time. His face, however, was a good color. He had fine, square shoulders. Lakeund was what the bartender had called him.

Lowell had a reverence for farmers. So often he had flown over their farms. Peering out of the small window of the plane, he would reflect on how every man had his square of land. Although he knew it was naive to think so, he liked to think of the farmer as the model man. It was he who most truly and simply made a life in nature. And wasn't it also he who had the best chance of maintaining his innocence? Because his tasks in life were basic and not so easily confounded by the many anxieties of civilization.

"Lakeund, that's your name, isn't it?"

"That's right." Lakeund turned.

Now Lowell could see his entire face. He wasn't wearing a mesh visor cap like the other two. There was something refined about him, something more sophisticated than the others. He had pale eyebrows and an aquiline nose. The kind of nose that princes were given in the illustrations of children's books. His skin was not rough from the sun, but it was aging, the most delicate lines traced down from the corners of his eyes around his cheekbones.

"I've been guessing that you're a farmer."

"That's one of my hats."

"Let me buy you and your friends another round," Lowell offered, not sure if he was offering this too soon, not sure why he wanted to do this.

Near the end of his second beer, Lakeund's whole body was facing Lowell. His knees were apart, his feet propped up on the rung of his stool. Lowell had already become very fond of him and was gratified to have been brought into such close confidence with a countryman. He was surprised at how much he already knew about him: the second son of a fourth generation dairy-farm family, he had married a local woman and was the father of four girls and a little boy. He was a certified cheese maker. That was the other hat he wore.

But it was not an art passed down from generation to generation, as Lowell had assumed. The truth was they had only learned twenty years ago. If there was a beauty in cheese making, Lakeund said, it was in the possibility of naming a price for their own product.

Lakeund brought his bottle near his lips and kept it poised there. Then, instead of drinking, he tipped it toward Lowell to make a point. "The government gave our milk a price, and after three years of finding a feed bill larger than our milk earnings, we were feeding the cows their own milk. Nothing left to do but think of something else. So Bernard came home one day from a university seminar all about agricultural diversification. Every night he and my dad would argue about Bernard's plan. My dad couldn't see beyond the cows and the work he knew. And I would be real quiet at the table because I was younger and wasn't sure what to think. But Bernard was set, and he brought me into it."

"Farmstead cheese," Peter said, pausing to light a cigarette, "means they use only their own milk for their cheese."

Lakeund reached into his back pocket and brought out his wallet. He spread out some family photos on the bar in front of Lowell.

The girl with the smooth hair had come up on her own to the bar. She wanted a pack of cigarettes. Peter talked to her in a soft voice. The sound of dice stopped.

"What, you showing pictures?" Harley called over.

"Never mind. You've seen 'em all." Lakeund spoke up.

He turned slightly away from the group, so Lowell did too. "You can see all my girls together here. This was just a year back."

"Is this your wife with them?"

"Yeah. You see they all have somewhat the same eyebrows. Kind of like question marks. Lord, if I don't feel like I'm in the middle of a lot of questions sometimes."

Lowell laughed, but Lakeund's face remained serious. Roman and Harley laughed too.

"Do you have a picture of your boy?"

Roman and Harley chuckled again. Peter leaned over to hush them.

"No, no, I guess not," Lakeund said. "But I can give you an idea. He looks like me, and he looks like her." Lowell looked down at a small picture Lakeund had slipped from a back slot of his wallet. A girl in her teens. Her style of hair was maybe from the fifties. It was a formal picture printed on something like magazine paper, only the gloss had been worn off. He realized that it had been snipped out of a yearbook.

"Who is she?"

"She's my sister."

Lowell took the flimsy square between his fingers. She had darker features than Lakeund.

"Is your son dark, too?"

"No, he's got my color. But around the mouth and chin—that's hers."

Lowell thought it was unusual, even a little alarming, for someone to hang on to such a picture. Had she died?

Roman leaned forward. "Hey, Lakeund, how 'bout some talk over here." Then it seemed Roman was embarrassed about speaking up.

"Roman wants to buy another round!" Harley smacked him on the back. "Don't you, Roman?"

"Where do you come from, Mr. Lowell?" Roman asked.

"Seattle."

"I think that's where my sister might be," Lakeund said very softly.

"What are you doing in these parts?" Roman kept on.

Lowell knew that no matter how he put it, his job would set him apart from the others. He decided to keep it simple. "They're expanding an airport in Prentice. I'm helping plan it."

"Huh," Harley said. "Must be good money in airports."

Lowell passed over that, was especially conscious of Lakeund. He was aware that he wanted the farmer to admire him. There had been a growing notion throughout the evening that it was Lakeund of all of them who knew what was important. Lowell said, "I like what I do." Then, maybe because he was high from the gin, he suddenly felt quite strongly about that.

"Huh," Harley said.

"No, I really do." Lowell looked at Peter.

"That's good," Peter said. "Lots of people can't say the same."

Lowell was drunk. He could feel his own sentimentality close at hand. It was like an embarrassing pet waiting at the door.

Lakeund's right hand rested under the dim light of one of the bar lamps. Lowell felt an unexplainable impulse to reach over and cover it with his own.

Peter said, "You never do exactly what you want. How're you even going to know anything exactly from day to day?"

"Day to day ain't so hard," Harley said. "But when you start talking about month to month . . ."

"Right, Harley." Roman put his hand on his friend's shoulder. "Today's big lake fishing, ain't it?"

"I don't think one has to know the absolute exact thing," Lowell said. "It might just be knowing at all. I read somewhere . . ." He tried to remember where. "Maybe it was on the radio. Anyway, someone said that knowing what makes you really happy comes about as often as a comet. It visits you, leaves its impression, and you spend a good deal of your life wanting to remember what it was like. But it's hard, it's very hard to know."

Lowell glanced in the direction of Lakeund and quickly looked away when he saw tears forming in the farmer's eyes. It's the liquor, he told himself. It's getting to him too.

"I remember what she was like." Harley smiled and tapped his bottle against his teeth. "Coleen Schlelein. When would you say that was, Roman, about 1961?"

Roman swatted Harley with his cap.

"You know what I mean. How about you, Peter?" Lowell asked, consciously moving any attention away from Lakeund.

"I was happy when I first got the idea of having my own business. I was working in the paper mill then, and I started reading all those how-to books. I just got to feeling more and more strong about how I was going to go ahead and take the risk."

Lowell studied the fact that Peter had eight customers on a Friday evening. But then realized that it was harvest time, which might keep the regular customers away.

"Do you remember a time like that, Lakeund?" Peter asked.

Lakeund was rubbing his hand over the base of the lamp that sat on the bar in front of him. The girl near the wall was shuffling in her purse, getting ready to leave. The men waited for Lakeund. No one else seemed to have noticed the tears. The farmer brought his hands together and gave the bottle a kind of squeeze. "When I was sixteen, my sister sent me a letter from Seattle. She was waitressing at night and studying music during the day. She sent me a picture of the island she lived on. It looked lush there, almost tropical. I was surprised to hear that Seattle had islands, let alone almost tropical ones. It was a good letter. She told me how big the ocean was. How it was like the sky turned over. She said the place was meant for me; in fact, there was even a road with the same name as mine, that she took her bicycle up that road to a swimming pond. But I still don't believe that part, the part about my name. I think I'm the only person or thing with that name."

"Would she have made a thing like that up?" Lowell asked. But the farmer didn't seem to consider his question.

He looked at Lowell. "I was going to say before, you see, I almost lived in your area. She wanted me to come. She sent me some of the money for traveling, and I was supposed to earn the rest. I was never so excited as I was thinking about that trip."

"But you didn't go?" Lowell asked.

"No. Bernard was just starting the cheese operation then. He needed me around."

The two pool players went out the door. Lowell could see

how dark it had gotten and could feel how the air came in cooler.

"Maybe that wasn't my happiest time after all," Lakeund said. "I bet it happened when I was younger—maybe too young to even remember."

Then he put his hands flat on the bar, thumb to thumb. His hands made a frame. "I wish I'd brought a picture of my boy. There's a fellow who's pleased with himself."

This seemed to Lowell like a digression from their present conversation. He noticed Peter look over at Roman, who was shaking his head.

"Funniest little guy. Not a care in the world. Doesn't even know when he's uncomfortable. This morning I found him standing up on a box in the cheese house in nothing but his underpants. All his skin was gooseflesh, and he was holding himself stiff to keep from shivering. I told him it was just too cold in there. But he shook his head no, like what I said wasn't true."

Harley gave a peculiar glance in Peter's direction.

"Aren't you forgetting about that fish fry with Eileen?" Roman said.

Lakeund shrugged, tipping his beer bottle to look inside.

Lowell could feel a slight shift in the mood around the bar. He realized he shouldn't drink anymore. He was in a hazy state. His mind was wandering a little. One moment he felt a familiarity with these people, and the next he felt on the outside—like he didn't understand something.

There were bound to be some vacancies in the summer motels along the road ahead. He could take a room, rather than driving the rest of the way tonight, maybe pick up a hamburger somewhere, take it to the room, and watch television.

Lakeund set his beer bottle down with a thump, and then Lowell could hear the girl's heels knocking across the floor. She went by them with a whoosh, her young man behind her, and the bar door shut after them with a hollow thunk.

"She was a pretty girl," Lakeund said.

"Yeah," Harley said. "I was just wondering about her little puss, how far I could take her. A lot farther than that young pony."

"Shut up," Lowell heard the farmer say in a strange, dry voice. Nothing like his voice before.

"What?" Harley said.

Lakeund had his fingers against his brow, shading his eyes, and Lowell wasn't sure, but felt that he was looking sideways at all of them.

"I won't shut up," Harley said. "Why shouldn't I say what I want? You've been yapping all night. My sister this. My sister that. Well, the one that just walked out wasn't your sister, and I'll talk as plain about her as I want."

Lakeund was quiet. His face had grown quite white.

"In fact, it's time one of us talked plain about Lucy. You've been putting her up to us for twenty years. So she wrote you a few times; then she stopped. You make her out to this visitor like she's more than she is, like knowing her makes you more than we are. All I know about any sister of yours is what every boy in town used to tell me."

"Harley, stop it!" Peter said.

Roman looked away from his friend.

"She was nothing," Harley murmured.

Lowell heard glass cracking. Lakeund held the jagged neck of his beer bottle in his hand. In one smooth movement he reached behind Lowell and pulled Harley over. Harley's stool clattered to the floor. He was gasping and seemed to hang from Lakeund's fist, which clutched the material of Harley's shirt underneath his arm. Lowell could see the white skin of Harley's upper arm exposed above the line of tan and freckles. Lakeund pressed the broken neck into that pale part of his skin.

"Christ! What's he doing?" Harley tried to jerk away, but Lakeund had the underpart of his arm in a firm grip. His strength surprised Lowell. Though Harley struggled, he looked as helpless as a small boy getting a vaccination. Roman pulled on Lakeund's arm, trying to relieve the pressure of the bottle neck being pressed into Harley's skin, and Peter reached over the bar and slapped Lakeund's face, once and once again. Lowell was off his stool, but at a loss for what part he should play. When Harley was finally free, there was a wound shaped like a star on his arm. For a moment the impression remained very clear, then the wound bubbled over with new blood.

"Enough!" Peter shouted.

Roman stood warily by Harley, as though he thought Lakeund might try something else.

"Goddamn son of a bitch!" Harley whimpered. He held his arm and looked away from Lakeund, as if it was he who should be ashamed.

"It's okay, Lakeund," Roman said. "We're all friends here."

Peter picked up some loose bills from Lakeund's place at the bar and handed them to him. "It's time to head home."

Despite his violence minutes before, they were all being gentle with him, almost conciliatory. Lakeund turned and walked away from Peter without taking the change.

"What happened?" Lowell asked Peter.

"Harley shouldn't have said that." Peter looked over at Harley, who was still blotting his arm with a bunch of cock-tail napkins. "In the first place, it wasn't true. A lot of fellas might have wanted to have Lucy, but you can be pretty sure they didn't." Peter leaned forward, his elbows on the bar. "The other thing is, Lakeund's got some problems, you know, mentally."

"He's usually okay," Roman said.

"That's right." Peter pointed at Lowell's glass, asking if he wanted another. "Lakeund is one of us. It's not like the city out here; we don't put people away so easily. We try to live and let live."

On his way out, Lowell had to pass Lakeund, who was standing by the door with his head down and his hands in his pockets. The farmer looked so lonely; he wasn't afraid of him anymore. Pausing, his hand on the door handle, he asked, "Anything I can do?"

Lakeund looked at him with an expression as clear and

direct as any Lowell had seen all night. It was the kind of face the chamber of commerce should paint on a highway sign to sell their state. So clean and alluring and good it was. "I don't think so," he said.

After Lakeund left the bar, he stood out back looking over the meadow. There was no moon, just stars, and the meadow was so black that there was no making out what were the hills and what were the flat places.

The last time there had been trouble about Lucy seemed a long time ago. It didn't matter so much if Harley and Roman never talked to him again. But when he thought about the city man, he felt ashamed. He had a feeling that Lowell was a connection to Lucy—that somehow, after making his way back to Seattle, he might meet her there. But what would he have to say about Lakeund? That he was a dumb hick who could barely hold a conversation. That he was drunk and crazy and cut people in bars. Maybe if Lucy heard that it was Harley he had cut, she would say to Lowell, "If I still lived on the same road as Harley Brandt, one way or another I'd end up cutting him too." That was a comforting thought to Lakeund.

But he wished he'd told Lowell more. Why had he missed the chance to tell him? Except that it was all mixed up, and there weren't any exact words for it. It was about what he wanted when he was a boy, before the cheese business, it was about real dreams, what Lucy used to tell him about them.

He remembered nights like this, lying on the hill with her, when the stars seemed held in a net over them, and the net had seemed so tenuous and insecure that it threatened to give way.

It was those nights, without the moon, when Lucy would talk about dreams. He was nine years old and she was thirteen. It was so dark on the hill, he couldn't see her. It was so dark that he had needed her to talk almost constantly, lest he stop believing she was there, start believing he wasn't there himself. Dreams. She knew about music, and that was how she had learned to explain things that were all too complicated for most people. There was a tone in real dreams, she said, that you learned to recognize. When he was nine, he didn't understand what she meant, but he needed to hear her voice because it was so dark. So he would say, "Tell me about real dreams."

They talked about it the way farmers discussed the weather and mothers discussed their babies' teeth. Lying on her back in the grass, she would say, "Any dreams yet? No? Well, I have one. I'm going to ride the bike straight up the pasture slope without stopping. And then, because I deserve it, I'm going to come rolling down again with my hair blowing back. Here's an important one: I'm going to play violin, not fiddle. I'm going to make serious music like nothing anybody's heard before. You and the folks can come to see me at the concert hall. A new symphony. People will sob—they'll be dumbstruck, it'll change their lives."

"You couldn't," he'd say.

"Yes." She'd grip his hands. "Don't ever say that. What's with you? You've the face of an angel, and you're smart. Can't you see anything out there? Not even a house?"

"On a mountain!" He'd begin to see the house he wanted. "No glass in the windows, birds could fly straight through it. I'd grow orange trees in the yard."

He found that he was capable of desiring things outside his life. And thinking about these things was similar in sensation to hunger: the way the smell of a turkey in the oven could suddenly make him ravenous, when only a half-hour earlier he hadn't been aware he had an appetite at all.

A dream was something you put your life into—even if only for a day—and what made the dream true was how close to a real want it was. The dream and the want needed to fit together to make a good sound. And if you started believing that you wanted something, it had to be for the right reasons, otherwise—you could hear it in your head—the tone would be off.

It was this tone she had taught him to listen for. When Bernard had talked at dinner about going to the university for two years, Lucy had looked across the table with just this question in her eyes: Is it a real dream? Lakeund had shaken his head almost imperceptibly. "No."

When their mother, after years of vegetable gardening, decided to devote hours of her week growing Floradora roses, they weren't sure. Then one day they found her behind the house, kneeling next to an open book about rose cultivation, the lap of her apron full of dirt. They had come to ask her a question, but she looked up at them so distractedly, so different from her daily presence, they would have been ashamed to interrupt her. "That's the want I mean, Lakeund," Lucy had said. "We can't listen to anything less. Like Mom with her roses—that's the way we are going to love what we do."

But he didn't know what kind of want came to him those nights they lay together on the hill. It was a more open want, and frightening, because there was no dream with it, only a kind of aching expectation. The two of them would leave the family after dinner, climb the hill, with ordinary conversation about relatives and school and the people in town. Behind the hill the sun would set, and they would turn on their stomachs to watch it, that brief aura at the end of the day that would tend to impress him more than her. Afterward, he felt irresolute. The light faded, and everything around him diminished, first in color and then in form. He would watch her face as they talked, until that too began to lose its lines, became a sort of gray, except for a more startling white from her eyes and her teeth. "I'm so glad I can talk to you, Lakeund."

They would lie there for hours. Some nights they would even sleep while they waited. But it seemed to him, after many times, that she had changed. It was really the dark she came to wait for—not the stars.

One night he had interrupted the silence by saying, "They're lit now, Lucy, every single one of them."

"They're always lit," she had said. "It's just when the sun's up you can't see them. That's the good thing about darkness. You can see things that you wouldn't see otherwise, and I don't just mean stars. There are things you can't even know about yourself until you're blind and afraid. People say the future's bright, but I'm beginning to think it's a terribly hidden thing."

He didn't like the sound of that. It had made him think of the crack between his bed and the wall. Made him think of their pastor's description of eternity, how it went on and on and never stopped. It was something he had been unable to think about. It had seemed to him that the future should be something you could see as clearly as a picture. He wanted to be able to see what he was going to be, and where and how.

That night Lucy must have sensed how lost he felt, because she had smoothed her hand over the short hairs on his head and said into his ear, "Lakeund. Your name is Lakeund. I know who you are."

But as he got older, she let him feel alone. And if she ever talked at all, it was never in the clear way she once did. She began to have trouble with the family. She stayed away in town, left her chores. Yet even when she was eighteen and he fourteen, they didn't stop going to the hill together. If there was a moon out, sometimes she would stand up, and he would watch her. She would move about, show him a dance step, pull at the grass. And sometimes she would just holler out over the pasture: swear words, the secrets she knew about a high-school teacher, or some other gossip from town. Mostly she would holler about the ocean and the coast, and places away from the farm.

She was restless. He wanted her to talk to him. "Why do you want to go to the ocean?" he would ask. "What would you do? Buy a boat, fish for a living?" But she would just lie there with her eyes open, saying nothing. There was always something she held just beyond his reach. If only she would tell him, he thought, they would both feel better.

She became so remote that he felt lonelier with her than he might have by himself. It seemed so long since she had talked directly to him about any dreams. And he had begun to dread that maybe she didn't actually know as much as he had trusted she knew. Lucy had raised his expectations. He'd taken her ideas as something akin to promises. There was the one where he could be a mathematician someday, be smart and calculate the meaning of things, the way Einstein had. Each new idea she had given him wore a deeper groove down the center of him. But then she stopped dreaming with him, and that groove came to feel only like a hollow place.

One night, after so much silence, Lucy had turned to him, and he couldn't see, but sensed, she had propped her head on her hand. "Things stop being simple," she said. "Sometimes I wish I'd never wanted anything. First you want something, and then you know about it. I read a book about a complicated man, and I fall in love with him. I can't be happy drinking beer with the fellas on the ball field anymore. I feel separate from them. I listen to a new record, and as hard as I try, I can only play half of the violin on it. Only half."

She rubbed her thumb along the dip below his eye, like he was a baby and there was a sleeper there. "What you know gives you trouble. You can't change what you know."

He pushed her hand away. "I don't know anything," he said.

"I think that you know I'm getting ready to leave here."
"Why?" he said.
"I'm afraid to. I don't want to, but I need to. You'll feel the same way in a few years."
"No, I won't," he said.
"Yes, you will."

Her insistence made him angry, suddenly, very angry. A moment ago he had yearned for her to give some form to the thoughts between them. And now he felt only mistrust. He remembered when Harley had insisted that the first time Lakeund was with a woman, he would tear something in her and make her bleed. He felt, then, that he was turned inside out, like he was the woman, and he could never let that happen. It was as though Lucy had led him to the edge of a cliff, stupidly, not knowing what she had been doing.

He grew very quiet, almost sleepy, and turned away from her. The sky was changing, and he watched it. He thought about mathematics, counting, and getting to the end of things—all the stars. But this, again, was too much like thinking about eternity, so he stopped.

He'd stood up and left her there, couldn't believe it as he was walking away. "Don't go," she said.

Just that one time he'd done that. But then he remembered waiting in the back hallway, hours it seemed, until she came into the house. And the air in the hallway was a little rotten with the smell of old potatoes. And every few minutes he wondered why he was waiting, feeling the dread that he did. Maybe he had hoped that she didn't really mean to leave and that nothing would be changed when he saw her. But she had come in, and looking at her face, he realized for the first time that he hardly knew her. He didn't know why, but it was like a twilight she had brought into the hallway.

He put his head down and realized after a while that she had sat down on the step next to him. There was a yellow bulb burning overhead. She had put her hand on his leg, said, "You're not a little boy anymore." It was a plea, something she needed from him. "I feel so very sad, Lakeund. Sometimes I wonder if there could have been a way to stay simple. Then I think, No, all it takes is one dream, and you're left with no choice but to be brave and go along with it."

He had stood up, letting her hand fall away. "I've got to get sleep for the morning," he said.

"I've got whiskey in my room," she said. "We both could talk."

"We both need sleep," he said.

And that he had always remembered as the turn of things. Why they had stopped going to the hill, why it didn't come up again.

It wasn't as if he had stopped loving her. But at that time even her name changed for him. There was a time when he heard it or said it and it had no meaning for him. It was like the smell of cattle or the continual rumble of plumbing in the house: it had been there since he was born. Now the sound of her name surprised him. The word meant *her*. She was something separate from him once she had decided to leave.

Looking out the upstairs window, a quietness would come over him. He would think her name, watch her cut her meat, bring it to her mouth, and eat it.

He learned how to tease her, the way she had always teased him. And they hardly ever talked except in this teasing way. Although sometimes they would be laughing, their fingers interlocked in some skirmish, and a sadness would take over her face, and he knew he looked the same way.

She talked about leaving a lot. She was growing out of the farm, and the town for that matter, she'd tell them at the table. The family would argue, and he'd keep quiet, refusing to picture where else she could ever be. And he'd hear that word *dream* again. Dreams, dreams . . . not really as though it had been said right there in the room, but as if the words were only faint sounds passing over the roof of the house.

He wasn't prepared for her leaving. Weeks later he heard the angry voices in his parents' bedroom—his father screaming something about the devil in her. That same night she had run out of the house and told him to follow. It was a moonlit night. She took him into the old silo, where the only light was what shone through the cracks where the wood was coming apart. She said, "I have to say good-bye to you." And once again she had him in the dark, except for the few dim fingers of light that fell on her face and shoulders.

"Lakeund, did you hear me?"

He felt suddenly as if he was in danger of some serious injury, that the rotten old silo might collapse or that he might be standing on a board ready to give way.

"It's so dark in here," he said. "Let's go back."

"Lakeund."

"You don't have to go anywhere."

"I have to."

She had moved closer to him, and there was only one patch of light on her chin. She took his hands in her own, said, "Grip them hard." He put all his strength into this, but weakened a few moments later, knowing this was her way of leaving him. "You mustn't be afraid," she said. Then she pulled her hands away and moved out of his sight. He had a hard time finding the silo door. His hands were full of cob-webs, and he felt that panic again.

Finally he found the light of the door, and once outside he thought he could see her by the house, stooped over to gather a bundle. He called and ran. And she ran, over the first field in the direction of the road. He had run through the field and up the shoulder of the highway, but she was out of sight, hidden, or already too far away.

Lakeund heard Harley drunk and ringing the bell out front. Listening to Harley made him angry all over again. He put his hands on the fence post in front of him and pulled it out of the ground and the weeds by his feet. He rocked with the post, straining, as if there was a chance he could pull the whole fence out of its place. Then he dropped it. If only Lucy would come home and see how it was for him. Sometimes he would imagine, if only she would get a grip of his hands like she did that last time and tell him what he was supposed to do. He felt so alone. He climbed through the wire and walked into the meadow. He kept parallel with the road until he saw the others pass by in their truck, then he walked home.

Bob Lowell found a motel forty miles up the highway. He'd turned the light on and found the room so dingy that he'd turned it back off. Then he had laughed at himself in the way you do when you've had too much to drink and watch your own behavior as if it were that of a stranger's. He turned the light back on and set the bag of burgers and a single bottle of beer on the bedside table. They were the classic, old-fashioned hamburgers wrapped in wax paper and smell-ing of butter and onions. But he noticed that the table was chipped metal enamel, covered with a film of dust, and it put the food in an unfavorable context. It reminded him of how greasy the grill had been at the tavern where he had bought them a few miles back, and this further reminded him that he had the tendency to unduly romanticize taverns and other such things.

He turned the television on, turned the light off again. As he sat on the frayed chenille bedspread to remove his shoes, he decided that staying in this motel was an atonement for his romanticism. It was a half-built place, like he'd seen in so many sections of northern Michigan, Wisconsin, and Minnesota. Places where he imagined people had come to live or people had always lived and didn't want to leave because they believed in the beauty of the land and further believed that the beauty would care for them. But the truth was, there is competition in the commerce of beauty: for every man who wants to build a pasty stand on the highway, two more will have the same idea, and many of them will be unable to make a go of it. And in his travels he had seen the beginnings of these enterprises: the abandoned framework of an outbuilding, the support timbers already gray from the weather, and a sign in the house adjoining that read: PIES FOR SALE, and beneath that one, KNIVES SHARPENED, and beneath that, SMALL ENGINES REPAIRED.

He watched a National Geographic program on television about a variety of oceanic wildlife only recently discovered. Until this year, oceanographers had lacked the technology to dive into the deep habitat of these beings. They were strange, blind, ephemeral organisms swimming under the lights of underwater cameras, and the narrator in slow, measured tones spoke about their origin, postulated that these species were older than any ever seen before by man, and through study of their primitive natures there was much to be learned about our own.

Lowell was reminded of another National Geographic article he had read several years before, an article about regions of the world where for some reason people were more likely to live into their hundreds. There were photos of elderly folk in the Ukraine, but the photo that left the most lasting impression was one of an ancient brickmaker in the mountains of Mexico who was 130 years old. The writers speculated that his longevity may have resulted from the continuous exercise involved in his traveling up and down the mountains, or from the altitude, or perhaps even from a diet of little fat and many starches.

Most shocking to Lowell was a photo of the man's feet. They had been utterly transformed—wide and gnarled, with the toes spread apart like fingers. This was because of the many thousands of days he had used his feet to mix mud in a large trough, kneading it over and over so it would be soft enough to shape his bricks. Lowell had remembered looking at the photo several times feeling a fascinated horror. Why? he kept asking himself. But it was really the man in the picture he was asking—Why did you do this?

And this made him think of Lakeund. He had been hungrily eating the first hamburger, but remembering the whole scene in the bar—the jagged glass being pressed into Harley's arm—tainted its flavor, and he set the remainder down on the napkin in his lap. What was wrong with Lakeund? What if they had begun the conversation in the bar in a different way? What if they had all begun by putting their cards on the table, begun by saying we are all very sad, even Harley is sad. And Lowell would have said, "I am, too. I make a career out of knowing what people want, and I'm always wrong. People don't know what they want. We get a glimmering sometimes, but we're fooled. The original sensation is too often replaced by what's immediate, what is available at the time."

When Peter decided that he wanted a business of his own, was it really a bar that he wanted? Or was the bar some shortcut to his basic inclination, something that he could imagine being possible? Lowell remembered driving along the highway and seeing the bell out in the yard. That was what had attracted him in the first place—there was something about that bell. What if it was the bell that had drawn Peter there too? What if the bar he had bought was only a distraction from the stronger feelings that bell had provoked, something he, Peter found easier to make sense of.

It seemed that people needed to keep track of those first basic inclinations, lest they lose sight of them and find themselves one day strangers in their own . . . Lowell looked down at the hamburger, which was half-eaten and cold in his lap, and snorted once through his nose. A little laugh at himself, because he was going on in his head like a philosopher. But then he felt sad again. Was it the brickmaker's dream to live 130 years? Was it his own dream to decide how many vending machines were needed in a small airport terminal? How did you ever know? They should have stayed together at the Meadow Bell, especially after Lakeund cut Harley. They should have talked and talked until they got to the meaning of that wound.

Because there was no moon, Lakeund wasn't sure what time it was when he finally got back to the farm. Perhaps it was 1 A.M. The minute he stepped onto the porch, he could feel his wife waiting for him. He opened the screen door, lifting it a little so it wouldn't scrape across the wood floor. In the kitchen it was too dark to see, so he stood at the door and planned how he would find his way upstairs. He thought about how Lucy's ocean would look at night, that if it was as dark as the sky, they would look like one thing. And yet Lucy would never feel lost in a place like that, not like he would.

He couldn't hear a sound from his children. He moved in the dark to a small room off the kitchen where he knew he would find Jimmy sleeping. He couldn't see him. The boy's breathing was light in the air, almost impossible to hear, and Lakeund was reminded of a whistle he himself had owned for a very short time. At one point he had learned to trill it like some afternoon bird. But for most of that week after his fourth birthday, he had simply lain on the hill with the whistle in his mouth and breathed through it. The sound could never have been called music. It was too singular and thoughtless—only a new sound that mixed in with the sounds of the heat and the crops, the flies and the road.

He paused with his hand on the stair railing, reminding himself again that he must climb the steps quietly. He began to say something in his head, and he realized that he was saying it to Lowell. He was remaking their conversation from before. He was saying to him, "Having a son is a way to start over, of being young and innocent. There is this most precious time when nothing is needed, everything is already yours." Lakeund put his foot on the first step. "But that changes. Lucy would say, 'First you want something, and then you know about it.' Do you know what you find out?" Lakeund needed to cover his mouth, realizing this thought had just come out in a whisper. "You find out that wanting is dangerous. You find yourself in the middle of wanting, and you can't go either forward or back. So I'm watching my son, and as soon as he starts to wish for things, I'll tell him he cannot go back now, he cannot be simple. And if he tells me he wants to make cheese, I'll tell him that only if, by some miracle, it is the driving wish in his heart. I'll tell him it wasn't for me, and how some nights, when I think about another day of cheese making, I feel I might die. And that is not a safe feeling. I thought I would be safe staying here, but I'm not. I should have trusted Lucy." That's what he wished he had told Lowell when he had the chance.

By the time he'd reached the bedroom, his eyes had adjusted enough to see the silhouette of their window, but he couldn't see his wife. He was quiet about undressing, and when he slipped into their bed, it was as if he were trying to make no impression with his body. She was so quiet that he knew she was awake, and he lay there with his hands on his chest, waiting for her to make some sound.

"Eileen?"

With no answer from her, his voice folded into the dark and left him unsure that he'd ever spoken.

"What?" she said, finally.

"Are you mad at me?"

She took a deep breath. She seemed so far away from him that if he'd reached out to touch her he would have touched only black air.

"I've been having lots of thoughts today. I want to make some changes. Eileen?"

She sighed deeply enough to cut him off. She had been

holding air in ready for that sigh. "Lakeund," she said, "are you going to go away from us again? Am I losing you again?"

"No, no. It's not like that Eileen. I was just remembering all the things Lucy used to say."

"She's gone. Don't think about her."

"Why does she make you so mad, Eileen?"

"Oh, Lakeund, you've been gone all night. If you'd just told me where you were going."

"I told Jimmy, Eileen. I told Jimmy to tell you." And then he realized, he shouldn't have mentioned Jimmy. This time he should have kept him safely in his head.

Eileen moved suddenly in the bed, and he could feel her leaning over him. Her voice was coming from above him instead of beside him. She said, "I don't want to go through this again, Lakeund. Listen to me. There is no Jimmy. We have no Jimmy. He's nothing but an idea, a fantasy you've . . ."

But her voice disengaged, floated up to the ceiling and then dropped away, a night hawk—that lonely thin sound. And Lakeund wanted to tell her it would be okay—he needed only a little more time—it was just a loss taking care of itself. But he couldn't make the words. He was a sleeping man, explaining a dream to his wife before he had stopped dreaming it. The dream of a boy and what the boy knows, about his heart and the bell and being brave. He would sing her this song, finally bring the sound to earth; it would not be lost again. Lakeund turned his head toward the morning still dim in the window, a blue-black sky, the shadow of the barn roof, the old pine bowing with sleep—anything he might find to be real and familiar.

DRINKING

A man and a woman have their lines in the river called the St. Croix. They're sitting under a tree. Their poles lie listless next to them, and little by little their lines have been pulling out with the current. But now her red and white bobber was hesitant, as if unsure any longer of its direction, and his bobber, which was all white, stalled too. Then they both drifted in the direction of the shore.

"It's a crosscurrent that's got them," Tim said. "They're bound to get snagged by the banks."

"Let them," Mary said, pulling him gently by the pocket of his shorts when he moved to get up. "Tell me about this first time you were here, about this woman."

"Well, it wasn't exactly the first. I'd been canoeing here with a friend before. But after that, I had it in my mind that I wanted to bring someone special."

"Was she special?" Mary asked, and for a moment she wasn't sure of her intentions or of her tone in asking. She might have made it seem she was jealous.

"I thought so at the time. . . ." Tim put his arms behind

his head and crossed his feet at the ankles. This pushed against the backs of his old tennis shoes, which made them splay at the sides and exposed the fairer skin on the sides of his feet. ". . . In that way you just don't think many people can be. You know, she wasn't going to turn around and tell me something I already knew." Tim was surprised to hear him-self put it this way, since this was an expression he hadn't used in a long time.

"Was she pretty?" Mary asked.

"Very, but fine, not necessarily sexy."

"Like me," Mary said.

"Yes." Tim smiled and looked out over the river.

"Except for the fact that I'm also somewhat sexy."

"Yes." Tim looked at the orange water and remembered how he'd waded into it ahead of the woman. He'd been quiet about how it felt, knowing she would step into the sand her-self, and it would feel to her a little more like a magical thing if he said nothing. The sun was just right. He hadn't gone in until he was sure the light would be even with their shoul-ders, slowly pressing down into the water around their waists.

"But you were drunk?" Mary said.

"Right, but trying to do it well."

"Of course," Mary said. "If you can't do it well . . ." She turned on her side listening to him. He was looking out at his story as if it were on the other side of the river. And she looked over to the far bank, at the birches and poplars and pine. There was a scrap of someone's bright yellow tent peek-ing through the trees. It was the kind of yellow they always used in cartoons for the sun.

"I had the proverbial Volkswagen van."

"Let me guess. Blue," she said.

He laughed. "Red, I'm afraid. I would have liked blue, though."

"Anyway, I'd met her at a festival, funky, very surreal, like Mardi Gras. And a friend of mine had just been talking about her. He'd just been telling me about this woman, someone he'd gone to school with, you know. She played the flute, orchestra employed. He went on and on—like she was this veritable paragon—about her impeccable character."

"And you met her just a few minutes later."

"Yeah, she'd been holding up one of these wonderful puppets, holding it up for someone in the parade. And when she gave it back, my friend, Ben, recognized her, but it was like I already knew who she was."

"I wish you'd tell me what she looked like."

"She was beautiful, good bones, good skin, good teeth. Ben said, 'I can't believe it,' you know, and so on, but it didn't matter. I was looking at her. I'd tipped some tequila just prior and, you know, there was charisma. I could feel it in my eyes."

"Right, Tim."

"Yes!" Tim turned to Mary and put his hand on her arm. "That does happen."

And Mary felt reprimanded. "I know," she said. And she did know, especially with tequila, she knew that brief peak, when you feel enlightened, more like marijuana, the illusion that light could be brimming over and coming out of your eyes.

"And you know," Tim said, "there was that element of destiny present. Ben had just sung her praises, and there she was. Her face was so peaceful, and it was like she could feel my look, but she wasn't going to take it any other way but within her own stride. She was with other people. We talked for maybe only a minute."

"But how did you finally get together?"

They were interrupted by a motorboat clipping past, its wake behind it. It wasn't long before it had rounded the bend, and they could only hear it. But the wake pushed the water up on the banks, almost covering their feet, and their bobbers were tossed on the reckless crest.

Mary pulled her legs away from the water.

It seemed to Tim that boats shouldn't be allowed to travel so fast in this part of the river. He put his head back against the tree, waited for the roar of the motor to die away.

ST. CROIX STATE PARK—he pictured the sign posted at the entrance. He passed it every time he drove Highway 8, and he wondered if there was ever a time he passed it that he didn't think to himself, If I could only. . . . What? That was always unclear. But the last time, he had decided he would bring Mary here. It was an almost half-hearted decision. Just a decision that had quietly culminated from all the times he had passed the sign and all the times he had begun to think, If I could only. . . .

"Bird-watching." Once the motor's noise had died, he was able to answer Mary's question.

"What?" Mary was incredulous.

"It's true," he said. "The very next weekend. I'd crashed at a friend's house. It was getting late, but we'd been on a toot. He'd been telling me that he had to knock it off, that he had to get up to go bird-watching with a friend, but I didn't want to leave, you know, didn't want to be alone."

"What was his name?"

"I don't know. I had such a multitude of friends back then. I was persuasive, as usual, and convinced him to stay up with me a little longer. I said I'd get up with him in the morning and go along."

"And you sat up the rest of the night talking about birds?"

"I think we did, as a matter of fact."

"I'm sure you were both quite expansive on the subject."

"I'm sure," Tim said. "But of course at that point I was blacked out. The next day my friend was horribly hung over, and he held me responsible. I had to wake him up. We both took showers. It was only 6 A.M. It was drizzling, and he'd thought maybe his bird-watching date wouldn't want to go after all. So he called her, used her name, but I never made the connection."

"Poor guy," Mary said. "Obviously she was set on going."

"Yeah. I drove his car. She was waiting outside her house wearing rain gear. I didn't recognize her until she pushed her head in the car. She looked a little sleepy."

"But more alive than the two of you, I'd expect."

Tim smiled, remembering. "I reminded her of our meeting, and she just settled into the backseat, smiled a time, and said, 'Yes.'"

"Yes, she already recognized you? Yes, she remembered now that you mentioned it?"

"I don't know," Tim said, but in fact he had always believed that she remembered him. They had driven to a kind of reserve. He would never remember the directions. The windshield wipers were going, an awkward squeaking against their silence in the car. His arms were heavy and his mind in a fog. But a special song had come on the radio, one that had been the theme song with a past lover, and that he still held very dear. The speakers were in the backseat just behind her head, so he'd felt that they were sharing a past, even if they didn't speak, and he was comforted by the remote certainty that they would become intimate.

"The land we hiked on was by a river, because I remember seeing trout fishermen when our path crossed it."

"And you saw birds?"

"Absolutely. But only the two of them had binoculars. I wasn't used to listening for them or seeing them. She, on the other hand, had a lot of experience, had been all over the country with her father since she was a little girl. She would just stop on the path, point without saying a word. My friend would raise his binoculars. I'd stand next to her, and she'd pass her binoculars with the strap still around her neck. She'd tell me the name and things about the bird. We had to whisper."

"Ooooh!" Mary said.

"Ooooh, yourself," he said.

"No, really," Mary said. "I love it: 'suspended passion,' the tension. Did your hand brush against hers when you were sharing the binoculars?"

"No," Tim said. "I didn't want to put her off in any way. And passion?" Tim said. "What if there was—would that have been so bad?"

He remembered how very quiet it had been on that path except for the light drizzle, the rustle of her rain jacket when she raised the glasses. He'd been wearing a trench coat, not the sort of thing one wears hiking. But he had had the collar up, and with the mist still rising from the ground, there was something right about that. He had felt that while she was showing him a world, he'd brought a slightly mysterious world of his own with him.

Mary thought back to their own courtship. How good-naturedly he had stood out in her new circle of friends, how unquestionably handsome he was. She'd always been glad that she hadn't met him in an AA meeting—that he hadn't been put in the context of metal folding chairs and Styrofoam coffee cups and the wash of rhetoric in some church basement.

The meetings had been necessary, but there was also a loss of feeling, a numbness that began at that time and even now lingered like an overdose of novocaine. She would listen to the others' stories, like the mother who drank steadily from a bottle she kept hidden behind the clothes dryer. "People at parties were always surprised at how low my tolerance was to alcohol," the woman would laugh. "Two drinks and I would be such an intense and passionate person. Sometimes it would take only one. One to upset the normal level in my blood. My husband always told them it was because I was so petite." She'd laugh. "My son once drove me home early from a family reunion." Her eyes would always fill with tears at this point. "He said I had kissed him on the mouth. He was nineteen." She always said this with complete horror, as if she hadn't already told them the story many times before. "And he never told me until years later when he was finished with school."

"You have to forgive yourself," people would tell the mother. Mary hoped no one in the group felt contempt for her, the way she sometimes felt toward this woman.

They all seemed to have their one special story. There was the insurance man who wore plastic gloves the whole first year they were in group together. He had disappeared for a week-long binge, telling his wife he had a convention. Then he came home on Monday night, lit the grill for dinner, and when the coals were white, picked them up in his hands and held them until he lost consciousness.

Mary often gazed at those gloves, which were a transparent green and always seemed to have some oozing substance bubbling under the surface of them. As grotesque as his story was, it didn't seem to bother her as much as some of the others. It was cruel, but also clean—a clean break. Whenever he looked at his hands, they would be both then and now. He didn't have to go deep back into his regrets to remind anyone what he was afraid of. His hands were always in front of him, horrible and simple.

Tim had been part of something clean and new the summer they first knew each other—picnics with a social group and bicycle trips. Like a teenager again, he seemed to throw himself into everything that was physical. He bought a sailboard and took it out every weekend, waving to them from the lake. He must have realized he was like an emblem for their whole experience, the sun glinting off his sail as it did, taking them back to a kind of adolescence where their possibilities were pure again.

Even their coming together had seemed unpremeditated and easy. He'd encouraged her to try the board, and she'd spent the afternoon out on the water, being dumped and swallowing lake water, bruising her legs against the board. But there was an elation, even in the pain, to be struggling with something so clean.

She finally had it sailing and took it for a distance, leaving him behind, laughing and treading water. But she couldn't bring it about and fell again. He had swum after her. Her suit had come down when she started to hoist herself on the board again. He brought her back into the water. As she'd tried to cover her breasts, he'd taken her hand away. He pressed carefully against her in the water, fitting his chest against hers and wrapping her legs around his hips.

They had been careful as lovers, as if neither of them could bear to show how experienced they really were, as if they were starting over. There seemed a silent agreement that drinking and love had been an all-too-integrated passion. So they were afraid, sometimes a little stiff and, Mary had to admit, sometimes a little bored.

The whole sailing incident had rushed back to her mind one day when she'd broken an apple open. The first of the season, so white—she was startled, even humiliated, to remember how equally white her breasts had been that afternoon. And she often wondered if Tim would ever have thought of her as a lover, if he hadn't seen them that one accidental moment. Maybe he had been as numb as she and had to be surprised into wanting someone again.

"Are you with me?" Tim laid his hand on hers. The sun had changed; it was shining right on the water closest to shore. The water was so clear in the shallows that she could see particles of light glinting from the sandy bottom. She could see where the river got deep farther out because it was a dark swath in comparison.

"Yes," she said. "Now tell me how you went from bird-watching to being lovers?"

"Well, we weren't ever lovers, not like you mean . . ."

This Mary had assumed and, somehow, now the story seemed more dangerous. It made her feel that it wasn't finished for him. That he still wanted the other woman.

"You haven't told me about the drinking. I thought this was a drinking story?"

"Just wait," he said. He poured her some tea from the thermos next to him. She could tell just from looking at it that it was merely warm. Cinnamon tea—she couldn't help associating it with their early romance. He had brought a package of it over on their second date. "Just smell this," he said. "Isn't it wonderful?" He'd brought candles, too, and put a tape on her stereo. Even then, so early on, it seemed he couldn't begin to be with her until he had created a certain atmosphere. And today she felt his usual insistence in making their time a certain way. Their lines were in the river not as much to catch fish, she felt, but because there was something ideal in the posture of two people with fishing poles beside them.

He didn't pour a cup for himself from the thermos, and

she decided there was no point telling him it was tepid. It didn't matter; there was nothing he could do about it.

"So we went to breakfast after the hike," he continued, "at a restaurant on the highway. We both sat across from her in the booth. My friend was feeling a little better by then, and it hadn't occurred to me that he might be actually interested in her himself."

"Good, Tim."

"Right. But while he was feeling a little better, I was feeling a little worse. I was cooking off some of the alcohol, and I felt really hot. He was keeping the coffee cups filled, like he intended to stay. But I was so hot, I could feel the flush, and I was sweating. I finally told her."

"Just her?"

"Well, them." Tim felt a pressure in his bladder and was surprised, since they had already used the facilities at the ranger station on the way in, but he ignored it and continued the story.

"She found a spigot outside, and even though it was still drizzling, she turned it on and let it run cold."

He didn't know how to tell Mary about his shirt, even if it was the part he always remembered most about that day. Because he was sweating, he was sure that she could smell the alcohol he was burning off. Yet she seemed to look at him so kindly. "Just rinse off," she had said. "You'd feel better." It made sense that he should take his shirt off. It wasn't that he was embarrassed about his body; he had a good body. In fact he had wanted to. He remembered this overwhelming belief that if he just removed his shirt, she would look at him and know him. It could be that simple. Sometimes he fantasized about the first time he would remove his shirt with a certain woman. It became, in his mind, such a momentous thing to do.

"I couldn't take off my shirt," Tim said.

"What?" Mary asked.

"You know, to wash up."

"Well, why not?"

"I couldn't be sure of anything."

"Sure of what?" Mary put her fingers around his thumb. She couldn't picture what he was saying.

"It seemed I could lose her right there if it wasn't the right time. It always seems like I have to wait for the right time to do something like that."

"What do you mean?"

He looked blankly at her, when she had expected this was a meaningful question.

"No, it had to be another time. I knew that much." Tim's bladder situation felt suddenly more insistent. "So I got my shirt all wet rinsing under the spigot, and my friend came out, pissed off, and asked me for my share of the bill right away. He wasn't very attractive about the whole thing."

"Well, you can be grateful for that, because eventually you were the one that took her out."

"Yeah. I called her, and we went out to dinner a couple of times. There was something almost prim about our conversations that I enjoyed. Only because I looked forward to breaking it down—to getting through to her."

"The river, Tim, can we please get to the river?"

But Tim was looking distracted. He got to his feet. "I have to find a bush or something."

He left so abruptly. Not that she doubted his reason, really. But for someone who valued outings like this so much, it was strange how suddenly he needed to eject himself from the middle of them, as though he couldn't stand living through what he had earlier so much looked forward to. He did this sometimes in restaurants, before they had even finished their meal. He'd say, "Let's go out for ice cream now or catch the 7:30 show."

She watched him walk over the park grass, which was mottled by splotches of shade from the many trees. He walked in and out of the pieces of shade until he eventually disappeared into a stand of bushes.

The river had taken on the flat glare of afternoon light. There was a long black log floating down the middle. It had found the main current, and she imagined it could have been riding that current for some time. It looked oblivious to time or change or the damage it had suffered. It made its slow progress through a patch of lily pads, their delicate edges ruffling against the coarseness of its bark, and then on it drifted into the distance, beneath the orange clay bluffs hunching over the river like great shoulders.

She thought of the log as a *she*. Automatically. Just the way one attaches gender to all sorts of things: dogs are he's; cats are she's; trees can be both. But this one was a she. She'll go on, Mary thought, out into the Mississippi, and then on some more, not feeling a thing.

Tim had found a small cove where the grass was growing tall around it. It was a place where no one on the shore or on the river could see him. He walked into the grass. It tickled his bare arms and legs. I'm sober, he thought—a statement he had made to himself in many other situations this past year. This time it was because he could feel the grass so sharply against his calves. And because it seemed very odd to be peeing out here when he wasn't drinking. It was strange because this was often the time when he would have been telling himself, I'm drunk. There had always been that benign first trip to the bushes, when he'd be standing there, listening to himself, trickling down on the leaves or the stones, or whatever was beneath him. And he'd realize that he was both inside and outside his body. The man outside his body would be sober and almost fatherly in his concern, his affection, his disappointment, standing just to the side with his hands on his hips, saying, Here you are again, you son of a bitch. And the inside part of himself would just be there, wherever he was. If it was a field, he would be buzzing a little like the bees and be sticky like the pollen and fuzzy like the grass. The first trip to the bushes was invariably happy. Then there would be a small period of orientation: yes, he was peeing; yes, he was doing it properly. Some accounting: yes, he'd had three beers and part of the bottle of whiskey; who was it that was waiting for him to finish; how much had they drunk; and were they waiting in anticipation for him to come back?

But now it was different. Now he was in possession of

himself. Strictly one person. And he and the grass were separate things. This was the St. Croix, a cool breeze was coming from somewhere. And he was impatient. Telling Mary this story, he wanted to get to the end of it. Sometimes you started a story, and then, hardly into it, you lost confidence. He was only continuing out of sheer willpower. He was already so very disappointed with the day. Why, he didn't know.

"Geez!" he murmured to himself. His shirttail was caught in the zipper of his fly. He'd heard a large fish plopping in the water nearby. "That figures." He thought of Mary looking into her fishless part of the river.

They'd been together over a year. He didn't know if they would ever be in love, the way people were supposed to be. He walked through the rough grass. And yet, there were these almost accidental times with her when she would make some awkward gesture, or laugh abruptly at him or herself, when he believed that she, more than anyone he had ever been with, knew the unspeakable things that get into people's hearts, that were in his heart.

Once he had answered the phone at her apartment. It was a man, a voice slightly tinny through a long-distance connection, but underneath that his voice was svelte, assured. "What do you want?" she had said before anything else. "No," she had said. "No." And then she had hung up. She was sitting on the carpet with the phone in her lap. She looked immovable, like a stone. Then he saw that her hand was clenched so hard around the receiver that it had turned white. He knelt down and pried it away, letting her grip his own hand. She began to lose the stony look and continued to squeeze his hand.

"That's okay," he had said, meaning she could squeeze even harder if she needed.

And then she looked up and said, "I'm never going to be the way I used to be."

"How?" he wanted to know.

"Hot and desirous and stupid and ugly." She'd turned away from him and spat the words into the room.

"Let's talk about it," he said.

And she'd snorted at him as if to say the suggestion was banal. She made him feel foolish. "What sense do we make of the dramatic details?" she said. "I'm tired of them," she said. "We both have our own groups. We can go on and on ad nauseam there. Can't we just be good to each other, without swamping ourselves in the details?"

"The river." Tim gazed over the water and remembered. "It couldn't have been more beautiful."

Mary looked around, thinking most anyone would find this place perfectly lovely now.

"It was a different kind of day from today," Tim said, "not just sunny. It was already late in the afternoon when we arrived. The clouds were moving, so the sun would come and go."

Tim had been rubbing Mary's hand absentmindedly with his thumb. It became irritating to her, she she slipped it out and rested it on his knee instead.

"I'd brought a picnic: good wine, bread, artichokes, tomatoes, . . ."

"All your favorite things," she said, "except the Wild Turkey."

"That comes later," Tim said. "But I have to tell you, the day was very different—it was like the river would look completely golden, and then it wouldn't and then it would because of the clouds. For a while the sun was below the clouds. Have you ever seen that?"

"No." But, almost immediately, she remembered that she did in fact see it like that once after a thunderstorm. She'd left a lot of people back at a party. It had gone into the morning. Those that were left had passed out. If it hadn't been for the thunderstorm, she would have continued sleeping. But she'd found herself in her Dodge Dart, hating her life, driving down the road. The farmers called it a "spent" thunderstorm—when the big, gray clouds are left without the rain. The sun rose underneath the clouds that morning so that all the houses she drove past were a deep orange and the sky above them a deep gray. She had almost made a U-turn back to the house so she could tell someone. But she decided that the phenomena would change before she even reached them, or whoever came to see wouldn't see what she saw.

"It's like the clouds are pushing the light down. That's when we went into the water. Mary"—Tim put his hand around her waist—"the water was so soft!"

"What did you do?" She let herself settle ever so lightly against his arm. And she realized there was a longing within her—she wanted to be in that water; but at the same time she felt repulsed, afraid that this was just the kind of wanting that tricked you.

"Water ballet," he laughed. "It was one of the things her mother had gotten her involved with in high school. She looked silly doing these pointy-toed things upside down in the water. It was as if she was sharing the more absurd side of being a princess. And I liked her even better for it.

"Afterward, we changed into dry clothes under a blanket. We were sitting on the top of a picnic table. She was already dressed, and I was leaning over, futzing with my shoes. The blanket fell off my shoulders, and my shirt was off. She put her hand very gently on my back and held it there like she was trying to sense something.

That's when I pulled out the Wild Turkey. It wasn't like it bothered her. She took a little in her glass. And for the next few hours, we watched the trees get dark against the sky, and we drank. We talked about everything, about my dad, and the time I was hit by a car running after my brother's school bus, and the time that Hank fell out of the chestnut tree in our backyard."

"I didn't know that," Mary said.

"Yes, nothing happened to him. He bounced. You know what she said? I remember, she said, 'You have a very physical family.' She told me things I hadn't thought of before. She told me about herself, too. As we got into it, the air was getting cool, like September, but we just wrapped in the blanket, and everything was changing as it should. The moon came out. We were trading secrets, back and forth. I wanted to make love with her and I almost . . ."

"What, Tim?" Mary had been stroking his hand.

"Well, you know how it is when you're talking to some-one, and you know they can tell you're getting drunk. But you keep drinking, and you keep watching to see if it makes a difference to them?"

"Yeah, I know," Mary said.

Tim uncrossed his ankles and brought his knees up to his chest. "Well, it made a difference. I could see it, like a cloud passing in front of her face."

Mary looked down at his gray sneakers, and the thought crossed her mind that he might have still had them as long ago as that day with the other woman. She looked at him. "You can't forever be ashamed about that, Tim," she said. And as soon as the words were out, she knew they were too simple, a phrase she would have given to any member of her AA group, something easy, and which she felt nothing about.

His face flooded with anger. "That's not the only thing!" he shouted. And instantaneously he imagined the park sign at the entrance to the road vibrating from the sound of the shout. And it became clear to him why he always had the impulse to return here: he was still looking for that perfect day. If only he could make a perfect day and still drink and drink perfectly with someone else, and they could drink too and drink perfectly. And if there wasn't that, what could he do? What could he want instead?

We're both still so sick, she thought. She didn't know what to do. She got up and waded over to where their bob-bers had floated into the shore and began to untangle them, pulling her hair behind her ear as it fell forward and got in her eyes. It was all awkward. She hated anything as frustrat-ing as these tangles almost as much as he did. That's why he had tried to prevent them from drifting in the first place. Still, he had let them, just like she had. And now the line was wet, and there were pieces of weeds clinging to the mess.

He was bending over her on the shore, his hands on his

knees. He was sorry he had shouted. He wanted to explain. "Mary," he said gently. "Don't you ever miss it?"

"What?" she said, coldly, not looking at him while she pretended to be working the little knots apart. But she knew he meant drinking. She still didn't know if she could talk about that. If she could say yes to that and still survive.

"Mary?" he said.

And when she looked up, behind the strands of hair that had stuck to her mouth, she was sobbing. He looked at her small shoulders, so bare and quaking they were like the two parts of a heart. And he knew even before he had done it that the next moment he would be in the water with her. That it would be cold: a cold shock and then a starting over again.

THE UNDERSTANDING

I'm a poodle."

That's what he would like to tell someone. Not that they didn't know that already. But he would like to tell them so they would know that *he* knew. Just once as the mailman came up the walk, instead of yelping and running from window to door to window again, he would like to wait patiently, even serenely, until the man had come to the first step. He would stand on his hind legs then, push the screen door ajar to show his face, and say, "Boo. I'm a poodle."

That would make an impression. If only there were a way he could express to someone that he was special—a poodle, but more than a poodle. The truth was that he'd changed in the last few years, though he continued to behave in much the same way he always had—pouting, running in circles, and being manipulative. Like the time he had defecated in the pocket of their neighbor's pool table. This had been his way of protesting being left there while the rest of the family went on vacation. That was years ago, but he'd do it again, given the same circumstances. Not because it was his nature, but because those were the means available to someone who had no hands and who couldn't talk. And yet, if someone could get inside his head, they would see that he understood much more than it appeared. They would see all the many things he had learned from living with Gretta.

Shortly, however, he was to be taken away from her, and a doubt had been growing in him about whether he really knew anything at all. He was afraid he might only know what Gretta knew, and once separated from her, the meanings he had come to recognize might just fade out, like radio music driving away in a car.

It was a slow, sunny day on the screen porch. Gretta held him in her lap, picking through his fur with one old hand and clipping it with the other. She didn't actually look at him as she did this, but felt out his long hairs, pulled them between the scissors and snipped them off, letting them float to the floor. There was comfort in her touch and in the quiet, and even in the snipping sound. Yet he was dismayed. He would be gone soon, perhaps even before the mailman arrived. He squirmed in Gretta's lap. She turned him over and began to clip the hair under his chin. Since she was nearly blind, he recognized this as a critical task and lay motionless, looking up into her face.

Gretta Ormson was 101 years old. She wore her hearing aid only a few hours during the day. The rest of the day she was stone deaf, and she sat with the stillness of a stone, like a Buddha, with her long, waxy earlobes, and her cataractous eyes. Her hands were particularly remarkable, hugely out of proportion as they curved over the ends of her chair arms. At rest there was still a kind of vibration under their loose skin, which, depending on the day or hour, changed in color from gray to a rough red to a purple cast. He loved Gretta's hands.

They shimmered with something a painter would ache to capture and never could. Except, perhaps, Rembrandt. Once there was a program about his paintings on public television; he couldn't tell if Gretta was able to hear what it was about, but she had fallen asleep anyway, and the sound of the narrator's voice mixed in with the sound of her breathing, which was the sound of old leaves blowing in the yard.

"There is a light," the narrator had said, "in each of his paintings, like a beacon, that draws one into them." And when
Binky had looked over at Gretta's hands resting on the arms
of her chair, he already knew how this could be true.

Two weeks ago, the day he had first heard the news, had
been the same warm kind of day on the sun porch. A flyswatter lay forgotten across Gretta's lap. Her hearing aid remained in the box on the kitchen table, and she barely
stirred at all. An airplane roared above. A fly was buzzing
behind her head, then around it in a circle, landing, lost for a
moment in her hair. It dropped down onto her hand, took a
walk along the blue, cordlike vein. Binky perked up, protective, and watched it take a pinch of her skin in its little chop-
sticks. Then he stood up to make it fly away. These were the
kind of daily activities they shared together.

After the fly left and boredom had set in again, Binky
had crawled over to the chair next to Gretta's and found the
spot under the springs that he had been digging at for the
past few days. He'd finally reached the stuffing; it was coming away in clumps, making him giddy as it sprinkled down
onto his chest and head.

Whack! the flyswatter came down on his belly. Whack,
whack, on each of his feet. "No! Binky!" she had scolded him.
She prodded him from under the chair with her swatter,
pushed him across the floorboards until he was lying at the
toes of her shoes, his paws drooping in the air like the heads
of remorseful ducks.

Later, she had reached behind her chair and raised the
window shade to put a patch of sun on the floor where he lay.
And forgiven, he fell asleep, dreaming he was a young dog
running after a scent, and the grass was bending around
him, and he had no words or thoughts, just the scent and his
running.

He had been brought out of his nap by the rumble of
Barb's Oldsmobile pulling up to the house. Barb was
Gretta's youngest daughter. All of her other children were in
their seventies or, some of them, dead, but Barb was a
latecomer and only in her fifties. There was always some-

thing breathless and earnest about her, as if she would never get over being the baby of the family. On his hind legs, he leaned against the porch door while his breath created a little circle of fog on the window. Gretta's chair was creaking a little, which meant she was watching her come, too. When Barb finally opened the door, he fell out through the crack, and she had to catch him with her knee.

"Ouch! Binky!" she said, because she had arthritis in her knees. She pushed him back into the porch. He jumped around her and yelped once before he jumped onto the footstool by the door so she could pet him. Then he whined. Then he jumped down and ran around her legs. Then he jumped onto the stool again. This was how he was with Barb.

She rubbed him all over with her long fingernails and said, "Oh, Binky! Goo'boy!" Finally, she had gathered him up and sat down in the chair across from Gretta. "Mom?"

Gretta raised the lids of her eyes a fraction and looked at Barb as if deciding whether she wanted to see her or not. "Hi," she said finally. "Are you already finished from work?" Barb worked part-time as a secretary. She visited Gretta every day.

"No, Mother, it's Friday." (Friday, Binky knew, Barb never worked.)

"Did you work hard today?"

"No, Mother, it's Friday. I'm always off on Friday." Barb leaned over to look in Gretta's ear.

"No, I don't have my hearing aid in. I can't hear a word you're saying. Is that a new blouse?"

"I got it today."

"What?"

"I got it . . . Mom, don't ask me questions if you can't hear me. I'll go get your hearing aid. I brought you a shake from Burger King," Barb shouted in Gretta's ear. Binky dropped to the floor when Barb stood up. She pulled a paper cup with a plastic top and a straw out of a bag. Gretta took it in both hands and immediately put the straw in her mouth. When Gretta drank a shake she looked like a Buddha drinking a shake.

"What happened to the chair?" Barb came back onto the porch pushing some of the stuffing into the corner with her foot. Binky had his paws tucked under and was avoiding her gaze. She handed Gretta the Indian bead box that always held her hearing aid. Gretta went through the ritual—opening the box, putting the battery in place, adjusting the dial, which caused a painful whistling. Eventually she placed it in the great hole in her ear and adjusted the dial until the whistling stopped.

"What . . . happened . . . to . . . the . . . chair?" Barb said loudly, each word a separate enunciation.

"He." Gretta motioned listlessly toward him with her big hand.

"Binky!" Barb leaned over and shook her finger at him. "Don't do that!"

Binky tried to look as dumb as he could.

"He needs a trim," Barb said. "Why don't you let me call the Poodle Patrol?"

The Poodle Patrol made house calls. Dogs were carried to someone waiting at the backdoor of their van. Inside they were clipped and shaved and powdered. Binky was usually given a number sixteen, which meant he got a hairpiece, resembling a shaving brush, molded on the top of his head. The rest of his body was shaved down to pink skin, except for his legs which were trimmed and left fluffy. Then he was returned with a ribbon around his shaving brush that said, "Poodle Perfect."

The whole tone of his day had changed when Barb mentioned the Poodle Patrol. He began to feel anxious and miserable. Just when he had achieved a plain comfortable scruffiness, he would be transformed into a fluff.

It was a great frustration. And he wondered as he did every time, if Gretta would bother with this, had her daughter Leslie not insisted upon it every month until the time of her death. In her lifetime, Leslie had succeeded in forming him into a parody of what one might find most ridiculous in people. Even now, when he was being finicky about his food, rigid in his routine, and generally snotty, he blamed Leslie.

When Barb suggested Monday, Gretta had said, "No. Costs too much."

"Mom, it costs as much as anyone else, and I hate taking him in the car."

"I'll trim him on my own," she said. "Then I'm giving him away."

Barb had plopped down in her chair, as if a little dumbstruck. She looked at Binky, and then back again at Gretta. "Well, okay, I guess," she said. "Okay then."

It seemed that Gretta had been trimming him for hours. He watched the little curls of his white fur make a larger and larger pile on the floor. He couldn't say he hadn't seen it coming. His bladder had lost its discipline over the years, and he couldn't hold out much past three in the morning. Last winter she had told Barb that it would be his last. It was too much taking him out on dark, icy mornings. Now it was September, and he supposed she had no reason to change her mind.

For days he had expected he'd get the news that they'd found him an owner. Barb left flyers with the Poodle Patrol, of all people, so they could circulate them to their customers. And though he'd heard no specific talk about it, he believed today would be the day. Perhaps Gretta would trim him badly enough that no one else would want him.

Sometimes he'd tried to imagine an owner other than Gretta, but the task made his head reel as much as trying to picture a color never seen before, or eternity, or being dead. He had to find her then, curl beside her in her chair, and tuck his muzzle beneath her hip. If someone were to ask her, she'd say she didn't own him at all. That it was always Leslie and Steiner that had owned him. And that he was just a living thing left behind.

There were even owners before them. He wasn't sure what he remembered: a lot of tumbling and disorder and then a stretch of being alone and hungry outside. Then he was inside again, which must have been this house. Leslie and her husband, Steiner, lived here then. They said that he was a stray—that Steiner brought him in to show Leslie and that she oohed and cooed. She was in love with him (or the idea of him) from that moment on. But Binky had never felt her love. He didn't feel anything like that in the world until near the time of her death. By that time she was just a dim remainder of a person. And so it wasn't her that had the love anymore but something persistent and steady in the air around her.

No, Binky didn't know what he could exactly remember of Leslie or what it was that he'd reconstructed from her artifacts. There were little coats she had made for him, crocheted in bright colors with matching hats. There was a raincoat, a rainhat, and a rayon sailor suit for formal occasions. There were her ashtrays and lamps, some rococo, the rest French Provincial. There were filigreed napkin holders, and goblets etched with palm trees, and, more than anything, there was a canopy bed. It was completely out of proportion to the small room that she and Steiner had shared in Gretta's house. In fact, the ceiling pressed against the canopy so that it drooped instead of arched.

The house filled up and overflowed with these things, and Gretta still kept many of them, as if maintaining her daughter's desires. But every once in a while she'd find something like a pineapple platter from Hawaii and dump it without a flinch, as if it had suddenly come loose of Leslie's pleasure, and without that turned instantly useless. And in his more anxious times, Binky wondered if he hadn't grown useless in the same way.

Gretta pushed Binky in her no-nonsense way off her lap. And he landed with a poof of dog curls around him. She began to rock forward in her chair, one, two, three, and four, until she had gained enough momentum to pull herself up on her feet. Binky waltzed backward, made little starts with his shoulders, as if he might jump into her arms. He wagged his tail incessantly—hoping—for what? To be let outside? To be fed? To be petted fondly? This he didn't know. The sudden desire for her to do something with him just came over him at times, and it always took him a while to guess what it was.

He circled around her legs as she hobbled away until she pushed him aside with her cane. He imagined suddenly that they could go on a vacation together before he had to leave. He had never gone along when the family went on vacation, and she hadn't traveled for years. Maybe it would be a good thing for both of them. They could go to Florida for the winter, and she could find a room with a balcony. He imagined the sun she would like and the seagulls flying over the beach.

He followed her with his small steps to the bathroom. But for the first time, he didn't follow her in. He just waited in the hallway and felt forlorn. He knew, after all, that they wouldn't ever go away together. And here he was in the hallway.

When Leslie was sick, he had been left there too. And it was those last days of her cancer when things had begun to have names and meanings for him. He didn't know what cancer was then, or even sickness, really. He only knew that he was no longer welcome in her bedroom and that he was treated roughly by Steiner, Barb, and Gretta, too, if he tried to enter. So he had slept on the rug that lay beween Gretta's and Leslie's rooms. A small light burned in the hallway and a small light near Leslie's bed. There was an endless procession by the others night after night from one light to the other. Their weight as they passed him on the floorboards was heavy and kept him awake. But still he never wanted another place for himself to sleep. It was as close as he could be without being inside.

Something happened. He began to distinguish between them better than he had before. He noticed that Barb would take her shoes off before entering the room, and the shoes had high spikes, and that sometimes, after she had left them, one of them would tip over and lie next to him. He noticed that Steiner would often stand in Leslie's doorway without going in, his hand just dangling there. And later Binky would look at the others and see that Steiner's hand didn't move as much as theirs did, but hung at his side as if heavy.

He began to know extraordinary things for a dog—not

just the feeling of weight or the look of size, but how one thing could be like another, and how they could be different. Gretta's step was the steadiest in those days. And it was for her mother that Leslie would call the latest into the night. Binky would hear the two of them talking in low tones. Their voices were the same as winter trees groaning together in the wind, and Binky, not knowing that it was a painful sound, was comforted by it and let the sound lull him to sleep.

One afternoon the family all gathered in Leslie's room. They went in and out. Barb came out with Leslie's purse and set it on the dining room table. Steiner made trips to the car. Finally Gretta came out with Leslie. She was wrapped in blankets. She walked slowly past Binky. He couldn't see her face, and it seemed that she couldn't see him either. Gretta, who was a stout woman then, held her from behind and by the elbow as they left the house.

They were gone for days, one of them returning only occasionally to put food in his dish and to let him out. And when they finally came home to stay, Leslie wasn't with them. But he remembered Barb coming in, and how she had again set Leslie's purse on the dining room table.

This must have been late summer, because the air was thick like a blanket over him. Many people visited during the rest of the day and into the night, some of them leaving later than the first bird calls. And he was overwhelmed with the density of them in that little house, their smells, altogether, like an invasion upon a peace that by this time he had become comfortable with. Little children had grabbed him up in their boredom, handled his parts, as if identifying them to each other, his paws, his legs, his pink belly. One of them would blow into his ear to make him shudder, then they'd laugh when he finally broke away to hide under the sofa.

When the house was finally quiet, Binky was the only one left awake. Barb had gone home with her husband and children. He had found Steiner stretched on the parlor davenport dead asleep. He climbed onto Steiner's chest, sniffed around his open mouth, and found the familiar sweet smell that Steiner had held in his glass all day.

He had traveled along the living room furniture, finding cake crumbs and the remainders of casseroles on paper plates. There were filled ashtrays, sweating glasses, coffee cups with red lip marks on their rims.

In the kitchen there was a drip from the faucet, a faint sound of something incomplete and not right in the house. The first light had only come up to the window, but not in— it stood there waiting like a stranger. And the whole house was gray with this strangeness. He was afraid of the quiet— the quiet left in Leslie's room; the quiet in the bathroom. And when he went looking for Gretta, he had found her door closed for the first time in months. But he could hear the rumble of her old air conditioner. He pushed against the door, and when it finally clicked open, he fell in through the crack.

It was cool and dry inside. Gretta was asleep on the single bed with her hand laid over her eyes. There were beads of water gathering on the underbody of the air conditioner, the dripping silenced by the drone of the fan. Light was slowly leaking into the room. An airplane vaguely roared overhead. He watched her sleeping. A bus shook the windows from two streets away. Light was creeping up the bottom of the bed, actually laying itself across her feet. The fingers of her hand fluttered, then slid away from her face. Her eyes were already open. There was nothing in them but the same languid feeling of the morning that had so far filled the room. And when she turned her eyes in his direction, he had stood up.

She looked past him as though someone had entered the room at the same time. And she looked as if, in the next moment, she would be either very terrified or very calm. But she was calm. He saw something in her gaze that he'd never understood before. It was memory. It reminded him of a full bottle poised on the edge of a table. She turned her eyes up, and he looked up, and the bottle trembled between them, then tipped over, silently; Leslie's black hair, how she looked while she laughed, and her perfume didn't spill out, but slowly dripped into Gretta's eyes and remained there.

Binky had stood transfixed, motionless as a hunting dog that has sighted something moving in the trees, excited and fearful too, that he might see it again and he might not. There was nothing he could do to see more. This was how he felt about his understanding: he was only on the edge of it. Looking at Gretta, he realized she wasn't seeing him now. Her eyes were closed as if she had fallen back to sleep, as if nothing had just happened in that room. And that's when he noticed her hands for the first time. They were gripping the sheets around her chest, as if they had somehow remained awake to keep her covered.

Today, Binky felt a similar tension—not simply about the fact that he had to leave. It was that he felt his chance to know things was ending. Gretta sat in her overstuffed chair, a few yards away from where he lay on the carpet. She was doing what she called her "handwork." Lately, she spent her time making pastel-colored pom-poms out of mesh. They were used to scrub dishes. She called them "chore girls" and gave them to all her visitors. "They are miraculous," she would tell them.

Every time she finished one she tossed it in Binky's direction, sometimes hitting him on the top of the head, sometimes not coming close at all. She could be playful in her own way. But it was that dull time of late morning, and he could smell chicken in the oven, reminding him of all the times he had smelled it before, and this made him sad.

Since Leslie's death, Steiner had died too. "Of drinking," Barb would say. And Gretta's son Darrel of a heart attack in North Dakota, and her brother Inver, finally, of just being old. All of her last friends were gone—Mrs. Burdon, Mrs. Matthews, Mrs. Johnson with the scent of schnauzer on her skirt hem that invariably gave Binky an erection, until Gretta would say, "Put that pink thing away."

All were gone except their neighbor, Mrs. Wood, who would do better to die. But "Meanness kept her alive," Barb

said, a confusing concept to Bin[...]
Gretta.

Wood, they called her. Ninety-six [...]
into the shape of an umbrella handle, she [...]
few days, down the sidewalk to their house [...]
her since she was given to generally poking and [...]
with her cane. Her hearing was barely keener th[...]
so much of their visit consisted of misunderstand[...]
other.

Wood would say, "My gas bill was terrible this mon[...]

"Oh! I don't blame you," Gretta would say. "It's bee[...]
over fifty years, and I miss my husband as if it'd only been a [...]
year."

"Mine's not over a hundred and fifty, but it's still a crime.
We're old women. They'd let us freeze if it came to it."

"I was forty-nine, standing on the window ledge, washing the windows, and Orrin came in the front door. 'Gretta, I
don't know what's wrong with me,' he said." Whether or not
Wood had heard, Gretta had told her this story many times.

"It's a scheme." Wood would pound her cane into the
floor. "Don't believe them. They call me all the time telling
me they should insulate my house, fix the doors and the windows. To save me money. Ha!"

Gretta would be quiet for a minute, resting. Wood would
gurgle and rattle deep down in her throat, trying to settle
something disagreeable in herself. They talked. "He was on
the bed," Gretta would say, never without holding herself
across the ribs and rocking the way he had. "He said, 'It
hurts so much,' and he was such a big man who never
complained."

Binky knew the script of their visits. Wood had many
complaints, and Gretta would stare out the window. Sometimes she had the look of a young woman, as if none of her
children had died yet, as if they hadn't even been born. Binky
could see her as a girl on the Dakota farm, the miles of
flatland stretching around her and her blue eyes full of the
sky, which she always said was the thing she had loved most
about the plains. Eventually she would look over at Wood,

which she already

to boil when Wood
visit, make tea for
e had offered coffee,

the table before her
oud enough to hear,
goddamn you."
"I came over yester-

l shout. "I can't just
ized. You know that
g clothes on the line.
Call me before you leave, and I'll let you in."

nderstanding

ly since it didn't apply to
years old and gnarled
would creep, every
. Binky dreaded
d swatting him
an Gretta's,
ing each
th."

But Wood rarely called. She had high expectations, Gretta said. There was a time when Binky would bark and jump on the arm of Gretta's chair to let her know Wood was there. But he had stopped.

One day she had come to the porch door and knocked with her cane. Gretta was taking her nap on the couch, her hand curled over her eyes, deaf. And Binky went to the porch where Wood stood behind the locked screen door. Rap! Rap! She banged the frame. "I'm here." But he didn't move. Maybe because her walk had been painful or because the sun was glaring through her thin white hair, she looked defenseless. "Tell her, dog," she said. But he didn't want her in the house.

Wood turned away and descended each step like it was a day. She came around the side windows, which were over her head. Binky watched the rubber tip of her cane bounce against the panes. She banged on the backdoor, and finally she was gone.

It was dinnertime. Gretta opened the oven door and the chicken spattering sounded like applause. "Grease is a great thing," the chicken almost seemed to say. Binky loved

Gretta's food. Years of it had left a lacquerlike film on the enamel of the stove and the yellow wallpaper. He could smell it everywhere in the house. If she did nothing else in a day, she still cooked. It wasn't Monday or Tuesday or Thursday; it was meatloaf or porkchops or roast. It was the substance of her day, her inspiration and her pleasure.

Some mornings, after dressing in the same knit pants and sweater she'd worn for days, before she'd even put her shoes on, she'd announce her menu plan, as if the whole family still lived in the house. *"Mashed rutabagas* and *potatoes.* Yes! Lord God, it's been a long time. It sure has." She'd go into the kitchen, dig two rutabagas and potatoes out, and thump them down on the counter with conviction. "I'll do that later for dinner," she'd promise.

Barb arrived as Gretta was setting a plate for her on the table. "Mother! What did you do to Binky?"

Binky stood up, alarmed.

"Doesn't he look better?"

"You missed trimming one of his legs. It looks like he's wearing a cast. Oh, Mother, can you see the bald spots? Poor thing." Barb picked Binky up, and he felt like crying.

"Worse things have happened," Getta grumbled. "Sit down now—we have chicken, creamed carrots, and rolls."

"Just coffee." Barb looked over at Binky laying on the rug. "My God," she said, shaking her head.

Sitting beside Gretta at the table, she opened the drawstring on the plastic bag that she had brought with her. "I washed some of his things," she said. And Binky, watching her pull out his vests and his small wool leggings, felt nostalgic for those sillier days.

"Good." Gretta fingered the material. "He'll be ready then. Have you talked to the man?"

"He said he'd call tonight."

What man? Binky's heart stopped and waited.

"What?" Gretta asked.

Barb leaned closer. *"He said he'd call me tonight about picking him up,"* she said louder and more clearly, exacerbating Binky's misery.

Gretta continued eating quietly. "Have some food," she said after a minute.

"Mother, I said no."

When Gretta had finally picked a drumstick nearly clean she tossed it on the rug next to Binky. He took it in his mouth listlessly.

Gretta dipped a biscuit in her coffee. "They say you shouldn't give chicken bones to a dog." Then she went back to eating. "I suppose one day he'll choke and die."

She stopped eating. "I'll miss him," she said. "I'll miss sitting with him."

"Yes, I know." Barb leaned forward. "But it's right. It's the right time."

Then Gretta looked up distractedly. "I'm calling Wood for dinner." She labored to get up.

"Mother!"

"She should be here; it's been a long time." She was finally on her feet; her napkin clung to her knee, then fell to the floor. "Dial her number," she told Barb. "Dial her number."

"Mom, I am."

"Hello," Gretta said as soon as she had the phone to her ear.

"Mom, she hasn't answered."

"Hello." Binky could hear Wood's voice sounding like an insect's over the line.

"I'm inviting you for dinner," Gretta said.

"I can't hear you. Who is this?"

And Gretta, who had her hearing aid in this time, said, "She can't hear me. Come to dinner!" she shouted one more time.

"Here, let me try." Barb took the phone. "Mrs. Wood. . . . *Can . . . you . . . come . . . for . . . dinner?*" But there was only confusion on the other end.

Then they were both shouting into the phone different things at the same time: "We've got food" and "You're invited." The way fans hopelessly cheer a losing team to win.

Then a click. And all three of them, including Binky,

watched in their minds as Wood walked from the phone to stand bewildered in the middle of her living room.

"You go see about her, Barb," Gretta said, "and Binky and I will stay here."

Early evenings, Gretta had to tend her garden. This was something she would do every day until the first frost. It was her constitutional. Tonight she looked over the narrow plot along the south side of the house that bordered the driveway and Binky stood on the concrete beside her. The mums were still healthy, and the bees were kicking their hind legs into them in that frantic way they have at summer's end.

It had been years since she had been able to kneel on the ground and ever hope to get back up again. But Binky still remembered those days. Now she managed by putting one hand on the house for support and reaching down with the other. She folded the wilted petal of a pansy back as if to look at its face. "Almost gone, aren't you?" she commiserated. "Pop your head off, I'm afraid." And she did, because the rule of thumb with pansies was to keep them thinned.

The pavement was still warm from the day, and Binky lay down. Gretta inched her way along the garden, pulling up weeds and dead plants and tossing them onto the driveway to be swept together later. Every few feet that she progressed, Binky would slide his body along to follow her.

The sun's angle had changed, and it seemed to lie like an arm around Gretta's shoulders as she leaned over her work. Her hearing aid had gone back into its box after dinner. And this time of day, when she was deaf, Binky felt deaf, too. The world took on a stillness in early evening, as if the two of them were together in a painting.

Binky rolled on his back. The sky was blue, and a plane passed silently, high over the treetops. He felt deeply peaceful. Dreaming, he had the sensation that the plane's shadow was covering him, and he suddenly felt very cold. No, it was a man's shadow. There was a man somewhere? Instinctively he rolled and found himself in a tense crouch. He was growling with that rumbling growl deep within his body that signified to him there was a danger even before he knew what that danger was.

Was the man really there? It was so strange. He stood, hands in his coat pockets, on the driveway not eight feet away from Gretta and said nothing. Was he the man who had come to take him home with him? No, Binky somehow felt this wasn't true.

The stranger watched Gretta as she continued to reach into the garden, searching out and grasping the roots of dead plants. And Binky watched her, too, with a great protectiveness. He loved the independence of her hands as they worked, as if through a century of sheer use they had come to possess a soul of their own. She moved quietly along the garden, the man standing behind her. Her face was smooth, and she seemed unaware she was being watched. As if to change this, the man stepped toward her. Binky crouched. He had never felt so protective of her in his life. His heart became huge in his chest; his lips drew back over his teeth; and he poised for an attack, growling louder and louder, finally leaping at the stranger. But the man disappeared, leaving Binky to attack thin air.

Binky, naturally, felt foolish, like the times in his youth he had zealously leaped at the mailman only to crash into the door between them. He knew he was whimpering as he went back to Gretta. And the fact that she couldn't hear him and didn't know what had happened made him feel utterly alone. He thought of Wood walking along this garden, trying to beat on the windows, and the loneliness of it. Gretta was slowly sweeping the weeds together in the driveway, and the light brushing sound was no more comforting than the sound of time passing. Why was she giving him away? What was going to happen to him?

Binky howled. He stood in the middle of Gretta's pile of sweepings and continued to howl. She tried to push him aside with her broom, but he wouldn't budge, and he knew that, eventually, if she looked at him, she couldn't help but see that he was calling out to her. She did finally, and she picked him up, held his head in her hand, looked into his face. He was trembling. "You're a troublesome little thing," she said. "Even so, I can't give you away today. I will though, Binky." She took his paw firmly in her large hand. "It won't be long before we'll just have to find another place for you."

"Now," she said, walking to the corner of the house, "there are just a few more things we should do tonight. We need to check the rain bucket." It was full, and somehow she managed to pour it into her watering can, still holding Binky. She set it back under the drainpipe. "It's bound to rain again," she said."You can feel it, can't you?" And he put his nose up to the air as if to show her he was listening. And sure enough there was rain in the air, coming from the west. Suddenly the fact that it was coming felt very immediate, as if he could see it beating against the western plains, like an army's march in their direction.

The rain was an oddly comforting thought. Somehow that Gretta was so sure of it made him feel safe again. He'd almost forgotten about the visitor in the driveway, but the thought of him came back again, quite simply. He understood. It wasn't earth-shattering. It didn't even change anything. Gretta had known the man was there the whole time. He was Death, wasn't he? And he had visited for years—he was in her windows and in her yard and in her morning cup of coffee. He would make no huge claim on her. She was peaceful with this, and Binky loved her for her strength, and for the moment he had the feeling they could live forever.

She walked slowly, carrying him back to the porch, occasionally stopping to knock a dirt clod back into the garden with her shoe, and he knew they would sit in her porch chair watching the sky darken in the west. She would have no inclination to go in until her expectations were met, until the thunder was in their neighborhood and the rain started washing across the street onto their yard and up against their windows.

FAITH

She stood with a family in the pew in front of mine. She might have blended in as one of their daughters, except that they were an ensemble of blazers, pastel wool coats, smoothly groomed hair, and she was not. She was a sort of jam session of clothing: navy opaque stockings, white slip-on sneakers, lime green culottes (something I hadn't seen worn since 1968), and a bulky pullover jacket that came nearly to the hem of her culottes. Her hair was closely, but unskillfully, chopped, leaving square edges around her ears. And the jacket, light enough, had a hood trimmed with long fur. The sleeves were also trimmed with fur and covered everything but her fingertips. I could see a few beads of a rosary wrapped around her fingers, and since very few people say the rosary anymore, let alone a girl her age, it struck me as odd.

She looked around frequently—at the stained glass, at the chandeliers in the dome of the basilica, at the candles burning in a dark foyer behind the altar, and at me. Her face was so superb, it diminished any prejudice her clothing or even the rosary had brought to my mind. She had that quintessential dark Irish look, the black black hair and eyes against clear white skin that I'd only seen before in movies or National Geographic.

I had hoped for a shorter ceremony. But I'd watched Kathy, the receptionist in the office I share with two other psychologists, escalate the event for months. Perhaps because I was the only other woman in the office, she kept me informed of the details as they compounded. "We got the basilica!" she'd squeal at me as I walked past her on my way to the rest room. "We are going to be in the absolutely most gorgeous church in town!" I'd hear through the restroom door as I washed my hands. And I'd wonder what the patient who was now in a session with one of my colleagues in the next room thought of this. Or, "Steve can't find enough groom's men to match my six," she'd tell me after our morning greeting in the waiting room. And after the many days of being included in her planning, I wasn't capable of making the excuses my associates had mustered for their RSVPs.

Now the uncle she had been afraid wouldn't be able to celebrate the service stretched his arms out of the wide sleeves of his vestments toward the crowd. "We are here to witness this precious union. Each of us has a special relationship with these young people. Our hopes for them are our gifts. And at this time of year"—he gestured toward the statue of Mary, where there were many baskets of tulips and lilies at her feet—"we can appreciate Mary and the special care she has for Stephen and Katherine." The mildest wave of revulsion passed through me. The dark-haired girl was up on her toes, trying to see the shrine, and I was reminded of those first May days in my girlhood parish when making the flower procession to Our Lady was the greatest honor.

When I was seven, still too young to be part of the May Day court, my mother gave me a smooth bisque statue of the Virgin. Her hands were open at her sides and her face was so peaceful and good that, after I had gone to bed, her image would float behind my closed eyes like a protective circle of light. In the enthusiasm of my first religious awareness, especially being enthralled with the folklore of Mary, I decided to make a retreat for her in my bedroom.

The service was my own innovation: I would spend the entire weekend shut away; I would only eat soda crackers; there would be a rosary involved. But I didn't have the monastic discipline required, and with so many hours to bear, I gradually relaxed, rather than giving up. I got off my knees. Later, I decided I could even nap as long as I lay next to the statue in bed. I'm sure I didn't last past dinner, but even a day is a long time for a child to be alone, and by the end I was in an almost trancelike state. I remember talking to the figure next to me, not as a friend—though her hands were kind and her face sympathetic—but as if I could indeed talk to light, and I remember feeling so grateful. There was no doubt in my mind that there was another presence in my room, that it heard me, even cared for me, and would never leave me alone.

Today, it seemed, they were incorporating some of the May Day traditions into the wedding ceremony itself. There was a considerable thumping of kneelers as a group of people in the front row got out and walked down the center aisle to the back. An offertory hymn began; two violins and a flute accompanied the awkward choruses of the congregation. Two girls, perhaps Kathy's sisters, brought baskets of daffodils and gave them to her. She in turn put them with the rest at the shrine of Mary.

This made me feel cynical and then somehow sad. I remembered that when I was finally old enough to be in the May Day procession in my own parish, I had grown too sullen to participate. As the other girls walked by my pew with their flowers that May when I was thirteen, I hadn't felt as superior as I would have liked. There was a part of me that shriveled in humiliation to think anyone might know how dependent I had actually been on the Virgin Mary.

"Holy Mother, take me safely," was a charm I used to have ready on my lips for any time of risk. It became so well used I eventually shortened it to just "Safely." "Safely?" A girl friend shouted at me one day as we ran across the street. I had said it too loudly, and even though I'm sure she had no idea what it meant, it was if she had flung open a door I'd been hiding behind.

The last offertory song was a solo by Kathy's brother. With a clear but soft voice he sang, " 'Tis a Gift to Be Simple." The dark-haired girl, at this point, was gregariously pointing out the verses in the program to the mother of the group who stood next to her. The whole family seemed to stiffen, and the woman nodded perfunctorily but did not bother to find the page. Though the girl didn't appear wounded, I felt a sudden protectiveness for her. Doesn't she see the girl is rather remarkable? I thought. And yet during the greeting of peace, when everyone shook hands with the people around them, and the girl turned to me smiling, offering me hers, every fingernail painted a deep red, I felt my own demeanor turn very cool and guarded.

I was weary of the long proceedings. The bridal party was standing together, waiting to receive communion. Somehow, Steve had recruited the extra two groomsmen. I flipped to the front page of the program to get his last name set in my mind. Wasserman—I remembered he was doing graduate work in chemistry. Kathy, who was working toward a degree in psychology (as many of our past receptionists had), spoke of Steve and his field with a reverence for something incomprehensible but complete. "Dr. O'Keefe," she said to me once when we went out on the street for lunch, "everything they have to work with is absolutely empirical. And in psychology nothing is—not really."

I have had a similar issue with the sacrament of the Eucharist. The more my religious instructors stressed that my entire faith hinged on the belief that this small white wafer was not merely a symbol of the body of Christ, but that, indeed, it *was* the body of Christ, the less I was able to accept it. Why was it necessary to choose such a clearly impossible phenomenon for us to embrace?

I felt numb as I watched the others go up the aisle, and most of them looked as numb coming back. Watching each face as they returned from the altar, I played the old guessing game: where do they have it—left cheek, right, already swallowed?

The girl, once she had reached the priest where he stood at the foot of the altar, took the host in her hand in the modern way. But instead of putting it in her mouth, she covered it with her other hand as if it were alive, like a grasshopper, and might escape. She walked away like this, and then, rather than turning down the aisle to return to her pew, she went straight ahead and pushed through the side door with her shoulder.

Though no one seemed to notice, it was a mildly outrageous act. In grammar school the nuns used to tell us stories of people taking the host home and cutting it with a knife to see if it bled, and how these defilers were inevitably punished in a supernatural way—being struck by lightning, or having their hands catch spontaneously on fire. It was made clear: though the host was given to us, it wasn't really ours.

I had already speculated about the girl's eccentricities. Now I began to scan my mind for the various psychological reasons she might do such a thing. But I found that I just didn't know enough about her.

The reception was held in a hotel across the street from the basilica. There was champagne, and then we were seated for brunch. I hadn't expected to see her again. Somehow the departure with the host had had a ring of finality. But I had no sooner placed my napkin in my lap than she was standing by my side.

"Oh, good, you saved me a seat." She had removed her jacket and was wearing an ivory lambswool sweater that, in contrast to the rest of her outfit, looked elegant.

"Yes," I said, playing along. I felt strangely relieved to see her and then quite sure I was making a mistake.

We sat at two of the eight places at a round table. There were three couples already seated, and I hadn't yet intro-

duced myself. My name card was there and then the place
with no name card that she had taken. I supposed it had been
reserved in case I had brought a date.

"I'm Tiffany Perrier." She held out her hand to the gen-
tleman on her left.

"Like the water?" he said.

"Exactly," she said.

"Jack Murphy." He leaned forward to also smile at me.
"And this is my wife, Ann."

"Peg O'Keefe," I said.

Soon Tiffany had solicited everyone's names, and we had
moved on to occupations. Jack was a lawyer. "Oh, I've read
the law extensively." She sipped from a glass of tomato juice.

"Really?" He smiled, blinking at a girl who couldn't be
older than fourteen.

"Really." She blinked back at him. There was a faint line
of tomato juice over her lip. "Criminal, Family Relations,
and Constitutional," she said. "That's the most interesting—
especially when it comes to freedom of religion. Church and
state and vice versa. How about you?"

"Corporate law," Jack said. "You need to narrow it down
a little if you want to make a living of it."

"Tell them what you do, Peg," Tiffany asked, not looking
in my direction as she reached for a roll.

"Perhaps you could tell them, Tiffany."

"Oh, no, I never get it quite right." She finally wiped her
upper lip with a finger.

"I'm a clinical psychologist; I have a private practice."

"Oh, that's interesting," the whole table seemed to say at
once, and then, as was customary, some of them began to tell
me about friends and relations who were having certain
"problems."

"I have a cousin," Ann Murphy said, "who gets pregnant,
has the baby, goes through a horrible postpartum, so she gets
pregnant again right away. She has eleven children, and now
her doctor tells her that her uterus is caving in."

"Like an old building," Jack Murphy said.

"Like an old launching pad," Tiffany said.

After we had eaten some sort of variation on chicken breast and rice, the bride and groom began to make their rounds from table to table. When Kathy finally came to us, she had that shell-shocked look of anyone on her wedding day. This was the encounter that I felt would end my obligation. "Dr. O'Keefe, I'm so glad you came." And then she looked at Tiffany. "I don't believe I know you."

"I'm with Peg."

"Yes?" Kathy said, still questioning.

"Visiting," Tiffany said, almost impatiently. "Her niece."

"I can see the resemblance," she said.

"Amazing, isn't it?" I said.

I was ready to leave, but Tiffany talked me into standing on the sidelines to watch the dancing. I thought it would be worth a few minutes to penetrate the sham she had created.

"Do you crash many weddings?" I asked.

"Only when it works out. Sometimes there's no place for me to slip in. You were great though. I knew you would be the minute I saw you in church."

"What's your usual routine?"

"I read the announcements in the paper. If the church is nice, I'm especially interested. I'm never quite sure about the reception. A lot of the time it's a sit-anywhere sort of banquet. I knew this would be tough because it was at a hotel."

"What if I hadn't cooperated?"

"You were watching me, though. You have freckles like mine—that makes you game. And your red hair—that makes you passionate."

We looked out onto the dance floor filling up with the first young couples. "Do you think they'll get to any polkas here?" she said, swaying a little to the music. "I bet they're too tight-assed. If they got into some polka, even you and I could dance."

"I don't plan on drinking enough to polka," I said.

"'We have piped unto you, and ye have not danced.' That's Matthew," she said.

"Just what I thought," I replied. There was something in me that wanted to get the best of her. "What did you do with the host?"

"The host?" For the first time she looked uncomfortable.

"With communion. You left with it in your hand."

"I went outside and ate it there. That's all."

"That's all?"

"You are a shrink, aren't you? Okay, try this—sometimes I want to be alone with it. I want to eat it and feel what it does."

"What do you feel then?"

"I feel better."

"Better?"

"Yes. It may not be obvious, but I'm a pretty sad person." And then she seemed to detach herself from our conversation, even from the noisy stimulation of the wedding party around us, and her exquisite eyes glazed over in the manner I had seen with countless clients in my practice—a look when all of an individual life becomes an event to be reviewed. What an actor, I thought.

"Tiffany?" I said.

"I'm dying. She tucked her hands into the pockets of her culottes. I looked at the back of her delicate neck and the lambswool over her shoulders. For a moment, I felt we were alone in a room, and I was her therapist. I could feel my eyes on her become still and attentive and guarded in the way they do when a client tells me something new and significant but not wholly believable.

"Tiffany?" I said.

She shrugged her shoulders, looked everywhere but at me, and then at me. "I have cystic fibrosis. Everything gets clogged up, especially my lungs."

"I know about it," I said.

But then she looked past me, as if disregarding that I knew anything at all, said, "Hey!" to a boy in oxfords and a blue suit, terror all over his face at the sight of her. And she asked him to dance, going directly to him and taking his hand. The words *cystic fibrosis* clattered to the floor in front of me, like large coins.

Now, as I watched Tiffany destroy every attempt that her partner made to lead her, I realized how unnaturally white her skin was—this, I knew, was one of the symptoms of the disease. It was too easy for me to look for the lies in people. And I resolved, at least for the next few minutes, that I would believe what she told me.

"I understand how sad you must be," I said later.

"I plan on making the most of it," she almost shouted, since the band and the noise of the crowd had become louder. And she reached over to the buffet table for a plastic glass of wine that was sitting there. "I think I'll get drunk."

"You don't want to do that," I said.

"Yes, I do." And she proceeded to gulp down three glasses in succession. If this was a way of showing off, I thought it lacked savvy.

I wanted to leave. She said, "Nice knowing you." Her face was flushed, and she already seemed to weave a little on her feet.

"Why don't I give you a lift?" I said, regretting my own words.

"Great." She picked up another glass of wine, but then left it once she saw I didn't intend to wait.

I asked her about the fur on her coat as we drove. She said it was wolverine, that it was good for not frosting up. And was her real name Tiffany Perrier? "Not the last one," she said. "My mom named me Tiffany after the movie, *Breakfast at Tiffany's*. I've seen it thousands of times. My mom thought Audrey Hepburn's name was Tiffany. But it's the name of the store. That movie is full of good stuff—like that goofy party where they're going up and down the fire escape, Andy Williams singing, 'Moon River, wider than the sea . . .'"

"Does your mother know you crash weddings?"

"My mother is mentally ill," she said. "Crashing weddings wouldn't seem like a very big deal to her."

"How about your father?"

"No such thing," she said.

"I suppose you're in school?"

"Yeah, I'm known as the Jesus freak there. I say to them, 'Don't leave out Buddha and Mohammed.' I figure if I'm going to be a freak, I might as well not limit myself."

"Tiffany, where am I taking you?"

"Hennepin and Lake. I have some things to do."

"I mean, where do you live?"

"Not far from there—just a few blocks."

I realized I was acting too concerned, and that this was probably what she wanted, drinking three glasses of wine and telling me that she was dying.

The intersection of Hennepin and Lake is recognized as the hub of Uptown. It's one of the trendier areas of Minneapolis, with its art and coffee and neon-lamp shops. The faces of the shops change every year to suit people's current tastes. Many fashionable people were sitting out on the sidewalks under café umbrellas and watching each other. And ironically across the street there was also a gathering of punks, most of them teenagers, most of them from the wealthier suburbs. There was a mob of them in front of the McDonald's, indulging in their own sort of café scene. Girls with the sides of their heads shaved and long feathers hanging from their earlobes; a boy sitting on top of a phone booth dangling his steel-toed boots over the side. It occurred to me that Tiffany might be dressing in their style.

"McPunks," she said, matter-of-factly.

"Friends?" I asked.

"Right," she said, which I took to mean no.

I pulled over at the red light. She looked out of her window and didn't move to leave. "What are you going to do now?" she asked.

"I'm having guests for dinner. I expect I should get things ready."

"What are you having?" she asked.

"Salmon. But, Tiffany, I shouldn't hold up traffic here."

"Give me your number," she said so authoritatively that

I immediately went to my purse and found myself ripping a deposit slip from my checkbook.

"Wait a minute," I said.

"It's not like I could be a rapist," she said. "It's not like you couldn't hang up on me if you wanted to." She seemed to be settling in for an argument.

People were honking their horns behind me. I was sorry I had driven her.

"Okay," she said, and left the car. The boy on the phone booth across the street drummed his hands against the Plexiglas and seemed to be shouting at her. She ignored him and walked in the direction of the library. She didn't blend well into the café crowd as she passed through them, but she seemed unconscious of this, as if the whole fashionable scene was having little effect on her. She waved at me as I turned the corner, but I pretended not to see.

I was out of town the next weekend at a conference. When I returned to my answering machine on Sunday night, there were many messages from Tiffany. With every one she gave me a different last name. "This is Tiffany D'Arc" she'd say, or Currie, or Martin. She liked French names. And then she called me again before I'd finished with my messages.

"Peg?" she said, sounding older than she had on the machine. "What's new?"

"I'm not good with those sorts of questions, Tiffany."

"You sound mad."

"It's just that I've hardly been home."

"Well, then I'll call you back when you're ready," and she hung up.

I was irritated. It was Sunday night, and I faced another week of clients just as needy as this girl. I'd spent the weekend at a conference, addressing several different approaches to the treatment of pathological narcissism, and every method was as muddled and futile in my mind as the next.

I'd slept there with a longtime acquaintance, a man I had always thought of from the first time we'd met as charismatic and untrustworthy. But it turned out he was as ordinary as I. We weren't especially compatible—found ourselves unable to go very far with our lovemaking. Instead, we got up in the middle of the night and poured ourselves enormous brandies. We sat for an hour or more across from each other in front of the closed drapes of the hotel window.

He talked about his divorce. His wife, he told me, said being married to a psychoanalyst was about as much fun as playing poker with a computer. "She said she didn't have as many emotions as I had answers for them. She said she had fallen in love with me because she thought there was some sort of spiritual connection. She tells me now that she thinks I'm a fraud."

I thought to myself that she must have responded in the beginning to the charisma he exuded. The very quality that had made me initially mistrust him. "You do have something about you, though."

"I think I know what you mean," he said. "I think I put on mysterious airs. I give people this sense that I have secrets that would be valuable to them. You have that same air yourself," he said.

"I don't feel I have any secrets," I said.

"But wouldn't you like to have them?" he asked, with a knowing look that I found irritating. "I mean, we put in a good many years working toward our doctorates, immersing ourselves in the study of the human experience. After all that, didn't you expect to earn a certain wisdom?"

"I expected nothing more than to become well versed in my field. The whole idea of psychologist as shaman was repugnant to me before I even entered graduate school."

"It was a popular image at the time."

"I know. I was involved with a spiritualist of sorts—we married, in fact. We finished our undergraduate studies and left, of course, immediately for Mexico. David really thought we were going to find answers—walking across the desert in search of a little, wrinkled teacher named Miguel.

"Did you find him?"

"Yes, the little monster. After a few weeks we found that we had much less money than we came with and that Miguel had come to have very much more. He was very smooth."

"Did you learn anything at all?"

"I learned that two people should not marry until they are each fully grown up."

"And when is that?"

"Well, for one thing, it is when one stops reaching into unreachable places for reassurance and meaning. And for another, it's when one stops relishing one's ability to make a fool of oneself."

"I can't imagine you having been guilty of either of those maladies."

"I wasn't, but David was. He insisted on staying with this fraud. Even when I told him I had to leave. He reasoned that feeling taken was probably just one of the tests the old guy was putting us through. That maybe the teacher thought feeling like a fool was a good place to begin."

"Did you divorce David?" I nodded. "And you haven't married again."

"No."

"This doesn't have to do with maturity anymore."

"No, I suppose it has to do with being very careful."

On some impulse my friend leaned forward and put his face very tenderly against mine. "Why is it that we are both so lonely?" he whispered.

I was afraid he was wanting to be physical again. "That's not something we need to get to the bottom of tonight," I said awkwardly. "Let's take a vacation from the deeper concerns, a little workman's holiday."

I think he was sadly relieved. Both of us have sat listening to countless stories of loneliness. There are only so many words to describe it. They get used up, and you find you can no longer use them for yourself. Instead, we drank more and got into the subject of fishing—something we have both always wanted to do. We talked about the patience it would take to coax the bass from underneath their rocks, about the elusive trout, and we decided at first that the bass fishing wouldn't be as hard as the other, but concluded that we just didn't know enough about it.

Two or three days later Tiffany called me again. "I've thought about it and decided I'd like you to be my Big Sister."

"How does that work?"

"You know, you would relate to me, be a good example, and take me out to experience things."

"I don't think it's common for a girl to recruit her own Big Sister. I'm not sure it's even appropriate. Doesn't one usually go through the organization?"

"What's the difference?"

"Tiffany, I feel like you haven't been completely consistent in telling me about yourself. There must be at least one adult that is responsible for you. If you could have that person call me, maybe we could start from there."

"What do you mean consistent? What kind of a word is that? How consistent are you?"

"But, Tiffany, it's you that's asking me to get involved."

"Forget it," she said.

I was angry after she hung up. It wasn't guilt. I'd like to think that doesn't bog me down much anymore. But to use a phrase one of my clients likes, she "got to me." There was something about her very nature that seemed to challenge my own. Even when she didn't say a word. When I was around her I felt square, flat in comparison to her; I felt like I needed to prove something.

Two days later Tobey Johnson, the director of her group home, called me.

"Is she really dying?" I asked him.

"Oh, of cancer?" he said.

"No, cystic fybrosis."

"I'm afraid not," he said. "Not of MS or lupus either. The first time she lied about an illness was an attempt to make her mother respond to her. Even when it stopped working, she continued to do it. It's become kind of a habit. She's not really a bother about it. It's just like a middle name that changes once in a while. One day you learn that it's something else."

"She changes her last name from time to time as well."

"The real one is Hale."

"She wants me to be her Big Sister."

"What do you think?"

"I don't know. One minute I'm drawn to her, and the next I think she's too disturbed."

"She is disturbed," he said, "and understandably so. She was raised by a manic depressive. You should meet her sometime—she's a beautiful woman, the same as Tiffany. But if it had been her sole goal in life, she couldn't have given Tiffany a more unreliable sense of the world. Mrs. Hale's an extreme case, no middle ground. One month they would be sailing around the Apostle Islands with one of her boyfriends, everything would be 'heavenly,' and the next month she couldn't face leaving their apartment, wouldn't answer the phone, wouldn't eat."

"I sense a kind of religious obsession."

"Oh, I don't know if I'd call it that. Her mother converted when Tiffany was only a baby, sent her to mostly parochial schools. I doubt if Mrs. Hale is even very involved anymore, but I think at least for now it's a source of stability for Tiffany."

I was quiet and for a moment there was some throat-clearing, which would indicate we were not agreeing with each other.

"She told me you were a psychologist," he said. "I can understand how you might see this as just another extension of your practice. She doesn't need that. She's had all kinds of therapists. She's a challenge; I think many of them have found her simply beyond their reach. She can be confounding in ways the professionals find hard to diagnose."

"What does she need then?"

"I think she's already told you. She needs an older woman, something positive."

"I think she's manipulative."

"Ruthless," he said. "She gets what she wants. If you don't work out, she'll find someone else like you."

"Now you're being manipulative," I said. But it worked, I wasn't willing to commit myself, but on the other hand, I didn't like the idea of being replaced so easily either.

So we arranged a trial outing. If it worked out, there would be another, but still on a trial basis. The plan was for us to have lunch at the new exhibition center downtown. But when I pulled in front of the stucco house, Tiffany was waiting on the step with another girl from the home. "This is Leslie," she said. Leslie wore very clean white tennis shoes and, in contrast to Tiffany's darkness, her hair and eyelashes were blond. Tiffany was wearing a cub scout shirt, a red skirt, and toeless sandals. "We're just going to give her a lift to the mall." I felt this was presumptuous on her part and things were already off to a bad start. I didn't want to be Big Sister to Tiffany's entire group home.

After we'd entered the mall, I caught Tiffany's eye. "It's just that Leslie needs some help with the escalator," she said. And sure enough, Leslie, who had not said a word in the car, hung back with a little moan as we came to the center of the mezzanine near the approach to the long, open escalator which led to the upper deck. "Maybe not today, Tiffany," she said. But Tiffany put her arm around her friend's shoulders and brought her to the entrance. The escalator was all glass. In fact, the whole high rise of the court was a collaboration of many glass panels, reflecting the city outside and the sky itself. It wasn't exactly an escalator to be taken for granted, and Leslie's inhibition caused me to hesitate myself. It actually did appear to be a free-floating stairway with no solid foundation.

"This is really hard for you," I said to Leslie, who seemed even afraid to touch the moving railing. "Tiffany, maybe a different escalator at another time would be better." I imagined any minute there would be a hysterical scene echoing in the middle of the enormous mall.

"No, this is the one that the two of us talked about last

night. And you said you wanted to try this one, Leslie. You told me this one might be worth it."

"But, Tiffany," Leslie began to cry, and I felt sorry that I had interfered, caused her to lose whatever resolve she must have accumulated over the night.

"It's just the first one that's hard," Tiffany said. "Remember, we talked about that."

Leslie stood for an interminable amount of time watching this first step roll out from the entry platform, flat until a seam appeared and then a new first step would rise.

"Just do it," Tiffany said.

Leslie leaned forward, looking for a sure place to get on, but it was always moving. Her shoulders were shuddering, too much time was passing, a crowd was forming behind her. The people were beginning to murmur, "Excuse me, can we . . ." They were moving closer—a kind of waving impatience swelling up to the escalator but waiting just that last second that Tiffany needed to put her arm around Leslie and effortlessly bring her on. There was a moment that Leslie swayed, then she was okay.

"We'll be helping Leslie go back down again?" I posed the question as we waited in line for a Shawirma sandwich basket at the Lebanese deli.

"It wouldn't be nice not to." She smiled.

"I'm into being a savior," she said later, as we sat on a wooden bench under palm fronds on the balcony overlooking the mezzanine.

"You're talking about the escalator?"

Tiffany was picking pieces of onion out of her pocket sandwich, setting them in her cardboard tray. "Small things add up," she said. "St. Theresa, The Little Flower, didn't actually do anything spectacular—she just stuck with it, made it her vocation."

Problems with grandiosity—I could see it already. "How would you describe your vocation?" I asked.

"Okay, not exactly a savior, but a guide to faith."

My therapeutic voice was rising—I couldn't really subdue it. "Such deep concerns are unusual for someone your age."

"Maybe not." She was looking at the small pile of onions in her empty tray.

"Who else do you think is like you in these concerns?"

"My mother, for one."

"Do you see her?"

"I saw her in the hospital at Easter time. She'd gotten ahold of some matches, and she'd been wandering the halls looking for vigil lamps. She had told the night staff that she couldn't go to sleep without a vigil. She told me the next day that when she is asleep, she spins like a turbine engine. That it's too much for her, and one night she will just shake apart."

"She sounds like a frightened person." I wanted to be careful how I spoke about her mother.

She didn't answer me. She looked into her lap and spent some time smoothing out the cheap napkin that had come with our takeout.

"Sometimes we feel like we need to save our parents," I said.

"Sometimes they need saving," she replied.

It didn't take long to recognize Tiffany's three major obsessions: her mother, her clothes, and Catholicism. And from the start, I think I was determined to diminish at least some of the stock she invested in each of them. I tried to impress upon her the need to discriminate between her mother's world and what was a livable one. "You grew up not being able to know what to expect," I would tell her.

"Maybe that's why I got into the *Lives of the Saints*," she told me one day, as we walked our rented bicycles up East River Road. "The saints didn't have to depend on the world being a certain way. And it's a good thing, considering how wicked everyone was to them. *They overcame the game*," she said, as if reading a T-shirt slogan from somewhere. "I mean, when there's something bigger out there to care about, everyday things don't hurt as much."

My bike had a flat, and we had a good distance left to walk. "But there have certainly been some painful aspects in saintliness," I said. "I'm going to dissuade you from boiling in oil, burning at the stake, and having your tongue cut out."

"I'm not into martyrdom," she said.

"Why do you say you're dying then?" This was the first time I had brought the subject up.

But she didn't appear to be taken aback. She had a small fluff of cottonwood in her dark eyelashes that she wiped away, then we resumed walking. "Sometimes I think if I don't die real soon, or at least think that I will, I'll live in a worse way. I would be like one of those zombies in the movie *Night of the Living Dead*. Sometimes I just look out of my eyes, and I can tell I only have a little of what I need left— that I'm almost out of it, and when it's gone, I'll change into a piece of wood."

This was said with utter sincerity. All the time she had been talking she had been looking at her feet, as if watching them walk. And even after she had stopped talking, I was aware of the sound of her footsteps and found myself watching her put one tennis shoe in front of the other. Finally she looked up. Her face with the sun on it looked vulnerable and white except for a few freckles on her nose.

"But, I don't understand what you're saying," I said.

"Don't you ever think about the fact that you're eventually going to die?" She was exasperated. "Don't you think that's natural, Doctor Psychology? Tobey does; he says I just speed up the time in my mind to keep me on my toes. That's kind of strange, I suppose, but not as strange as all the people walking around who act like they don't expect ever to die."

After a few weeks the trial period had ended, and a system of equality was established between us. It was Tiffany's idea that we should take turns planning our outings. She called it "designer of the day." The other one was the "client." It wasn't simply the event the leader controlled, but the experience itself. The client had no say whatsover. I'd felt caught off guard when she had first made her proposal. It didn't seem prudent for me to go along with just whatever she might fancy doing, considering her capable imagination and the energy of her obsessions. But I found I couldn't quite object either. It was a challenge. I agreed on the condition that we could leave religion out of it.

I took her to the races once, Shakespeare-in-the-Park, and on a city canoe trip through the channel of lakes. Tiffany took me to the first established church of Minneapolis, located on the river, where we ate meat pies distributed by the French Canadian sisters. (She insisted, and I had to agree, this was not a religious experience.) Initially, our designer days were mild.

But one rare weekend evening I found myself across a cocktail table from her in "glamorous dress," as she had requested. She had made herself up quite successfully as an older woman. Through some miraculous treatment, her hair was swept back and smooth. Her dress was a black strapless, not unlike the kind Audrey Hepburn wore in the sixties. A light pink lipstick and fine black eyeliner completed the effect.

"Marvelous!" she panned, looking out at the view of the city. We were in the Orion Room, a revolving restaurant and cocktail lounge on the sixty-seventh floor of the IDS tower. The tilt of her head, the line of her neck—a "just so" pose— caused me to cross my legs in an elegant way. I felt an excitement that I could only associate at the time with a kind of espionage. "Two champagnes," she said to the waiter, "and tell me"—she beckoned him closer—"if there is a peach to be had—we would both adore a sliver in our glass."

All I could think about, while we waited for our drinks, was the consequences for contributing to the delinquency of a minor. But once the champagne was served, each with a slice of peach, I was happy again. "My mother could dress like this," she said, "like a jewel in a box, even while we were so poor. It was a way to make me proud of her." After we finished our wine, she set the glass down and smiled. "This was easy, wasn't it?"

And it occurred to me later that the whole evening had been both a tribute and a parody of the kind of romantic magic her mother was capable of. Perhaps by being able to imitate it, Tiffany was dismantling the power it had always had for her.

I found myself spending more and more time with Tiffany. At first I set fairly strict limits—seeing her every other weekend. But my limits expanded almost unnoticeably until one day in August I looked up from my gardening and watched her adjusting the position of the sprinkler on my lawn.

I realized she'd gotten more than a toehold in my life. And I realized that I didn't mind. I minded a little that she would drop by when I had guests. Always, there was an initial consternation regarding her unique ability to control a conversation—any conversation. My friends would look askance, wondering when I was going to take the reins in hand. But I knew she would draw them in soon enough. They would be comparing computer technology to waffle irons and the possibilities of telephones for dolphins, and there wouldn't be a shred of banality left in the room.

It exasperated me that she took pleasure in exposing my more personal feelings, asking me about my "boyfriends," or whom I was jealous of in my family, who loved whom best. After she had grilled me relentlessly, she would explain simply that she was a "Therapist's Therapist."

I objected when she tracked down my office phone. But as if she understood what the real limits were, she never pushed that one. Yet even without her calling, I found her to be strangely present in my work. "That's not enough!" a middle-aged man had roared at me during a session one day. I had just finished saying that the important thing was that he needed to feel good about himself. On any other day I might have responded with "It may feel that way" or "You just have to trust me on that." But instead I felt winded, disoriented. Something, I realized later, in the challenge of knowing

Tiffany was rattling the very detachment and confidence I had always felt was necessary to work with my clients.

"Most everyone loves me," she once said while pulling a cake we had made out of the oven. It occurred to me this was her way of telling me that I should love her. But it was more than that—something in the warm kitchen's air must have actually made her feel this was true. And now she was just repeating it, making it into a certainty.

But the absence of her mother was a hairline crack in her optimism, and some days when she remembered something awful, or when just the accumulation of time was a reminder that she had been left alone, the crack would fracture into a chasm. Then I would find her sitting on the picnic table as I pulled my car in the driveway. And I would know because she was unsettled, and at a loss for what to do with herself. There was no chance of our talking, no chance of my leaving her alone, so I would go on with opening my mail or whatever else was at hand, and she would stay, sometimes pulling the curtain away from the window to look outside, as if it were raining and she was waiting for it to stop.

In the next few days she would give her hair another blunt treatment, take up jogging with a competitive marathon in her sights, or I'd find a regular smorgasbord of garden vegetables she had arranged at the mouth of the rabbit hole in my yard. Food for a rabbit we had seen neither hide nor hair of in weeks.

At the end of the summer Tiffany entered what at the time I couldn't help but diagnose as a manic phase. She began to wear her scapular, with the small image of the sacred heart, on the outside of her shirt. She had gray rings under her eyes, and I suspected she wasn't sleeping at night. She was constantly running her hands through her hair, so that it stood up in tufts on her head. When she would visit, she would talk, she would talk and talk, as if it were the equivalent to breathing. "My mother isn't doing very well," she'd say. "They say she's speeding up. I think I know what it is," she'd say. "She's speeding up for the wreck. I don't think she's gone this fast before."

I was afraid it might not be her mother she was talking about, but herself. I called Tobey Johnson.

"What is happening with her mother?" I asked.

"We hear she's in a manic episode. Pretty bad, I guess. They don't think it is good for Tiffany to visit her."

"But Tiffany knows about it."

"She saw her once. I guess that was enough."

"I think Tiffany's in serious trouble, Mr. Johnson. You understand, even at this age it's not impossible for the illness to kick in."

"Dr. O'Keefe, I know it's hard not to be afraid of that. But I've known her for a few years, and I've seen similar behavior before. Somehow she seems to have her own way of getting to the other side."

But the next weekend we attended an office picnic together. I had invited her several weeks before, but when the time came, told her that in light of her recent behavior, I wondered if it was a good idea for her to go. "I'm not crazy," she told me once again in the car on the way to the park. She had a large watermelon in her lap. I had assured her she didn't need to bring anything, but she had insisted from the start that she wanted to bring a melon. She was wearing a sleeveless, lemon-colored undershirt and her earrings were little plastic oranges and bananas. I realized she was following a kind of fruit theme.

My partners and their families had found an area of picnic tables under a pleasant stand of elms. Once we arrived, Tiffany immediately began to slice the watermelon and pass it to people on paper plates. The adults were drinking beer, waiting for the coals to get hot on the grill. The children were off playing Frisbee. Kathy and Steve had brought out their wedding pictures, and there wasn't much room on the table. "Maybe we should wait with the melon," I said to her gently.

"I just thought, . . ." she started to say but stopped. I knew she felt humiliated.

One of my partners, Keith, set his dead pipe down and reached for one of the plates. "I wouldn't mind a little," he said, and smiled.

Kathy looked up from her pictures. "It looks wonderful," she said. "As soon as we finish boring everyone, we'll have a big plate." She said this with a tone one uses when talking to a child.

Steve hadn't even looked at the melon. All I could see was his blond well-groomed head bent over the pictures. "This one should go into the reject pile," he said, putting a photo to one side.

"But I like that one!" Kathy said.

The pictorial tour of the wedding went on.

I had never seen Tiffany so reserved in a group before. She sat picking seeds out of the watermelon on the plate in front of her. She did this methodically, stripping one slice and then, without eating it, going on to another. Her pace began to pick up, and eventually she had a large stack of seedless melon slices and large pile of seeds on another plate. There was going to be trouble.

"Why don't you eat some of it?" One of the children, a little boy, had come up to the table behind her. She didn't answer him.

"If they could invent a seedless watermelon," Keith said lamely.

Tiffany finally looked at the child. "This is for you and the other kids," she said, handing over the soggy plate that was almost collapsing under the pile of melon slices. The boy walked carefully away, holding the plate well in front of him so the juices wouldn't drip down his front.

She quietly watched him make his way to the others lying together in the shaded grass. For a moment I had the impression that she was peaceful. But when she turned back to the table, her face was a mask of stony contempt. "What's wrong?" I mouthed the words to her. She ignored me and stared ahead. The other adults had barely noticed her this whole time, except for Keith, who I sensed was sharing in the tension I was now feeling.

Tiffany had her hand in the plate of seeds beside her. She was rubbing them between her fingers, though she still looked straight ahead.

"Are you in high school yet, Tiffany?" Keith asked, while dipping a match into his pipe.

Keith's wife looked at Tiffany, aware that she wasn't answering.

My other partner and his wife were still obliviously looking at pictures with Kathy and Steve.

"Keith asked you a question," I said.

She acted as if I hadn't said anything and slid nearer the group around the pictures. She took a picture from the pile and appeared to study it intently.

"*Ha!*" she laughed, causing everyone to look toward her. I sighed heavily, as if I thought the sound of it might change the course of things. Everyone else had become very quiet. "Look at the romantic couple." The picture was upside down for me, but I could see across the table that she was pointing at the bride and groom in one of the church pictures. "And who is this?" She pointed one of her long, thin fingers down in an exaggerated manner. From the speck of lime green under her finger, I guessed she was pointing at herself. "This is the only one in the church who's praying."

"Tiffany." I put my hand out toward the picture.

"Auuugh!" she screeched, and pulled the picture out of my reach. Kathy jumped. Steve had his chin leaning in his hand, the hand covering his mouth, which made him look like he might either burp or yawn. Keith was still holding his pipe to his mouth, but he wasn't drawing from it. I imagined he was giving her some sort of diagnosis. I could almost see the possibilities rolling through his mind, like the music grid in a player piano.

The little boy with the watermelon had returned. I could see the other children were also coming toward us. She got up and held the picture up to the boy, who was standing at the other end of the table. "If we could make this into a moving picture," she said to him, "you would see everyone was only going through the motions. You know"—she looked at

Kathy—"genuflect, cross your forehead, splash some holy water on your head, get into the *modern* guitar."

"Who?" the boy asked.

"Like Peg here." She pointed to the tiny figure that must have been me. "You're all going to be damned!" She was standing on the bench now, her orange and banana earrings jiggling, and she seemed to be shouting to the kids who were only a few feet away.

"Hey now!" Keith's wife said.

"That's enough." I stood up.

"You all think that if you just remember a little of it, it will save you. Like hanging a No Pest strip on the porch." She had her arms up, her fingers running through her black hair. I could see her navel and the white skin of her small belly. "But you've got to believe as much as me, as much as me." There were little specks of spit flying out of her mouth. "Or you might as well forget it. If you don't really believe it's out there, then there will be nothing out there to see you. You'll be completely invisible. Like my mom."

She looked me directly in the face. There were tears in her eyes. She was so unhappy and so beautiful I didn't know what to do. I wished I'd taken her hand and, instead of standing outside of the scene, as if I had nothing to do with it at all, looked up at her, saying, "Maybe you should come down now, maybe I should take you home."

Tobey Johnson and I kept in closer touch. Tiffany, on the other hand, was mostly not interested in seeing me. She was going through an "isolation thing," Tobey said. "Was she depressed?" I wanted to know. He thought that was probably true. And maybe a little ashamed, he said, about the thing in the park.

I wrote her a letter. I used the most guilt-producing argument that I could think of. "I gave you many, many chances before I even knew you. We have a relationship. How is it you can count on me, but I'm not allowed to count on you. . . ?" I also made a point of reminding her that she had left off owing me at least two days where I was allowed to be the designer. I don't know if guilt persuaded her or not. She accepted, but when Tobey called to tell me, he said, "She's going through a sullen stage. I don't envy you."

I arranged a weekend at my family's lake cottage when none of the relatives would be there. I was hoping that being alone would make it easier for us to talk again. It was a designer weekend. Fishing was the one and only activity. My plan was to fish on the lake until we caught something over twelve inches. "If it takes all day and night," I told her, not believing it would. I had borrowed some books at the library on the subject and rented equipment at a sports shop in the city.

Tiffany was dangling a night crawler over the water as if any moment a walleye might sit up in the lake and beg. This was her response to my asking if she wouldn't maybe like to start using the pole that I had paid twenty-five dollars to rent.

After about five minutes of this, I built up a feeling of righteousness. "I'm the designer," I said. "You have to fish."

"Do I have to talk?" she said.

"No, but I might say a word now and then."

The lake was everything I would have wanted it to be for someone who had never been there before, dark but crystalline, like the deep-colored marble we used to collect. And farther out the light lay on the surface of the water and rolled along as if it might eventually reach us. I was used to days when the cloud cover constantly changed overhead and the wind slapped water against the boat so that even while you were anchored you were pushed like a whirligig in circles. But this day was still.

The loons were out fishing, creating a sense of camaraderie. They were a pair of black shapes on the glaze of light in the distance, and I wondered if we were the same to them.

"Watch when one of them dives," I said.

But neither of them did. Instead of facing me, Tiffany faced the back of the boat. Her line was dutifully in the water and that was about all.

She had grown a little taller since I had first met her, she was wearing her hair longer, she had rolled up her T-shirt sleeves. There were a few specks of lake water glittering on her forearm. A smudge of sunburn was darkening on each white shoulder and I thought how I might have to remind her later to cover up.

"I can only imagine that the worm on the end of that line, Tiffany, has died of boredom." She was quiet. "I mean you have to play with your line a bit."

She turned around, her hand shielding her eyes from the sun, which was shining behind my head. "You don't know that much more about it than I do."

"Ohh, ho." I was determined to be good-natured. "Fish catching—and I've done some significant research—is the simple result of a precise combination of factors: where, when, what, and how. Sometime today, one of us has to hit it right."

But something went wrong. The loons disappeared in the afternoon and came back in the early evening for their dinner, craning their necks back and swallowing it whole. It was getting very dark, and still neither of us had even a glimpse of a fish near our boat. Tiffany was silent, and this added to my sense of foolishness.

We'd eaten all the sandwiches. Everything in the cooler was warm. "I suppose you would like to go in," I said.

"It's up to you," she said, without expression.

I started to row back, forgetting to pull up the anchor. And there were a few awkward slaps of the oars which splashed water on her back. She reached around with her hand and quietly wiped it away. I set my mind to an efficient rhythm of rowing, but I couldn't avoid the discouragement I felt, like an ache, as we approached the shore.

In the twilight, with her knees drawn up to her chin and her arms wrapped around her legs, Tiffany looked like one of those gray cocoons you find broken away from its branch. Everything that I had known to be alive about her appeared to be wrapped and dormant. When we finally bumped against the shore, she was upset in her seat and had to reach for the sides of the boat.

"The day's not over," I said. And I felt like you might feel when your lover has left, and you still believe you could somehow make him love you.

There was no electricity in the cottage, and while lighting the kerosene lamps, I anticipated the trip we would need to make to the outhouse. "Tiffany, I have another plan," I said.

"You want to frighten me," she said, when I told her.

"I'll have a flashlight, and I'll be right behind you."

"No," she said.

"You don't have a choice, though," I said, and she knew this was true.

Even before we had come, I had thought of the outhouse as a new experience for Tiffany. When I was a child on our weekends at the cottage, the nightly trip there had always been a kind of odyssey. It was a necessity and yet something terrifying because of the woods we had to travel through to get there. One of my parents would always lead me with the flashlight. But somehow they didn't have the power to dispel the phantoms I saw silhouetted in the undergrowth along the path.

"If you had a flashlight," I said to Tiffany, "it wouldn't be the same as it used to be for me. It looks different when you don't hold the light yourself."

On our way, she stopped dead in her tracks, and I bumped into her. "What?" I said.

"Didn't you see that?" she said.

"What?" I felt exhilarated that this was working so well.

"Let's keep moving," she said. "Keep the light in front of my feet, for God's sake!"

Every few steps I'd twist the beam into the foliage along the path, just barely, knowing that my parents would never have done this to me. Her indifference had vanished. She had her hands out at her side, she was listening to everything.

Then, when we finally reached the outhouse, and after she had taken her turn, I made the mistake of giving her the flashlight. Before I was finished, everything went dark. When

I stepped out, she placed the tube of the flashlight in my hand. "Here you go," she said.

The batteries were gone.

"Now nobody has a light." She was cool and still. She had taken my power away.

The trees were looming over us, shuddering erratically in the wind. We found our way to the cottage only because we could hear the lake lapping against the dock.

Before I went to bed, I took the lamp into her room. She was lying, still in her jeans, on the top of a bedspread that used to be mine when I was young.

I sat down on the edge of the bed. "You should cover up." I felt awkward, reaching over her to pull up the blanket when she hadn't asked.

"Tiffany, I wish we could talk."

She looked sleepy. She had her arms behind her head, and her eyes were just barely visible under her lashes.

"I was wondering," I said, "if I were to tell you something, would you tell me something similar in return?"

I could see her eyes go sideways, under her eyelashes. "Is this a designer thing?" she asked.

"Yes, I guess it is."

She shrugged her shoulders.

"Okay," I said. "When I was in second grade, I used to talk to a statue of the Virgin Mary."

"Is that it?" she said.

It seems there were to be no bounds to my humiliation this weekend. I realized this was a tame admission to be making to someone with her experience. So I paused, trying to think of a way I could express it better.

"But, you see, when I talked to her, I absolutely believed someone out there could hear me."

Tiffany had the back of her hand on her brow and appeared to be yet unmoved.

"And now I could never do that. When I think back, I think that was the saddest loss in my life."

She had her hand over her eyes.

"What I always wondered," I said, "is when you take the host outside, do you talk to it the way I talked to the statue?"

She still had her hand over her eyes. But her lips were stretched more tightly, and I could see just a little of her teeth. She was trying not to cry.

"John, Chapter 16," she said.

"What?"

"That's what I would recite. 'Behold, the hour cometh . . .'"

"I don't know it. Tell me the rest."

She rolled on her side, facing the wall. "It doesn't matter," she said softly. "I don't say it anymore, and I don't take the host."

Tiffany spent the month of September in a day treatment program. Tobey Johnson said she was on medication for depression. We went once for a Friday fish fry at a Perkins near her house. She was changed; the medication gave her a sleepy look in the corner of her eyes. She ate little and didn't even use the catsup, which she used to adore. She said that the psychiatrist was hopeful that the depression was reactive, rather than chronic. She needed some time away, Tiffany said, and she would call when it felt okay.

Then in the middle of October, when Tiffany was already back in school, I came out to the reception room between clients and Kathy Dade looked up at me in an unusually expectant way. "Tiffany phoned," she said. "Her mother died this morning."

"How?"

"I don't know, but I knew you had only one client left this afternoon, so I told her to just come over." Kathy looked uncertain.

"That was absolutely right," I said gratefully.

Waiting in my office for my next appointment, I found myself trying to recall the last scene in *Breakfast at Tiffany's*. It is pouring rain in New York City. In a cab, Audrey Hepburn is confronted by her lover for being a fraud. She opens the door to the cab, her cat runs out, she runs after her cat. Then I can only remember her crying, on a doorstep in the middle of the city, wearing a little sweater, the rain running down her face.

When I heard Kathy speaking to someone in the lobby, I wasn't sure if it was my client or Tiffany who had arrived. But it was Mrs. Carrol, a woman my age who had been struggling with depression. She didn't look good. Of all the maladies I treat, depression makes me the most weary. It is like trying to talk to someone underwater, knowing they can barely hear you.

"Sit down," I announced too loudly. And I realized how truly agitated I was. Even Mrs. Carrol seemed a little stunned by my tone, and her face, which had been smooth and lifeless, took on a wary attention.

I went over in my mind the notes from her last session. "Continue with her introverted anger . . ." had been the plan for today. I would let her talk. Yet I found myself moving my chair into a position of confrontation. There was barely a distance between us. I knew that it was almost certain that Tiffany's mother had killed herself, just as Mrs. Carrol's mother had. Statistics were unrolling in my mind—an enormous number of children of suicides will eventually end their own lives. I heard the door to the outer office open. "If your life depended upon it, Mrs. Carrol, what if anything would you have faith in?" I had almost shouted this at her. Yet she kept her head lowered, and only the smallest furrow in her brow indicated that she had even heard me. "I mean, if you were to die because you didn't believe in something, what would that thing be?" She was motionless for some time. It seemed I wasn't using any kind of judgment in the tack I was taking. If she didn't respond, I didn't know how we could proceed. It occurred to me that if she didn't respond I might just somehow pick her up over my head and shake her. She looked up slowly, not really seeing me, and then she began to cry.

"Outside my window," she said softly, "in the morning, when I'm lying in bed, I can hear the traffic. It stops at the traffic light, I can hear the cars idling, and then when I hear them pulling ahead again, I know the light has changed." She laughed, crying at the same time. "You must think I'm crazy."

I shook my head no.

"I mean, it's more than the light, it's the sound. I mean, not the sound, but as if there's something behind it all that keeps it going."

"You need to believe that something won't let it stop."

"Yes," she said.

"I do, too," I said.

I couldn't read Tiffany when I was finally able to see her. Her school clothes were uncharacteristically traditional—a wool skirt, a blouse. My throat ached once I noticed she had stuck pennies in the slots of her loafers. She was holding a Styrofoam coffee cup that Kathy had given her, probably not knowing what else she could do. The coffee was to the brim and obviously cold, and she handed it to me when I came out as if she'd been holding it for me instead. I had an urge to tell her about the progress I had just made with Mrs. Carrol.

"Tiffany?" I said.

Her eyes went sideways in the direction of Kathy, letting me know she didn't want to talk there. She uttered the beginning of something. I leaned closer. "I'm the designer," she whispered.

She took me to Loring Park. It was still too early for the after-work crowds. But there were some regulars lounging on the grass or fishing in the lagoon. It was late afternoon, and in the October light the trees in the park glowed like lamps. Many of the orange and gold leaves had already accumulated along the sides of the path where we walked, and the sound of them under our feet became rhythmic.

"Tiffany, did she . . . ?"

"No!" Before I could finish, she swung her fist to the side, connecting with my diaphragm. I had to stop to catch my breath, and I grabbed her arm in a gesture of defense.

Her voice was very tight, "Please, let me just do this."

"Okay," I said, "what do you want?"

I was still holding her arm, and she put her hand on my forearm. She looked at me, then lowered her eyes. "I want you to be her for a little while."

"Okay," I said softly, and relaxed under her hand.

We walked up the slope of a grassy hill. We were close to the center of the city, the freeway was a white roar, I could see the dome and other patches of the basilica through the trees. Children were running home from school over the lagoon bridge.

"Over here." Tiffany took me under the yellow canopy of an enormous oak. "We used to have picnics here," she said.

We walked up to the trunk. She leaned against it, touching it with her white hands, her fingers disappearing in the deep crevices of its bark. "There's a spirit under this," she said. And when I looked at her face, I felt, miraculously, that she was safe. "Lean against it," she said. Once I had leaned my back to the tree, she seemed embarrassed and couldn't look at me, but leaned her side against the trunk and went back to poking her fingers in the bark. "Close your eyes," she said.

With my eyes closed, the air smelled stronger. "Autumn is the season that remembers," a client once told me. It could have been any autumn I smelled now. I saw my first school shoes as I walked down a road in Wisconsin, and the yellow trees were bending over me, as if they did after all have spirits, knew me, and would continue to know me.

I felt Tiffany's hand touch my ear. "Mother," she said. I remembered I was to be her mother today. But I liked thinking of that road in Wisconsin, and now Tiffany was the girl, and I imagined I was her mother, and we were walking down the road together, both in our cloth coats.

"Can you hear me?" I heard someone ask. It seemed like the tree, but it was Tiffany, very close to my ear. "'Behold, the hour cometh,'" she was reciting. "'Yea, is now come, that ye shall be scattered . . .'" I could see us walking down the road. "'. . . Every man to his own, and shall leave me alone: and yet I am not alone,' Mother," she said. "'These things I have spoken unto you that in me ye might have peace. In the world ye shall have tribulation: but be of good faith; I have overcome the world.'"

And we were walking down the road, and the trees were bending over us.

ACKNOWLEDGMENTS

I thank my editor, Jane von Mehren, for her careful, firm, and loving guidance. I especially thank my friends, Mark Cox, Mei Mei Evans, Ellen Lesser, Laura Cripps, and Janet Wigfield for helping me craft stories that at first were always awkward. And I thank my brothers and sisters. In addition, I am sincerely grateful to The Loft, the Pen American Center, the Edward Albee Foundation, the Minnesota State Arts Board, the Robsons, and the Bush Foundation.

ABOUT THE AUTHOR

Mary La Chapelle's short fiction has appeared in many magazines ranging from *Northern Lit Quarterly* to *Redbook*. She is the recipient of numerous awards, including a Whiting Writers' Award, an Edward Albee Foundation Fellowship, a Minnesota State Arts Board Grant, a Bush Artists Fellowship, and the PEN/Nelson Algren Award. She lives in Minneapolis, where she is working on her first novel.

VINTAGE
CONTEMPORARIES

VINTAGE
CONTEMPORARIES

Now at your bookstore or call toll-free to order: 1-800-733-3000
(credit cards only).